STAT

MICHAEL SHEA ~~~~~~~~ ~~~~~~~~~ thrillers
in the 1970s under the pseudonym Michael Sinclair,
but stopped writing novels when he became the
Queen's Press Secretary, a position he held for a
decade. He now combines writing with a wide range
of business interests, dividing his time between
Edinburgh and London.

Praise for the novels of Michael Shea

Spin Doctor

'Michael Shea knows all about political intrigue and
makes fine use of his expertise in *Spin Doctor*, which
dashes enjoyably around the corridors of influence.
What gives *Spin Doctor* its cutting edge is the fact
that Michael Shea has been a spin doctor himself. His
fiction bears a disturbing resemblance to fact.'
Sunday Times

'A gem – a taut thriller of political intrigue and skul-
duggery that fairly belts along. A chilling portrait of
the Machiavellian world that lies behind the corridors of power in Westminster and Whitehall.' *Today*

The British Ambassador

'This intriguing novel makes full use of Michael Shea's
inside knowledge . . . a gripping ingenious tale . . .
engrossing and informative.' *Glasgow Herald*

'Michael Shea has produced another first-class thriller
in which his experience at the heart of government is
put to excellent use.' *Sunday Telegraph*

MICHAEL SHEA

STATE OF
THE NATION

HarperCollins*Publishers*

HarperCollins*Publishers*
77–85 Fulham Palace Road,
Hammersmith, London W6 8JB

This paperback edition 1997

1 3 5 7 9 8 6 4 2

First published in Great Britain by
HarperCollins*Publishers* 1997

ISBN 0 00 649878 7

Set in Linotron Sabon

Printed and bound in Great Britain by
Caledonian International Book Manufacturing Ltd, Glasgow

To Mona
and
With thanks to
Robin and Trish Crichton,
Corinne Lea and William Russell

For convenience, the events in this book can be thought of as taking place some few years hence. But this is in no way a futuristic book. The action could, in different circumstances, be taking place now.

The book is very loosely based on the novel, *The Dollar Covenant*, published under Michael Shea's pseudonym, Michael Sinclair, in 1973.

Treason doth never prosper, what's the reason?
For if it prosper, none dare call it treason.
                                    Sir John Harington

Hulse City, New Jersey, population 613, is still a place on the fringes of nowhere. A little further south one soon reaches pleasant, rolling, open countryside. To the north, however, the horizon is broken by a festering landscape of obscene towers, pipes and scaffolding, like some demented modern sculpture, that is the first of a thousand chemical plants, fertilizer factories and other inventions of man, created to better the environment anywhere but there.

Hulse City itself was not a bad place to live – neat houses with carefully swept yards and a newly painted little church that was well attended on Sundays. A railroad line used to run through the middle of the city, parallel to Main Street, but it had long gone.

That day, two years back, could have been much, much worse, but it was Superbowl time and most of the inhabitants were inside, sunk in front of their TV sets with stacks of Schlitz and Budweiser beside them. Even the filling station and the Pizza Pie Factory were closed that afternoon. But Floralove Skeen wanted to go outside, as did Dusty the mongrel. Neither was much interested in the Superbowl. No one watched as Floralove, a little bored, played first with the dog and a ball, then started breaking all the rules and made a fine mud pie in the dirt on the side of the backyard. Floralove was only five. She was a pretty little girl with well-brushed ringlets of fair hair, and that day she was wearing her favourite pale blue dress with the lace trimmings, which her mother had made for her last birthday.

Maybe it was the mud. Maybe she was going to get a smack for playing with dirt. Her eyes started to sting and she began coughing and then Dusty began keeling over like her father had last New Years. The dog staggered and fell, and so did Floralove.

Later, Mrs Skeen, a precise if kindly lady, who'd become suspicious at the lack of all noise from outside, suggesting that her little treasure might be up to no good, pulled back the net drapes and looked out into the yard. The sound of her screaming was almost immediately drowned by the alarm sirens from the chemical plant and the bullhorns of the emergency vehicles, their loudspeakers blaring warnings to the good people of Hulse City to stay indoors and shut their windows, as they tracked the monstrous yellow dust cloud, which drifted south on a gentle, so gentle wind.

1

The State of the Nation

Today is the fourth anniversary of Scottish Independence. But who is celebrating? Look out of your windows. Where are the Bravehearts, once so vocal? Where are the bands, the flags, the parades, the bread, the circuses, the proud speeches from our nation's leaders? Where indeed is that feeling of nationhood? We believe it exists but it has been buried deep beneath what has happened to Scotland in the last four years, the strikes, the poverty, the unemployment and the civil unrest. The opposition parties accuse the Government and above all the Prime Minister, Keith Sinclair, of a failure of leadership. But that is the easy option. Surely we all must share the guilt and the blame.

(Editorial in the *Herald*, St Andrew's Day)

Clydebank, Scotland. A rhythmical spiral of water poured from a fractured gutter tight under the grey slates. It made little impression on a century and a half of engrained grime as it hit the projecting lintel above the doorway. Most of the water drained away in rivulets down to the flagstones but enough was retained to provide nourishment for the bright green crops of moss that flourished along the crevices where sandstone fitted unevenly against rotting doorframes.

Aided by the teeming rain, the heavy grey of the clouds, only one shade lighter in tone than the surrounding buildings, blurred into uncertainty the line where rooftops met sky. Each surface was decaying and slimy to the touch; the rain, rather than cleansing and refreshing as it fell, became immediately infected by its new environment. Running among the cobblestones to the blocked drains by the kerb, it encouraged the polluted pools to stretch out and form a barrage across the street.

The high walls of the squalid tenements provided an all too effective trap for the small band of marchers. That wet Saturday morning was both St Andrew's Day and also the fourth anniversary of Independence, which was why Clydebank's Republican contingent was making its sodden, tartan-bedecked way through the deserted backstreets to meet up with the main procession for the big rally in George Square.

Constable Wright, brought in by bus from his rural beat in the Campsie Hills to help a hard-pressed City Constabulary for the day, was one of the regulation handful of police escorts. He would submit his incident report later. He was an honourable man, always well turned out; his style was unpolished and unimaginative but he missed little of the detail.

The party faithful were far fewer than in previous years. The organizers comforted themselves by telling each other that the rain had kept people at home and that Celtic were playing away. But they knew in their heart of hearts that twelve percent unemployment and the general strike meant that not many had the passion for celebration.

There were still sufficient numbers for the march to fall into disarray though, particularly when they had to ford the flooded street. The three pipers at the head of the procession neither faltered nor broke step, but those behind them were less resolute and the procession ground to a halt while discipline was reintroduced to the ranks. The police escort took advantage of the delay to find a moment or two's shelter in a doorway. PC Wright, reluctant immigrant to Scotland that he was, privately cursed the weather, the squalor and the stridency of the pipe music with equal vigour. The respite was brief. The procession moved

4

hesitantly forward once again. Pulling the collars of their capes up around their necks, the policemen returned to their duties and to the rain.

By the gates of an idle, deserted factory the marchers turned a corner into another anonymous street lined with boarded-up shops. For a moment the rain and the misery obscured their view. Then the Republican leaders saw the men waiting for them: a crowd of some three hundred Reunionist strikers, spread across the street ahead, standing silent, black and yellow industrial helmets glistening in the rain.

The police sergeant in charge shouted an order. PC Wright spoke urgently into his radio. At Constabulary Headquarters alarm bells sounded.

By now only fifty yards separated the two groups, the Republicans outnumbered by at least four to one. The Reunionists were not there by accident; they would not willingly clear a path. Both knew their enemy; it had happened before.

'Keep on,' shouted the procession leader, a dedicated man in his fifties in an ancient, well-used kilt. 'Keep on. We've a right tae march; the polis will see we're a'right.' The man's look belied the confidence of his words. Half a dozen policemen would not go far.

Only ten yards separated the two groups before the procession hesitated and juddered to a stop. The pipers continued to blow resolutely, marking time, awaiting instructions.

PC Wright, flanked by his colleagues, moved forward in an attempt to clear a way through the motionless wall of men. Tension was at a breaking point, but the pipes played on. High above, a few anxious female heads watched from tenement windows.

'Move along there. This is an authorized procession.' The sergeant addressed the strikers through his loud-hailer. No one moved at first. Then, unexpectedly, with some shuffling, a narrow but orderly path opened up ahead. PC Wright muttered hopeful words of commentary into his radio. At Headquarters the alarm bells continued to ring.

The small group advanced deep into the crowd, pushing its way along a reluctant path between the silent men. The policemen were a few steps ahead. The pipers kept manfully in tune. Even the rain seemed to ease a little.

When the procession was about halfway through, PC Wright heard, from his left, a shrill, deliberate whistle cut in above the sound of the pipes. At once the strikers closed in. The music died instantly and a set of bagpipes flew incongruously through the air. Wright raised his radio to his lips but strong hands grabbed him from behind, a sack was thrown over his head, and he felt himself carried like a child through a mass of surging bodies. He heard muffled shouts, a scream of intense male agony close at hand, and the clattering of steel-capped boots on cobblestones.

Wright realized he was being borne away from the main crowd, but with arms and legs expertly locked by several pairs of hands he was unable to resist. He felt one of his captors stumble, heard a door slam somewhere, then the sound of shouting became fainter.

'We've got no great quarrel wi' the polis.' A deep voice penetrated through the sack. 'But only move and ye'll get the same as they Republican scum.' Thrown roughly onto a floor, Wright felt his hands being bound behind him. Further whispers followed, then there was silence.

He sensed he was alone. Gently he tested the ropes. He had been hurriedly and unskilfully tied and he easily worked himself free. He reached up and cautiously pulled the sack from his head.

The bare room was empty and almost in darkness, though a little light filtered in from a skylight above the door. At a guess he was in what had been a coal cellar. He felt for his radio but it was gone. He stood up shaking, and as he did so, his foot scraped against something metallic: the crushed remnants of the radio lay on the dirty stone floor. He abandoned it and moved towards the door. Jammed rather than locked, it gave easily when he ran at it with his shoulder. He emerged into the close of one of the tenements and from there into the street.

Blinking in the dull light, he arrived back on the scene at precisely the same moment as the first of the squad cars. The sodden street was littered with bodies and broken banners. Not a striker was to be seen. Wright stumbled towards his colleagues as they emerged from their shiny black cars. On his way he accidentally trod on a set of abandoned bagpipes which let out a low moan of sound. At last the rain had stopped.

The police were slow to recognize the scale of the Clydebank riot, otherwise they would have insisted that the Prime Minister leave by a rear door after his official lunch with the Chamber of Commerce in Glasgow's Merchants' Hall. The Reunionist strikers, kept well back from the Republicans' St Andrew's Day rally, were better informed; they had, after all, planned the ambush. Their blood was up but there was a sinister lack of heckling as Keith Sinclair emerged from the building at the corner of George Square, and started to make his way, escorted by police protection officers, towards his Rover Ecosse. Beside it, his official driver, Ingram, and his Private Secretary, Robert Guthrie, stood waiting. Around him, the Prime Minister could sense that the police, many of them in full riot gear with helmets and visors, were tense and apprehensive. Why were the strikers so silent? It was as if they were waiting for some signal. Then a young constable who was standing closest to the Prime Minister suddenly looked up and over the heads of the dense crowd. The missile, thrown with great strength and accuracy, followed a graceful, curving trajectory against the background of the steel-grey clouds. The constable shouted a warning, *Look out, sir. Behind you!* But it came too late.

Abel Rosenfeld had also been at the lunch in the Merchants' Hall. The forty-one-year-old New Yorker was Strategic Director of the mammoth US multinational, the Unity Corporation, and he had gone more out of duty than enthusiasm to hear Prime Minister Sinclair speak about how his government intended to deal with the economic problems currently facing Scotland. It was, as he had expected, a subdued occasion. Gone was most of the nationalistic bombast he had heard on previous St Andrew's Days since his dynamic and highly demanding chairman, James Fulton, had first sent him over from Manhattan to Scotland. Rosenfeld had been charged with setting up a Unity branch office in the big castle they had bought north of Perth, a strange assignment to give a Jewish boy from the Bronx. He had never been to Europe before and couldn't even find Scotland on the map when he had first been given his mission. He had demurred only slightly when Fulton had summoned him to his New York penthouse office and told him what was intended. But you didn't both argue with Fulton and stay with Unity for long. Abel Rosenfeld was a free agent with no family ties, he liked his job, liked the huge salary hike even more, and had come to Scotland – God, almost two years ago now. It was a challenge, he kept telling himself, and, above all else, Rosenfeld loved challenges.

Rosenfeld also loved conspiracies. He was in many ways a latter-day Machiavelli, who manipulated his carefully tended network of influential contacts with polished cunning. A dedicated professional, he knew whom to speak to and on what terms. Secretive to a fault, he seldom consigned his thoughts to paper, strongly believing in the flexibility of choice, action and opinion that not having things confirmed in writing gave him. He believed in being particularly pliant with his superiors, which some of those who worked closely with him called sycophancy or worse. In fact, Abel Rosenfeld always knew exactly where he was going and what he wanted from life. He was a man for all seasons. Many saw him as effortlessly smooth and overridingly ambitious. If he was the latter, his ambition was less to do with money than with the excitement he got from influencing those more powerful than himself. He had a need to win. He schemed and conspired with purpose and that purpose was, for the time being at least, to do James Fulton's every bidding.

The moment the Prime Minister left the Hall, Rosenfeld pushed through the crowd of fellow guests and darted out after him. Before the lunch he had taken the precaution of finding his way around the building. He knew exactly where to go. Now he raced up a flight of stairs to the next floor and entered the empty office that overlooked that corner of George Square, by Queen Street railway station. He arrived just as the Prime Minister emerged from the main entrance and so had his intended grandstand view of what happened next.

Portable telephone in one hand, he was already talking into it. 'OK,' he yelled. 'What the hell are they waiting for? It's now or never.' He rang off but immediately wished he had not, because he quickly spotted the solitary brick come from the depths of the crowd, and sail soundlessly through the air until, arching downwards, it struck the Prime Minister with great accuracy on the back of the neck. He saw Sinclair's body fall forwards and witnessed the subsequent pandemonium as police and others crowded around the body.

'Shit,' Rosenfeld swore to the empty room. 'This was just a frightener. Last thing we need is a fucking martyr.' He tried to get through on the number he had just called but this time there was no reply. He pressed his face against the window pane, trying to get a better view. At that precise moment, the Prime Minister's Private Secretary, Robert Guthrie, waiting for the ambulance to force its way through the ugly, rioting, chanting crowd, looked up on some instinct and glimpsed Rosenfeld surveying the bloody scene. For some reason that briefest of visions became firmly locked in Guthrie's memory.

A few months previously, Robert Guthrie had been inclined to turn down an invitation to lunch at the restaurant at One Devonshire Gardens in Glasgow. As a senior civil servant and someone as close to the Prime Minister as he was, he was always cautious about leaving himself open to lobbying while being entertained at such luxurious establishments. And lobbying it would be. Why else would Abel Rosenfeld, the Strategic Director of the Unity Corporation, have wanted to meet him if not to build up his web of influence? But a telephone call from Ian Campbell, the Minister of Finance, to the Prime Minister himself encouraging the meeting in the furtherance of Scottish–American commercial relations led to that not disagreeable occasion those few traumatic months ago.

A darkly handsome, medium-built man of thirty-eight, Guthrie's slightly off-putting terseness concealed a shyness of character that was balanced by a conscientious, quietly efficient approach to his work. His immediate colleagues tended to like him when they got to know him; his wry good humour and his lack of pomposity were surprising for someone in such a key position. But others found it difficult to get through to him which, coupled with his tendency to be something of a workaholic, was the probable reason for his never having got married. After gaining a doctorate in company finance at the Harvard Business School, he had intended to find a teaching post at one of the older Scottish universities. But his prospects of making it in academia had been damaged by a hard-hitting exposé he had had published in the *New Statesman* about administrative and financial incompetence at various well-known seats of higher learning. As the world of business had little appeal, he found the civil service a challenging if conventional alternative. It was the perfect environment in which to deploy his increasingly well-honed tactical skills.

His private life was a closed book even to those colleagues who thought they knew him best. They tended to see him socially only at Christmas parties and the like and even then his abstemiousness verged on boring. He was sometimes spotted at theatres and concerts in the company of a slightly older, immaculately turned-out divorcée, the cavalier suggestion being that he was her occasional walker or toy-boy. In truth she was a rich cousin who had a huge mansion in East Lothian, and his real past passion, which had endured for nearly a decade, had been with a married woman whose husband had spent most of his working week with the European Commission in Brussels. Recently however, the man had been posted back to Edinburgh and Guthrie's love life had subsequently faltered, and then died, as the lady in question opted to return to the convenient safety of her marriage. This threw him back on his own devices and particularly to his tendency to work very long hours, something that was extremely easy to do in the hothouse which was the Prime Minister's private office. In by seven-thirty each morning, he was usually still at his desk at the same time each evening. He, after all, was the filter through which everything came to and went from the PM himself. There was nothing that Guthrie did not know of the views of Ministers and civil servants as they fought for their budgets, their policies, or for the promotion and the patronage that was in Keith Sinclair's sphere of power.

As the Janus-like keeper of the outer office, Guthrie also controlled all access to the Prime Minister. He kept his appointments diary and the confidential record when there were meetings with Ministers, and he listened in on his special extension to all official and most unofficial telephone conversations with the great, the good and the not so good. He combined these reactive roles with skilled use of his innate negotiating talents. He knew that power and influence were very different commodities. In real life, few, even the Prime Minister himself, had much *power*: his boss's decisions always had to take into account the views of his Cabinet colleagues and the electorate at large. But influence was another matter: knowing what to say to whom and when, was, as his lunchtime host Abel Rosenfeld also knew, the key to getting a message or a strategy through the Byzantine network that was the decision-making process of Scottish public life. Robert Guthrie had developed this process to a high art form. He knew instinctively what to say, when to make a phone call, when to go public with his views, when to hold his peace. He was seen to be indispensable: he knew who really got things done and who were mere title-holding place-fillers. He was the Supreme Mandarin.

When he really relaxed, he relaxed alone. He would go right away from the inward-looking, incestuous world of Scottish politics, climb into his one extravagance of life – his BMW – and drive three hours westwards to a modest mountainside croft he had bought some years ago, on a side road between

Lochgilphead and Crinan in Argyllshire. There, in that tiny, three-roomed building, which he was slowly restoring and improving, he would unwind. Gone were business suits and ties. He would put on his oldest clothes and take out hammers and nails and saws and put politics and strategies and other people out of his mind, as he gradually replaced rotting doors and windowframes, rebuilt open fireplaces with stones from the surrounding mountainside and, with only minimum help from a local plumber, put in a basic hot water and central heating system. He took no one to that croft. There, by choice, he was alone.

But that late-autumn day, in that Glasgow restaurant, he was at his most sociable. The two men had met briefly before, and so were able to recognize each other at once. They sipped spiced-up tomato juice in one of the hotel's elegant drawing rooms before lunch, then were ushered through to a discreet corner of the dining room. There, largely hidden by tubs full of flowers and heavy hanging drapes from the view of their fellow diners – a famous conductor in one corner and the chairman of Scotland's best-known malt whisky distillers in another – they began to size each other up.

As with all the most effective lobby lunches – Guthrie had guessed correctly – no business whatsoever was discussed until the meal was almost over. They reached the coffee stage. Neither man had drunk anything other than mineral water during the meal, and neither accepted the offer of a cognac at the end. It was not that they were particularly wary of each other nor of the carelessness that could be injected into confidential conversations if alcohol interferes; it was simply not in either of their career-conscious characters to drink at lunchtime.

Guthrie, with his experience of living in the United States, was not unfamiliar with nor unsympathetic to the cynical approach to life that Rosenfeld appeared to adopt. He assumed, correctly, that they would hit it off well enough. Their conversation ranged over theatre and music and the state of the contemporary novel, subjects on which they had remarkably similar, old-fashioned views. They talked lightly of that strange cultural phenomenon, those deep-seated Edinburgh–Glasgow rivalries, which, Guthrie argued, had actually increased since Independence.

'Kinda crazy,' Rosenfeld smiled. 'Came as quite a shock when I first got here: thirty-nine miles apart, yet totally different life-styles, attitudes, humour, sociability –'

'Historic jealousies. You must have your inter-city rivalries too.' Guthrie sipped at his coffee.

'Sure . . . but here it's like war at times, without the fighting.'

'There's even been a bit of that,' Guthrie shrugged. 'Been to any football games?'

'Keep my viewing of violence to TV,' Rosenfeld laughed agreeably. 'How do you explain the politics of it?'

Guthrie paused thoughtfully before replying. 'Before we moved from devolution to full independence, I used to argue that Scotland wouldn't be able to stand the strain. We'd fall apart. Our regions are all so varied. Way back in the days of Burns and Scott there were two nationalities: highlanders and lowlanders. It's even more distinct now. North and south of the Highland line; the east–west divide, and just ask the Orcadians and the Shetlanders, or anyone in the Borders for that matter, what they think of the current Edinburgh Government.'

'Every nation has a natural distrust of central government,' Rosenfeld prompted. 'France, Germany, the US –'

'I was wrong in many other ways,' Guthrie went on. 'I thought a majority of the trusty citizens of Edinburgh would oppose the whole Independence–Republican movement, and that Glasgow would be rock-solid for it. Look how it's worked out.'

'Not sure it's the traditional people of Edinburgh who are pro,' said Rosenfeld perceptively. 'The ones I meet with at least. With the Scottish National Assembly and a hugely expanded Civil Service came the legions of hangers-ons. Your capital has become a magnet for those who want Scotland to succeed as an independent nation. That's where power resides . . .'

Guthrie nodded his head in agreement. 'True enough. Leaving the Glaswegians, and those in Aberdeen, Inverness and Tayside, wondering what went wrong. You've seen it: that's where the Reunionist revival is strongest.' He paused as a waitress approached to refill their coffee cups.

'I've been here a while, but because I'm an American who's really interested in what's going on here, people still tend to tell me what they really think.' Rosenfeld threw Guthrie a slightly perplexed look. 'If I were a social historian, one thing I'd be studying would be this strange new Reunionist Alliance. How do you explain the common cause shared between the traditional landowners, the professional ascendancy – the lawyers, financiers and so on – and the trade union activists, the left-wing cadres and, above all, the industrial belt's unemployed?'

'Is that so strange?' Guthrie responded. 'Self-interest, historically, always produces odd bedfellows. The political spectrum, the traditional left–right, doesn't run in a straight line. It's egg-shaped. Extremes meet round the back. That's why the French wisely seat their deputies in the National Assembly in a semi-circle. We Scots have tried to follow suit rather than aping the Westminster model of two opposing sides confronting each other, House of Commons style, with a huge variety of attitudes on the cross-benches. No . . .' He paused and carefully selected a chocolate from a small plateful on the table in front of him. 'I see nothing at all peculiar in some of our grand Dukes coming out, as they have done recently, in support of the strikers. Scottish landowners may have driven their crofters into exile in previous generations, but now they see it's in Scotland's best interests to get work for as many as possible. And that, to many of them, can only mean going back into some sort of reunion with the rest of the United Kingdom.'

'It was a good move by these old landlords – the Clearances, I mean,' Rosenfeld said. 'Been reading up on them. Historically good for the US, Canada and Australia I guess. Otherwise we wouldn't have had the Carnegies, nor even my own boss, James Fulton. He's strong on his Scottish roots. American Scots like him have always taken a lead in driving our country forward. I, as an unbelieving Jew, understand the Scottish diaspora only too well. Fulton's got a tough bunch of colleagues on the Unity board, and a couple of them are also of Scots descent. His vice-chairman, Carlyle, is tough. Really tough. And mean. Grandfather came from Dundee, I believe. He's good...' Rosenfeld added approvingly.

'We've always exported too much talent,' said Guthrie vaguely. 'At one time I thought I might emigrate, even if it was only to London...' He laughed. 'That was a few years back, when I didn't like the way Scotland was drifting.'

'You weren't an ardent Nationalist?'

'We civil servants are impartial.' Guthrie knew it sounded a touch too grand, so he softened it with a grin.

'The hell you are,' Rosenfeld laughed back. 'On the surface: apolitical. Underneath: more politically adept than anyone. Unless Scottish civil servants are different from all others I've come across,' he teased.

'You know what I mean,' Guthrie continued in a serious tone. 'I'm into good government, whatever the party. Who is going to be best for the efficient running of the country? Who is going to be the most effective leader of a determined team?'

'Civil servants run things, whoever's in power,' Rosenfeld responded with a shrug. 'I bet you tell Mr Sinclair what to think.'

'Not true. Perhaps it's because we're so newly independent. We can try to guide Ministers away from their more absurd policies, but in the end they get their way...' He hesitated as if wondering whether to pick up the bait and explain Keith Sinclair's strategies.

'Which is why you're in the mess you're in, is that what you're saying?' Rosenfeld prompted.

'That would be disloyal...'

'But accurate...'

'There are lots of other factors.' Guthrie became defensive. 'Not just political ones, which have led to what we call, rather pompously, our "national predicament".'

'Which is why you may, proud nation that you are, need more outside help,' Rosenfeld said quietly. 'A nation at war with itself cannot see the fire for the flames. It needs arbitration and support.'

Guthrie did not follow up on the remark straight away but asked, 'How are Unity's relations with the US Embassy in Edinburgh?'

'Formal. Polite. Inconsequential.' Rosenfeld shrugged disparagingly.

'Can you explain?'

'We have little to do with them.' Rosenfeld was vague. 'Steer clear. My reading of their function is that they're still little more than an adjunct to our embassy in London. Grosvenor Square makes all the running as far as Washington and the State Department are concerned. The Ambassador here is OK as far as he goes. The American who really wants watching is William Torrance.'

'Really?' Guthrie was surprised. Torrance was the grandly titled Special Commissioner of the Federation of American Caledonian Societies, and was resident in Glasgow. He'd met the man at parties once or twice, but presumed his interests were more of the cultural, Highland dancing, mod-attending variety. Torrance always seemed to be in the company of kilted Scottish clan chiefs and not particularly concerned with the political or business life of the country.

'Don't be mistaken. He's shrewd. He's a potential power for good or ill as far as Scots–American links are concerned. He's got quite worked up about some half-baked ideas of how to help Scotland. I've tried to sound him out a bit, but he's not my type. 'Fraid we didn't hit it off.'

'He's got ideas on how America might help?' Guthrie prompted, making a mental note to mention this part of his conversation to the Prime Minister later. He glanced at his watch. It was nearly two-thirty but the conversation was developing well. It gave him a new perspective on a lot of the problems that were piled high on his desk back at St Andrew's House. They could wait. He might deal with them more effectively if he let his lunch with Rosenfeld run on a little longer. 'What did you mean a minute ago when you talked about us needing more 'outside help?' Now he chose to follow up on the remark.

'Maybe, if you found it useful, I could explain how I see the various strands of potential Scottish–US support?' Rosenfeld looked across the table questioningly.

'The truth?' asked Guthrie. 'The transatlantic view of us is surely like looking through the wrong end of a telescope.'

'Right in a way,' Rosenfeld responded. 'It's like that remark about how you worry less about what people think of you when you realize how little they do . . . think about you, that is.' He laughed. 'In the great scheme of things, there is one diplomatic service officer in the State Department in Washington who deals with the former United Kingdom, plus Ireland, plus a lot else besides. You are, to official America, if you don't mind me being frank, a very small dot on the world map. The US Embassy in Edinburgh is a remote outpost, only of significance in terms of what it costs the US taxpayer to maintain it.'

'Blunt, but doubtless true,' said Guthrie reflectively.

'OK. That's the official side. But there are other elements: let me spell out the two that *really* matter, on the unofficial side . . .'

'The Federation of American Caledonian Societies being one?' Guthrie asked.

'Right. A loose-knit umbrella group that pretends to tie together the misty-eyed Scottish diaspora . . . You really don't mind the facts, do you?' Rosenfeld paused as Guthrie shook his head. 'They are the ethnics. Some of the earliest Caledonian groups in the States were, admittedly, like labour unions or friendly societies, hard-nosed organizations set up to protect their fellow Scottish immigrants against threats to their livelihoods from other invading tribes – Irish, Germans, Hungarians – in the bitter, highly fluctuating job markets of the new world. Now, however, the Federation claims to represent the unrepresentable: everything from the numerous Caledonian Societies – fifteen thousand of them at a last count – plus Clan Societies, St Andrew's Societies, Burns' Clubs, Highland Games organizations, Scottish Country Dance groups, even whisky appreciation societies.' He laughed again. 'Trying to tie that lot together is an impossibility. Deep down, Torrance is the first to realize it. He's an ambitious and energetic fellow, his heart's in the right place but he's not going to get very far the way the Federation is presently structured. We're seeing how we can help –'

'We?' Guthrie interrupted.

'Which brings me to the second unofficial element that really matters: the Unity Corporation. We've offered the Federation a bit of organizational support, if they want it. Speaking personally, I doubt if it's worth the effort for us. You see, Robert, in terms of serious financial backing for Scotland, you can forget the US Administration: you don't even feature at the bottom end of the Richter scale of their attention and the Federation is largely a bunch of hopeless do-gooders, whatever Torrance may be dreaming up. No, Robert,' Rosenfeld smiled, 'I don't know how much you know about the Unity Corporation . . .'

'Not much,' responded Guthrie. 'I thought, when you talked about external help, you were on about the IMF or the World Bank, or yet more assistance from the European Community . . .'

'Not my field,' said Rosenfeld softly, still smiling. 'I'm talking about us giving you substantial private sector assistance.'

'A multinational company helping a country?' Guthrie was dismissive without being impolite.

'Not an absurd scenario. We're a very big company and growing fast. Chemicals, construction, distribution, shipping, oil. You name it, we're there. Our turnover, it may shock you to know, is not all that short of Scotland's total gross domestic product . . .'

'Goodness . . .' Guthrie was impressed, despite himself.

'And, if I may say so,' Rosenfeld continued, 'Unity, thankfully, doesn't have your magnitude of debt burden, nor the continuing strain on resources that you have in order to pay out on national insurance, unemployment benefit, medicare, substandard housing . . .'

'Don't tell me,' Guthrie sighed. It was the sour bread and butter of his daily work. 'So, explain,' he asked.

'We're in the process of developing an exciting new global

strategy,' Rosenfeld began cautiously. 'It's well advanced but I can't share the details of it with you yet. Mr Fulton is keen. It could involve Scotland in a very significant way.'

'You've been using your cheque book quite a bit over here already.' Guthrie had noted the frequent press reports of Unity's interest in and purchase of a number of Scottish retailing and construction companies.

'It could be just the beginning. We see a mutual advantage in our expanding in Scotland. We've some hard, well-formulated ideas and the cash and resources to back them up, not like the amateursville ideas that are coming out of Torrance and the Fed. Mr Fulton may want to come over sometime soon, once we've finally honed our strategy. Would a meeting with Prime Minister Sinclair be a possibility?'

It was the first piece of hard business in the whole lunch. Guthrie felt no need to be cautious. He was growing to like Rosenfeld. He knew what the PM's reaction would be. 'I'm sure Mr Sinclair would be more than happy to meet Mr Fulton,' he said. 'Give me plenty of warning, will you? His diary tends to get very full, a long way in advance.'

Rosenfeld summoned a waiter and paid the bill. It was a quarter past three. 'I don't usually take such a long lunch hour,' he said apologetically.

'I don't usually take lunch.' Guthrie smiled back. 'Sandwiches and a glass of milk at my desk is my usual fare. Thanks very much. Most enjoyable. And interesting.'

'Must do it again soon.'

'Glad to,' said Guthrie, meaning it.

It was only then that the slightest shadow was cast over the occasion. As they stood briefly outside the hotel before getting into their cars – Guthrie had driven himself, while Rosenfeld had a new Mercedes with a uniformed chauffeur – the American turned and said, 'If there's anything I can help you personally with,' he was still smiling, 'I know the civil service pay has been frozen for years now, do please get in touch. We at Unity are always ready to be helpful . . .'

They parted company, shaking hands warmly. In the quiet of his car as he turned onto the M8 motorway back to Edinburgh, Guthrie reflected on Rosenfeld's last remark. Had he misunderstood or had a discreet opening been offered to him? Was there a hint of a possible bribe? Then he shrugged and put it out of his mind. He was not a moralizer. It was lonely on top of integrity mountain. Most big companies had slush funds; they were, if anything, merely a routine if corrupt part of international corporate life. In any event the whole Unity idea seemed to have exciting potential. He'd liked a lot of what he had heard from Rosenfeld. Public–private sector initiatives were, he had long believed, the only way forward for Scotland. He'd monitor the idea carefully from now on and give it a firm push where he could.

Thirteen-year-old Piggy McNeish was playing on his own. He wouldn't normally choose to, but his one close school friend, Boffin Humbie, was away on holiday on the Costa del Sol and most of the other children around would only spend their time teasing and tormenting him. He hated school, he hated the holidays, he hated his nickname, he hated his father, which was why he had built a secret hide high up on the hillside, amid a small clump of woods overlooking the loch. Each day he would disappear straight after breakfast, after his father and mother had left for work, taking with him a substantial lunchtime picnic and a battered copy of *Jane's Fighting Ships*, to climb, gasping and perspiring, to his hidden eyrie. Piggy was, as might be guessed from his nickname, more than a little overweight.

That cloudless day at first promised to be very warm. He thought of taking his shirt off but he had always been wary of exposing his chubby white flesh just in case anyone should see him and laugh. He realized it would be difficult if not impossible for that to happen, concealed as he was in his hide with its walls camouflaged by broken branches and carefully interwoven with dried grass, but he took no chances. Piggy had two special items of kit there, buried in a hole at one side of the hide. Wrapped in plastic Tesco shopping bags, to protect them against the rain, were some old WD wartime binoculars, which his dearly-missed grandfather had given him two years earlier, just before he died. Then there was a school jotter with lined pages in which he kept a log recording every time he saw a ship or small craft pass by the head of the loch where it met the wider expanse of the Firth of Clyde beyond.

He wrote each entry with care: the date, the time, the direction in which the vessel was sailing, the type – tanker, fishing boat, tramp, tugboat, pleasure steamer, yacht, and occasionally, to his especial excitement, a naval vessel. When the latter appeared, he eagerly consulted *Jane's Fighting Ships*. If physically he was not well-endowed, he, like his friend Boffin, had an alert mind and he usually managed to accurately distinguish frigate from minesweeper from fishery protection vessel. Sometimes, as the peak of excitement, he spotted submarines, some with just their conning-towers exposed, some gliding like sinister grey cigars on the equally grey waters of the loch, their presence given away only by the white of the bow wash. Piggy had made submarines his speciality. He knew them all, supplemented by information from Boffin's father who had once worked at Faslane and had given his son a list of the recognition numbers of those ships that usually patrolled the peaceful waters of the Clyde.

That particular day was fairly boring. There was little marine activity of any interest. But later the weather changed and heavy black clouds built up in the western sky. Piggy decided it was time to pack up, but dallied a while longer, reluctant to abandon the security of his hideout in exchange for an uncertain evening with his quarrelsome parents. The sky darkened considerably, the wind picked up and troubled the surface water of the loch. So it was fortuitous that, with the last sweep of his ancient binoculars before putting them away in the safety of their plastic bag, he caught sight of the small submarine turret, as it briefly appeared then vanished below the surface of the waves. There were two things wrong with the sighting: one was that he did not immediately recognize the class. That upset him. It had a minute conning-tower and a surrounding superstructure which

21

he was certain he had never seen before. The other oddity was the course it appeared to be taking: not up the secure centre of the loch, but at right angles to the shore, as if wishing to destruct itself against the cliffs and the rocks beneath. He caught one last sight of it, memorizing how it looked as it disappeared beneath the grey foam-flecked waves.

Late that night, in the partial safety of his tiny bedroom, Piggy McNeish scanned the relevant pages of *Jane's Fighting Ships*. No British class of submarine matched the superstructure as he remembered it. Perhaps, he thought with brief excitement, it was some rogue Russian submarine, there to threaten Scotland's security. But again nothing matched. The closest he came to it was one of the American mini-types, though they were all meant to be serving in US waters and not on this side of the Atlantic, which was away out of their normal range. And what of its strange route? Piggy thought about it, then put it out of his mind. After all, as his father kept telling him, he was far from infallible.

2

PM in coma – death toll rising

Over one hundred and fifty Republican and
Reunionist demonstrators were arrested in the
George Square area of the city today, following the
brutal massacre in Clydebank. No specific charges
have yet been brought against anyone for the attack
which has left the Prime Minister, Mr Keith Sinclair,
in a coma. He is in intensive care, in the Royal
Infirmary in Glasgow.

(Reuters tape)

For a crisis meeting it began remarkably placidly. The Commissioner of Police, Sir Jimmy Mactaggart, took his tea without
milk or sugar. He had it served in a glass, tea leaves carefully excluded by a little silver strainer, so that it took on the
appearance of a pale malt whisky. It was an affectation in
peculiar contrast with his short-back-and-sides appearance,
his clipped military moustache, his abrasive manner and apparent
lack of any of life's subtleties. The others present were
served with instant coffee, so perhaps the Commissioner had a
point.

It took place in an agreeable office on the third floor of the
new Police Headquarters, with a bright, open outlook down to
what the Edinburgh city planners had left of Princes Street. The
Permanent Secretary, the Under-Secretary in charge of the division and the Secretary to the Cabinet were already there talking

to the Commissioner. Robert Guthrie hovered in the background. By rank he was the most junior man in the room but he was one of the most influential.

They all stood up as the imposing, statesmanlike figure of Sir Alexander MacDowall, the Minister of Internal Affairs, paced into the room.

'The score?' he asked impassively as he took his seat at the head of the table.

'Five dead. At least twenty seriously injured, Minister,' said the Commissioner grimly.

They were all quiet for a moment. It was by far the worst incident yet. MacDowall turned abruptly to the matter in hand. 'Police morale, Jimmy? What's it like?' These busy, intelligent men all wanted to go on talking and analysing the reasons for the riot. MacDowall saw little point. It had happened, they knew why, that was an end to it.

The Commissioner launched into his usual diatribe about crime and punishment. MacDowall saw his mistake. He should have set the agenda and tone of the meeting, introducing his own ideas from the outset.

The Commissioner was brashly confident. The police were ninety-nine percent loyal to authority; the only problem, in his view, was the political one of ensuring that that authority did not change. That was not his problem, he added impertinently. One percent was unreliable because some Section Houses were under direct pressure from local Reunionist groups. They and their families felt threatened and a lot of the younger officers doubtlessly secretly sympathized as well. The Commissioner emphasized that he had things well in hand. He had already appointed a special Review Committee within his personnel department to investigate cases of insubordination and to cross-post drastically where necessary. Two constabulary subdistricts had already been broken up and restaffed.

The Police Commissioner sat back in the heavy leather arm-chair and sipped at his glass. To most of the others in the room he appeared far too complacent. Special Branch reports suggested much less contentment in the Section Houses. Would the Minister burst his self-satisfied bubble?

Leaning forward across the polished mahogany table, Mac-Dowall pursed his lips into what might have been intended as a smile. Under the shock of flowing grey hair his rimless half-moon glasses, at once fashionable and unfashionable, perched themselves precisely in the middle of his long drooping nose. They were glasses to be looked over rather than through and they symbolized the man. Tall, imperious, Sir Alexander MacDowall, the sole tenant of his office since Independence, was a man who ran the country more than any other. MacDowall, the awe-inspiring old soldier of the Scottish independence movement, whom the press had dubbed the Father of the Nation, had held on to office long after lesser men would have retired because it was seen to be his by right and no one felt strong or sure enough to take it away from him. He was a man of whom the vapid Finance Minister, Ian Campbell, had suggested in an unguarded moment that underneath that cold exterior there beat a heart of ice. It was not entirely true: underneath that glacial intellect, warmth and compassion could sometimes be detected.

'We are making dangerous assumptions about morale by assuming present conditions will prevail in the future,' he began remotely. Guthrie recognized the tone and foresaw that the Police Commissioner would take offence later when he realized the veiled criticisms behind the pedantic words. But not yet; Mac-Dowall was being diplomatically obscure.

'It may be,' he went on, 'that the five – I'm sorry, did you say one – percent discontent within the Force can be successfully dissipated. But, as you yourself recognize, Jimmy, the political climate is highly volatile. We are in a rapidly deteriorating situation. We need to formulate some tougher measures to ensure that there is no more violence like this. All agreed on that?' He looked round enquiringly as he always did in Cabinet. Seldom did he reap a dissenting voice.

He did this time. 'I'm only a simple policeman,' began the Police Commissioner.

Guthrie watched MacDowall's lips mouthing, 'Quite so.' No one else noticed. MacDowall was too used to bullying the Cabinet; he should show more discretion at a time like this, Guthrie thought to himself. Widely held to be a shrewd and percipient judge of character, Guthrie was always a welcome addition to any senior civil service selection board; for years he had scrupulously kept, weeded out and promoted names from a list of the important figures of Scotland which was kept in the Prime Minister's office to feed the boards, committees, institutions and other quangos that make a significant contribution to the good governance of almost every modern democratic state. That was why, when he watched his hero Sir Alexander – yes, he admitted that was what Sir Alexander was to him – he admired so much about the old man. Pedantic to a fault, sparse in style, over-discreet, infuriatingly cautious at times, he was hugely courageous and of great moral conviction. He was, in the Scottish Government, the only one in the Grand Master class, even with his little failings.

'I have the utmost trust in the good sense and discipline of the Force,' the Commissioner continued. 'But we need strong political backing. We need more resources, men and equipment.'

'I fully subscribe to that sentiment,' MacDowall retorted, 'if only we, and the Treasury, had the money.'

'If I could break in . . .' When Robert Guthrie spoke, he was always listened to, since he was known to have the fullest confidence of his boss. Those more critical of Keith Sinclair had on occasion suggested that most of the PM's thinking and attitudes in fact emanated from his cleverly determined Private Secretary. 'I know that the PM, when he's ready to take charge again, will want to be sure of one thing: in the worse scenario, with a general breakdown of law and order, could we cope? There's precious little of an army left to provide back-up for the police, and calling out the Volunteer Reserve would, I'm sure everyone agrees, be foolish in the circumstances.' The Volunteer Reservists were Reunionists to a man and would only inflame the situation.

'That's a political decision,' replied the Police Commissioner smugly. 'Discipline will break down elsewhere – in the civil service for example – before it does with us.' He glared with hostility at the officials as he spoke. 'To answer your question, Mr Guthrie: we can cope – especially if the Prime Minister arms us.'

'You know that's impossible,' MacDowall broke in with growing irritation. His long-standing lack of respect for the Commissioner was beginning to show.

The Commissioner stared back coldly, and then, as if deliberately trying to provoke him, went on. 'All things are possible, Minister. If only we had been armed this past year, a lot of things might have been very, very different.' He paused. 'Take today's riot. Five is a hell of a lot of dead.'

He was making a direct challenge to MacDowall's well-known opposition to giving the police more weapons. Everyone looked at the Minister, who flushed and started to erupt. Guthrie saw the clash coming. He chose the moment carefully. Moving his chair abruptly forward he upset a coffee pot as if by accident. In the general confusion, everyone gradually subsided. But from then on the meeting was a dead loss. Each official said his bit, but, in the end, nothing was agreed except that they should meet on a daily basis until the crisis abated.

MacDowall and Guthrie left the meeting together. 'Accident or deliberate?' the Minister asked the younger man.

'Sir?' Guthrie responded innocently.

'You're a bright lad, Robert. Too smart for your own bloody good sometimes.' MacDowall paused as they reached the front entrance of the Police Headquarters. A duty policeman saluted them as they passed. 'You knocked that coffee over to stop me blowing my top with that pompous git . . .' He looked at Guthrie with a half-smile. 'Anyway . . . what's the latest on the PM?'

'Conscious, as you know, Minister. Complains he's got no feeling in his legs. Doctors are more worried than they will admit. He's on heavy sedation.'

'The press?'

'We're holding the line: slight concussion and he'll be as right as rain in a couple of days.'

'I can go and see him?'

'No, sir. Intensive care. I haven't even been allowed –'

'Nora . . . his wife . . . how is she taking it?'

Guthrie dropped his voice to a whisper. They were outside the building now, waiting for the official cars to turn up. 'All these hours since the attack and we . . . er . . . haven't been able to find her. So unless she sees it on TV or listens to the radio news . . .'

'Doesn't know? You're joking.' MacDowall was genuinely horrified. 'Where the hell is she?'

'I don't want to make a big thing of it.' Guthrie hesitated. 'There is no way we can alert the police that she –'

'What the hell are you on about, Guthrie?' the old man suddenly exploded. 'The Prime Minister of Scotland is seriously injured. And you tell me that his wife doesn't know yet. *And* you don't want to make a big deal.' The Minister was outraged.

'Sir, please,' Guthrie pleaded. 'I wouldn't be any good at my job if a certain amount of gossip didn't come my way. I think I know where she could be. It's a long shot. Are you sure you want to know?'

The telephone on the bedside table rang and kept ringing. Nora Sinclair, naked, heavy, pendulous, sat up in bed and looked down at the sweating man beneath her. 'You said no one knew you were here,' she said accusingly. They had been interrupted at the peak of their passion. 'Damn, damn, damn,' she said. The telephone kept ringing. They were going to have to answer it.

'Nobody should know,' said the man, reaching across reluctantly and picking up the receiver. 'Hello,' he said cautiously. He did not give his name. He listened in silence for a moment, then handed the phone to Nora. He was white and shaking. 'Robert Guthrie . . . it's for you,' he whispered, holding his hand over the mouth piece. 'How the fuck did he know?'

By the main gates of the National Assembly building, a news vendor's placard carried the latest unemployment figures, the highest since the thirties. Another billboard for that morning's *Herald* proclaimed PM'S CONDITION: LATEST in huge letters. At the emergency Cabinet meeting, the suggestion that both stories be played down until after the debate had met with little support. The Secretary to the Cabinet put up a shocked defence of open government and democratic practice and that was the end of it. One or two Ministers had briefly argued that there were occasions such as this where the 'national interest' clause in the constitution could well be utilized, but it was decided to delete any reference to this in the final Cabinet minutes.

The meeting continued as it had begun: not one of them was certain what to do next. Even MacDowall was lacking much of his usual decisiveness. He had brought Guthrie to the meeting with him, he explained, so that when the PM regained his strength, his Private Secretary would be fully up to date on the Cabinet's thinking. Besides, just before the riot, Guthrie had already been detailed by Sinclair to travel to New York to explore the potential of a proposal that had, as Rosenfeld had indicated it would, come from the American Federation of Caledonian Societies. Even Ian Campbell, the Minister of Finance, who had been last to arrive at the meeting and might have been expected to argue that this was a task for the Treasury rather than for the Prime Minister's office, surprisingly re-approved Guthrie's mission with a cursory and dismissive nod.

As an opener, Guthrie was instructed to tell the Ministers about the meeting which the Prime Minister, with him in attendance, had had the previous Friday. While privately sharing the views of Rosenfeld about the amateur nature of the Federation and its ability to deliver anything worthwhile, Guthrie reported without comment that William Torrance, the Special Commissioner of the Federation, had, after the initial pleasantries, indicated that the Federation was ready and willing to try and drum up massive financial help for Scotland. The man was obviously trying to be helpful but whether he was capable of delivering anything worthwhile was another matter. Sensing this, the PM had deliberately played for time. Guthrie reported to the Cabinet that Sinclair's non-committal attitude had obviously unsettled Torrance. The PM, not wishing to offend him, had then become more positive and had said how much he appreciated the Federation's enormous generosity. He was confident his Cabinet colleagues would be equally encouraged. As a measure of its importance, he volunteered to send his Private Secretary to New York to meet with the Chairman of the Federation, Liam Anderson, to see how matters could be progressed.

When Guthrie had finished, MacDowall cleverly steered the Cabinet as it debated how the offer should be handled. On the face of it, the proposal was indeed generous. Via Torrance, Anderson was offering both to launch a major fundraising campaign amongst the Scottish diaspora in the New World and to provide backing by placing a major Scottish Government Bond Issue on the New York Stock Market. This might not, the Americans accepted, solve all the country's long-term problems but, taken together, such measures would help overcome the current economic crisis.

At the end of an acrimonious two hours, the Cabinet remained deeply divided, with Guthrie privately tending to agree with Campbell who warned his colleagues that the Treasury was far from convinced that the Fed's idea would do much good even in the short term. 'Holding out a begging bowl in the US is not the way to solve Scotland's basic problems,' Campbell argued plausibly. 'It makes us look even weaker and more dependent than we are already.' MacDowall, by contrast, said that Scotland was not in a position to look gift horses in the mouth. In any event, Anderson and the Federation, who in many ways were more Scots than the Scots, would be deeply offended if the Cabinet turned the offer down flat. The Cabinet's eventual decision was a holding one – they bought time. They would await Guthrie's report on his return from the States. He was instructed to find out what timescale Anderson envisaged and what strings were attached to an operation of this scale before they decided whether to go ahead or not.

As Guthrie left the meeting intending to return to his office to prepare for his trip, he was handed a message by a secretary: Prime Minister Sinclair was conscious and was demanding to see him.

Another crisis, another place. But the setting and the style could not have been more different. The skyscraper, a gleaming tower between Park and Madison in New York, was faced with huge sheets of mirrored glass. Those inside could watch the world go by; those outside saw mere reflections of themselves or, at street level, the suite of long black limousines parked nose to tail by the sidewalk.

Inside, the huge foyer stretched seven storeys high with a magnificent feeling of space and light. Through the walkways, garlanded with hanging plants at each level, walked efficient, well-dressed men with firm missions, and immaculate women, coiffeured, manicured and doubtless smelling to perfection. The apex of corporate America was going about its business with dedication, energy and verve.

The decor in the penthouse boardroom had been selected by its very expensive interior decorators to blend with the stunning skyline views in order to promote a sense of tranquillity and reason. Judging by the mood of the current meeting and the tension felt by each of the ten men and the one woman secretary, who was feverishly trying to keep a record of the occasion, that attempt, for today at least, had been a costly failure.

The tall, cold figure of the Chairman of Unity Corporation Inc., James Fulton, was, as was his wont, quoting his favourite American politician, old Joe Kennedy, JFK's father.

'Politics is like war. Business is like war. That was Joe's belief. That's what made him so successful.' Fulton's words spilled out in a deep, gravelly voice. 'Sometimes I don't think you guys get this. You're too nice, too fuckin' amenable. I have had enough.'

Fulton got up so suddenly from his chair at the head of the long rosewood board table that it fell backwards and crashed on the floor. Everyone jumped at the sound. Towering over his colleagues, he looked at them, one by one, then went on.

'Gentlemen, this is war. The gloves are off. No more Mr Nice Guys. You understand me?' He looked down at them all in turn until he had captured nine nods or signs of agreement. Then he righted his chair and sat down again. 'OK. Joe Kennedy was a bastard. People hated him. But he was clever and ruthless. Everything he got, he bought. Know what he said?' Faces stared blankly back at him. When James Fulton was in this sort of mood the last thing he wanted was answers. He demanded silent, uninterrupted attention.

'Know what Joe said? And God did he have it right. He said it took three things to win. First, money. Second, money. Third, money. And he won. Just like we're going to, gentlemen.' Fulton stood again and paced over to a sidetable to pour himself a glass of mineral water. Every eye in the room watched his move, waiting expectantly for what was to come. They all owed their jobs to Fulton. Even the hardest men round the table would not have dared to disagree. They had been summoned to hear Fulton's grand strategy, as to Moses with the tablets. His idea of a good management team was one that did only and precisely what he said. James Fulton was far from unique in hard-nosed corporate America. There were a lot of very rich hard men around, running huge companies, who would not have disagreed with much of what he said. In terms of single-minded endeavour and an unflinching belief in himself, he had few equals. But even his most violent detractors admitted that it was Fulton, above all, who had built the Unity Corporation into what it was today.

'You know,' he continued, fixing his colleagues with a flesh-stripping glare, 'I kinda sympathize with some of these Waco siege types, free rangers, anarchists, who take on the State and Federal authorities. America never got great with too much government. We need fuckin' permission to breathe these days. The Washington administration is sucking Unity's lifeblood away, not just taxing the shit out of us, but regulating us right out of business. Ever since that damned Hulse City incident. One kid and a fuckin' dog, for crissake. Each state where we have anything going is after us, waiting on the outcome of the New

32

Jersey case, licking their lips, salivating in anticipation of vast damages. The politically correct environmental lobby will be the death of American industry. I didn't build this great company from nothing over these twenty-five years to see those bleeding-heart regulators steal it from me. They've got a great conspiracy against us. I am not going to stick it any longer, gentlemen.'

Now, alarmingly, Fulton had begun to parade around the table like some despotic schoolmaster with a class of errant pupils. Some turned to watch his every movement, others stared straight ahead, nervous of what would come. With Fulton, cruelty and anger were seldom far apart.

'They want pawns to knock around? They're not going to get them from me. They want us to get down on our knees and beg for mercy? That's not me either. Those no good Washington lickspittles can go shaft themselves. And we, gentlemen, we're going to make the move. Where money talks, truth can damn well stay silent. We're going to call in all our friends with all their chips. They have favours to repay.'

'Cayman or Bermuda, James?' To everyone's astonishment the oldest member of the board, an old friend of Fulton's father so it was said, dared to interrupt the great man's flow.

'No, Luigi. Not Cayman, not Chile, not Manila either. We're going a lot better than that.' Fulton wheeled round to the old man, anger burning in his eyes. Then suddenly he laughed. 'Climate may not suit old men like you quite so well. You wait and see.'

3

Government planning massive tax rise

In the continued absence of Prime Minister Sinclair, the top rate of income tax is to be raised to 75% under plans being considered by Ministers according to documents seen by the *Scotsman*.

The Social Democratic Coalition Government's plan was attacked last night by Republican Party leaders, who claimed it would drastically reduce the incentives available to Scottish management and endanger the prospects for more domestic investment from the United States and the Far East. A Government spokesman refused to confirm that the proposal was being discussed, dismissing the report as pure speculation. He said the increasing number of US companies opening up in Scotland showed the high regard foreign companies still had for Scottish skills. One example was the Unity Corporation's rapidly growing stake in the personal computer and semiconductor market, following its purchase of the Nippon Data site at Bathgate.

A statement from the Reunionist Party said the proposal was yet another sign of the failure of four years of go-it-alone policies . . .

(Lead item in the *Scotsman*)

A combination of injury and the sedatives he had been given caused Keith Sinclair to drift in and out of consciousness. He remembered little but did have a brief period of lucidity marred only by his wife Nora's visit. Surrounded by doctors, she came in, wearing suitable clothes and a matching expression of deep concern. She was particularly alert to the presence of press cameras, as the next day's newspapers would demonstrate. She was always especially nice to the journalists she met, courting their editors assiduously, which was doubtless one reason why her dangerously indiscreet social life was almost never reported in the newspapers. As always, editors, particularly tabloid editors, were ready to expose the follies of the rich and famous, but they too had their cronies and, as in the days of the Government in Westminster, some scandals, well-known to a select few in public life, never saw the light of day as far as the mass of people were concerned. This veil drawn over intimate aspects of Nora's life was greatly helped by the fact that the Scottish Parliament, only last year, had passed a far-reaching privacy law which now prevented the more obscene intrusions by the tabloid press. Occasionally the less-regulated English press were unkind to Nora Sinclair, suggesting that she was less than faithful to her husband, but she shrugged such reports off with reckless abandon.

When the medical staff left them briefly alone together, it was immediately very different. Even in his groggy state, Sinclair could sense the aura of recent sex hanging over his wife. To understand that was to understand Nora. Their twenty years of childless marriage had lurched from indifference via infidelity to deep hostility. But it had, until then, suited them to keep up the pretence of marriage. She liked the privileges that being the Prime Minister's wife brought; lacking a family, it gave him the illusion of having a stable background, at least as far as an ill-informed electorate was concerned. In the distant past, Nora had always had a good eye for a young politician on the make, and, he had to admit, she had chosen him rather than the other way round. For his part, he had mistaken a brief physical desire and a fascination for a woman whose name so frequently appeared, even then, in the society gossip columns, for love. They both discovered their mistake in time: thus, no children.

Sinclair, a well-built, flush-faced man in his early fifties, had few friends. He was a solitary person, genuinely preferring to spend the larger part of his time in his own company. He liked to do things when he wanted to, not when it suited other people. It was a matter of refusing to make the compromises necessary for friendship. It was a weakness but it was the way he was. He suffered fools badly and knew that people considered him bad-tempered. But, he argued to himself, if he were not bad-tempered, he would be remote and even more difficult to work with than he was. But Nora, in terms of basic unpleasantness, had always had him beaten. Even now, when she asked him how he was, it was only so that she would be able to answer questions from friends and from the press. Not one hint of genuine compassion showed. Indeed, when, in a moment of weakness, he admitted to having no feeling below the waist, she responded, *So what's new?*

Sinclair was saved from her further company by the arrival of Robert Guthrie. His Private Secretary, recognized and unchecked by the duty police guard stationed outside, came into the private hospital room, saw Nora and immediately made to withdraw. 'No, don't go,' they both said, almost in unison. Guthrie watched remotely as Nora bent down towards the pillows and pretended to plant a consoling kiss on her husband's cheek. They had never liked each other, Nora and Guthrie, but Sinclair thought he noticed her throw him an especially hostile look as she left them alone together.

'Glad you came,' he said. 'Clever of you to track Nora down.'

Guthrie ignored the hint. 'Perhaps I should have waited –' he began.

'You did well,' Sinclair said warmly. He had a lot of time for Robert Guthrie and his loyalty. He depended on him a lot and always talked to him with particular familiarity and openness.

'How are you, Prime Minister?' Guthrie asked cautiously.

Sinclair told him about the total lack of feeling in his legs. But then, 'Enough of me,' he said. 'I want a full update. What's top of the list?'

'Your speech to the Scottish CBI tomorrow, sir.' Guthrie hesitated, pulling up a chair and sitting down by the bedside. 'Ian Campbell has agreed to give it for you.'

'Fine,' said Sinclair. 'Mind's in a complete mess since the attack. Give me a run-through of what he's going to say. From the beginning . . .'

'Very well, sir. Here goes.' Guthrie pulled some sheets of paper from his briefcase, shuffled through them, then began to read: 'Four years of Independence, ladies and gentlemen, and Scotland remains a member of the Commonwealth with The Queen as Head of State. As you know, we are full and generally cooperative members of the European Community, more so than the current English Government at least. We have established excellent diplomatic relations across the Atlantic and with other major countries like Japan that are of immediate economic concern to us. The European Community has been extremely generous in allocating funds for regional development within Scotland. Something like 700 to 800 million pounds has come our way since Independence, and so we can hardly complain. But now Brussels, understandably, won't go any further. I understand that: they have to be seen to be even-handed. They are obliged to adopt a level-playing-field strategy in dealing with us as against other less well-developed parts of the Community. We therefore cannot expect any more major help from that quarter. Here in Scotland itself, there is some good news and a lot of bad.' Guthrie hesitated. 'Sure I'm not boring you with all this, sir?'

'I insist, Robert. And I want Ian to stick to the text once it's agreed.' The Prime Minister had closed his eyes and his head was resting gently on his pillows, but Guthrie could see that he was still attentive.

'The good news is that Scotland's financial institutions are working well. Billions, not only of Scotland's wealth but England's and a lot of Europe's, are still managed by our experienced fund managers and investment banks in Edinburgh and Glasgow. North Sea oil, you all know about. We have more than the London Government thinks is our fair share but even that is not sufficient to allow us to pay our way. The other good news is that American companies are coming in and investing in a surprising way, including in particular the Unity Corporation. These are all signs of hope. Ladies and gentlemen, US multinationals would not be coming in if they did not think highly of our skilled workforce and our potential for the future. Unlike some of our critics, they don't appear overconcerned about the political instability that has, I accept, frightened a lot of other people off, especially the Japanese, who, admittedly, have enough economic problems of their own these days. The bad news on the industrial side, as you all know, is that the early boom years have gone and the whole Silicon Glen phenomenon has largely evaporated as a result of world overproduction on the computer front.'

'Enough of all that, Robert. What about the political scene?' interrupted the Prime Minister. 'What have we agreed to say on that?'

'OK, sir,' said Guthrie, glancing down at his notes. 'In brief, he'll remind his audience that politically we have perfectly good, if coolish, relations with the Government in London and with the rump of the old United Kingdom in Cardiff and Belfast – I'm summarizing here, of course. The English, naturally, don't want to get too involved with us given the unhappy nature of the break-up of the union. That said, we still manage to play "British" on a large number of fronts. We still field British teams at the Olympics and elsewhere. It's not terribly tidy but it's worked so far and there's not too much criticism even from die-hard Republicans. The problem, however, lies in where we go from here. We're running very short on budget: we've problems over our public sector borrowing requirement and where to get the money to improve our sub-standard housing, expand health and educational services and so on, now that we don't get the extra support from the London Exchequer. We need help.' Guthrie paused. 'We're still working on the text, Prime Minister, but it will go something like this: as I said, it's not going to come from Europe. Which is why we're looking hard at America on a number of fronts, both at the old Scottish diaspora through the Federation and, on a much harder-nosed commercial front, at companies like Unity and its ilk. If we don't get that aid with the problems that we currently face internally then we are going to go nowhere fast. The Apocalypse scenario which the Reunionists keep warning us about, that we'll either have to go crawling back into the Union, if London will have us, or starve in isolation and go under, overstates the case to a ridiculous extent. But the World Bank and the IMF have been as generous as they possibly can be and we can't expect more hand-outs from them at this stage. For far too long the begging bowl's been seen as Scotland's national symbol. It isn't good for us; it isn't good for morale; it isn't good for the government. It cannot last.'

'Solutions, Robert. What solutions are we giving them?'

'Your speech stresses that the solution lies across the Atlantic, sir. Have no doubt about it.'

'I think . . . I agree,' Sinclair said with a brief but weary confidence. As he did so, he felt the painkillers beginning to work again, dulling his mind. Guthrie had also noticed that his boss's attention was slipping away.

'We're working hard at it, sir. Everything else is in hand. Nothing to worry about.' Guthrie lied a gentle lie, then, soon afterwards, he left the Prime Minister to sleep.

Republican Party in poll turmoil

A confidential opinion poll commissioned by the Republican Party has revealed that 64% of party members are in favour of Scotland retaining a hereditary monarchy rather than an elected President. The poll's findings, leaked to the *Scottish Telegraph*, have deeply embarrassed the Republican leadership since they undermine the whole reason for the party's existence. Commissioned as part of a consultative exercise on the draft Election Manifesto, the poll . . .

(Page one news item, the *Scottish Telegraph*)

The skylight was unfastened as they had promised it would be. The man in gloves produced a small oil can and gently applied it along both of the protruding hinges and waited a few moments till it penetrated the rust. Then, inserting his fingers under the rim, he raised the hatch carefully. There was hardly a sound. He rested the heavy frame back against a concrete chimney stack.

He climbed up, hung lightly over the hole, then lowered himself easily into the darkness. There was supposed to be a table, down and slightly to the left, which he would be able to reach with his feet. For an instant he swung precariously in space till his feet felt the promised foothold, and, finding his balance, he let go with his hands and softly eased himself from the table to the ground.

A pencil torch shed a thin beam of light round the little room. The walls were lined with old newspapers neatly arranged on steel racks. The glass door was open and a chipped sign stencilled on the nameplate read PRESS CUTTINGS SECTION. There was a dust-laden smell in the air.

He went out onto the linoleum-covered landing, then down two flights of stairs. He remembered to step over the second top step of the lower flight because it creaked badly, though it shouldn't have mattered because the building was meant to be empty.

He decided he must be on the correct floor. Plush brown carpet had replaced the noisy linoleum and the walls were hung with stark modern American paintings. The large double door facing him had to be the one. He went up to it and examined it carefully, confirming his instinct. He bent down low.

Placing his torch on the floor so that it shone at the base of the wall, he produced a small screwdriver. Holding it in his gloved hands, he eased away a small square of skirting board which fitted, almost unnoticed, at the bottom of the doorframe. It came away easily. Behind it, screwed to the wall, was the junction box for the high-tech alarm system. He noted the disconnected wire that had already allowed him to pass through the skylight unannounced. He took his screwdriver and carefully disconnected two of the other points. Marked with red blobs of paint, they fed the circuit round the double door and also covered the safe in the room itself. Whoever had defused the skylight had not been able to neutralize this part of the alarm, since it was always checked by the guards last thing at night. For the tenth time, the man in the gloves hoped that the Special Task Force had prepared their ground well.

He double-checked his instructions, straightened up and faced the door, holding carefully a key he had been given earlier. The business end of the key was oddly shaped. He had never used one quite like this before. Inserting it gently into the lock, he found it turned easily. There was no sound as he reached for the handle.

For a moment he thought something had gone wrong, that there must be another lock. But he had misjudged the weight of the reinforced oak door, which swung open at the second attempt.

It was an elegant room, dominated by a rosewood desk in the centre. Steel and black leather armchairs were scattered around a low marble-topped coffee table by the fireplace. In the corner, the only thing out of keeping with the other furnishings in the room was the safe, a squat, ugly steel box, well bolted to the floor. The dials of the two combination locks were set into the door, one above the other.

The man took off his gloves. Setting the correct combination would require a light touch, and he had a specially impregnated cloth in his pocket to remove any fingerprints afterwards. Holding the pencil torch in his mouth, he took a piece of paper from his hip pocket and reread the numbers on it. He turned the top dial slowly, alternately clockwise and anti-clockwise. He dialled a different set of numbers on the bottom dial, pulled the lever handle and the safe door opened. If all safe-breaking jobs were as easy as this he would now be a rich man and not just out on promised permanent parole from Peterhead gaol.

File number XK 1739 was a red folder on the top shelf. *Top Secret* labels were stuck diagonally across the front. The title read *Correspondence with the President of the Federation*, just as they had said.

The man replaced his gloves, took out the file and moved across the room to the desk. He opened up his dark bomber jacket and from a small plastic bag suspended round his neck took out a tiny camera. He adjusted it briefly, still holding the torch in his mouth. Then, extinguishing the torch light for a moment, he went across to the windows to make doubly sure that the curtains were tightly closed – he didn't entirely trust the flash on his specially-equipped camera. Back at the desk, he began to photograph the contents of the file, page by page, turning them carefully by the very tip of the sheet as they had shown him. He did not try to read the letters. That was not his business nor part of the deal with the men who had come to his cell and who had so startlingly promised him freedom in return for his specialized services.

Half an hour and two changes of film later, he had finished. He returned the file carefully to its precise position in the safe. As he did so, he noticed the black steel cash box on one of the lower shelves. With an effort he ignored it – not out of scruples, but because he knew his contacts would be waiting for him outside to account for his every move.

He shut the safe and twirled the dials till they locked. Then, having wiped away any fingerprints, he deliberately retraced his steps, checking each action as he completed it. He left the room, relocked the door with the odd-shaped key, reset the burglar alarm, replaced the section of skirting board and climbed the stairs to the top floor once again.

The last stage was the most difficult. He had to get from the tabletop out of the skylight. Standing on the table he could just touch the ceiling. He needed more height. He looked round desperately. Had they slipped up? He thought for a moment. He would risk it. He took a bundle of old newspapers from one of the racks and piled them on the table. When they came in the morning, they would take it that someone from the senior staff had been up looking for something. He took off his shoes, tied them by their laces around his neck, climbed up and, with effort – for he was out of condition after months of confinement – pulled himself out onto the roof. Putting on his shoes again, he carefully shut the skylight, wiped the protruding hinges clear of the remains of the penetrating oil, then rubbed some roof grime back across them. Only the closest inspection would reveal anything and there was no reason for them to be suspicious. He rested briefly against a chimney stack to catch his breath, then, because he was a real professional, went through each action once more, rechecking before it was too late. He had always been a careful operator. It had always been others who had let him down.

Along the rooftops to the next house then down the fire escape, just as he had come. Halfway to the bottom he spotted the man in police uniform and instinctively froze. Then the officer looked up, saw him and signalled with his arm to his colleagues who were waiting unseen in a nearby car. The man climbed to the ground, reaching it as they came towards him. What it was to be on the side of the law.

Princess Royal opens English High Commission

> The Princess Royal yesterday opened the new English High Commission offices in Regent Terrace. For the last four years the High Commission has operated from temporary premises in Queen Street. The High Commissioner, Sir Terence Shackerly, said that, given the historic links between Scotland and England, it was appropriate his office should be close to the National Assembly Building. It is next door to the United States Embassy and is now part of the diplomatic centre of Edinburgh.
>
> The Commission, which has a staff of twenty, represents . . .
>
> By our Property Correspondent
>
> (News item from the *Times of Scotland*)

The Campsies, a range of green hills that stretch in an undulating belt to the north west of Glasgow, had been chosen a few years earlier as the site for the main Communications Monitoring Station. Prior to Independence, it had been an outstation of the highly secret GCHQ based at Cheltenham, which eavesdropped on all external communications between Britain and the world and much else besides.

At that time of night, the high-security, barbed wire compound that enclosed the station was shrouded in mist. There were floodlights and a state of the art system of alarms around the huts where the technical and monitoring staff worked. But the complex field of directional aerials, satellite dishes and other antennae were less well guarded because of the huge space they required.

Back to his uneventful life at the Lennoxtown station where a couple of drunks on a Saturday were the high spot of his week, PC Wright, fresh from his ordeal at the riot amid the Clydebank slums, switched off the engine and jumped from the comparative warmth of his Range Rover. He produced a powerful torch and swung its beam back and forth across the high mesh fence around the outer compound. All seemed in perfect order. The garbled message via the newsroom of the *Evening Times* about a threatened break-in was obviously a load of rubbish. A few years ago it would have been different, and every communications centre in the country had been under constant military guard. Now the violence was confined to the city streets. The countryside was at peace.

PC Wright checked in with the security nightwatch inside the base itself and told them that he would do a routine sweep along the perimeter wire, if only for the benefit of his police log book. They too had just completed a routine patrol, they informed him. After ten minutes he was confident it was a false alarm. He climbed back into the Range Rover, switched on the radio and put out his routine call sign. He told Control there was nothing amiss. Control came back straight away about a second anonymous call, this time to the *Herald*. He was ordered to do a further check. 'Would you like assistance from Lennoxtown, ZF One?' the voice over the radio crackled.

'ZF One. No need. Over and out,' Wright replied irritably.

Back to the gate and then round the fence once again. His inspection was even less thorough this time. He stopped occasionally, peering through the mist, his torch beam cutting a reassuring swathe into the night. The windows of the operations huts were all firmly shut, and nothing, not even a rabbit, stirred.

Back at the Range Rover, he reported once again to Control. They were being bloody difficult. He was told to wait and watch for a further half hour, to be on the safe side. Wright asked them to ring his wife and let her know he'd be late. Then he switched off the radio, looked at his watch, yawned and prepared to do his duty. Half an hour but not a minute more.

He gazed vacantly out of the windscreen. It had been an enormous relief to get away from the filth, hate and violence of Glasgow. He was a straightforward, uncomplicated man. He liked the countryside and had always been lucky to have escaped a posting to any of the big metropolitan forces. It was the friendliness of the people in the country: they were kind, even to an Englishman like himself. It was only the climate that continued to depress him after twenty years of exile. His roses fared worse than he did. He kept telling his wife that one day they'd go back home to Devon. There, a garden was a garden . . .

PC Wright did not see the man in the blue overalls run up to the fence at the side of the compound furthest away from the buildings. But he saw the burst of flame as the canister the man had lobbed hit the ground beside the big complex of antennae. A bright, harmless flare lay burning among the sodden tufts of last year's grass. The policeman sat forward urgently in the driver's seat and seized the microphone. He gave his call sign, and briefly reported the fire. He told them he was going in to investigate. He asked them to alert the guards inside the central compound.

Acting as it had been intended he should act, Wright got out and walked across to the fence. As he went he opened a sealed packet with the keys to the gate at the far end of the compound that were held for just such an emergency. He found the Chubb that fitted the locks and swung the gates open, then

45

ran across the compound towards the burning canister. His sudden burst of speed caused the two men who were coming silently up behind him to misjudge their attack. One of them tripped slightly. Wright heard the sound and turned. A brief hesitation, then they both came at him together. Instead of the silent knockout blow that had been intended, there was a brief and vicious fight. He broke away from them and made for his Range Rover and the radio.

One of the men started to run after him. The other, a young, hard-faced man with sandy hair and a wisp of a beard, stayed still. He had something in his right hand. The noise of the shot was swallowed up by the surrounding mist before Police Constable Wright's body had time to hit the turf. From the ugly gash in the middle of the back of his uniform jacket, the blood was already beginning to flow.

'You bloody lunatic. *Christ*. You've sodding done it now.' The man who had started to chase the policeman had stopped in his tracks and, white in the face, was screaming at his colleague.

'Belt up will you,' the younger man hissed back. 'What's the police ever done for you? We've got work to do.' The hardness of the voice quelled further dissent. The other man turned hesitantly and then ran rapidly in and out among the radio masts and aerials, pulling the fuse wire and the interlinked semtex parcels behind him.

Inside the Range Rover, a voice from Control was crackling incessantly, 'Come in, ZF One. Come in, ZF One. Are you receiving me? Repeat: Are you receiving me? Over.'

Twelve miles away, Control had just put out a general alarm call when they heard the sound of the multiple explosions.

The old joke had it that England was a country ruled by Scots. In many ways it had become even more true with an independent Scotland; the power elite, the financiers and the leaders of English, European and North American industry included many who were Scottish by nationality or descent. Talent still travelled to where opportunity was greatest. Thus the shuttle flights between

Edinburgh, Glasgow and London were packed daily with an inordinate number of key players on the international stage. The scene had changed little over the years. Briefcase-carrying identi-kit men and women, the younger and more upwardly mobile all with their portable computers, filed into executive lounges, checked in, helped themselves to coffee or drinks and then, when their flights were called, wheeled out again to board their aircraft. There was little more hassle, little more glamour than in strug-gling onto the Colinton bus or boarding the 7.19 train from Linlithgow. There were, of course, other travellers around – tour-ists mainly, groups of curious Japanese or holiday makers bronzed or palely anticipatory, bound for Morningside or Benidorm, who, less experienced in the ways of the shuttle, tended to be herded to the back of the plane.

This sizeable number of expatriate Scots – people who held key positions in the London media and in publishing, in City finance houses, investment trusts, insurance companies and mer-chant banks – were constantly being thrown together to talk, conspire, negotiate and do deals in these executive lounges. Hug-ging their briefcases, their complimentary newspapers, their coats, their overnight bags, it was still probably the most impor-tant internal route in the entire British Isles, unsurprising since Scottish financial experts estimated that a large proportion of the wealth of England, Wales and Ireland was still managed by canny Scottish institutions.

Today, as Guthrie waited for the early-morning London shuttle to be called, he watched clusters of these movers and shakers conspiring and negotiating. Many faces were familiar to him. In one corner he identified a Jermyn Street-shirted group of Edin-burgh and London bankers whispering together over some new deal. Sipping their coffee, they were certainly not chatting about golf or the latest cricket results. He spotted one senior partner from Flemings, a bank that continued to make much of its Scot-tish antecedents, who had once personally boasted to Prime Minister Sinclair that he had opened and clinched one highly profitable deal on the short one-hour air journey itself. The executive lounge offered a sense of release, free from the confines of status-laden offices and boardrooms, where people rubbed shoulders in equality on classless flights. Each traveller no matter how mighty was briefly levelled by identical boarding passes, security checks, and the same amount of legroom and space to put their bags and briefcases in the overhead lockers. Lobby, negotiate, wheedle, ingratiate, bond, gossip – whatever the agenda, political, social or economic, the executive shuttle lounge was a deal-making place for all seasons and conditions of human kind.

It was also a dangerous place. Secrets were hard to keep. Everything could be overheard. When people spoke loudly to one another it was usually only an irritation to the other travellers. When they started whispering in such close confines or tried to speak softly when using their portable telephones, then something important was being said.

Guthrie looked at his watch. He hoped there was not going to be a delay or he would miss his onward connection from Heathrow to New York. He was sitting on a couch, browsing through an early edition of the *Scotsman*, one that had gone to bed much too early to carry news of the Campsie explosions. Had it done so or had Guthrie turned on the radio and heard the headlines, which he had failed to do in his rush to get to the airport in time, he might have made more sense of the brief snatch of conversation he overheard.

His couch was back to back with another, in which a man, face unseen, was talking on his mobile telephone. The voice was distinctly American. 'Good,' the voice said. 'Total wipe-out?' There was a pause as the man listened. 'OK,' he continued, 'if you guarantee it's safe, arrange the conference call and pass the strategy electronically. Even if they're listening Stateside, it don't matter. It's over here that some of the . . . er, deal . . . you know what I mean, would set the sirens going.'

The flight was called and Guthrie stood, briefly curious about the identity of the person he had overheard. But the other man had already moved rapidly towards the exit door and Guthrie never saw his face.

4

Reunionists seek new Party Chairman

Chairman of the Reunionist Alliance, the Hon. William Donaldson, is to retire in the spring to spend more time looking after his Berwickshire estate. The hardline landowner and former Edinburgh banker has led the Alliance since Independence. An Old Etonian who hunts with the Borders Foxhounds, he has been a surprisingly popular leader but his likely successor, the neo-Communist union leader, Mr Todd Mackay, shows the change that has taken place in the composition of the party. It now has more unemployed strikers among its ranks than members of the landowning and professional classes.

Mr Donaldson was briefly arrested some years ago when he chained himself to the railings outside the National Assembly on the day of the inaugural sitting.

By political correspondent Donnie Lea
(From the *Scotsman*)

With long experience of transatlantic flights, Guthrie altered his watch to the time at his destination point immediately he boarded the aircraft. Heathrow to JFK was some seven hours' flying time, seven hours in which to adjust his system to the change of time and pace.

Like many long-haul flights, it was three-quarters empty, and he could spread himself across two business-class seats. The first hour he spent digesting the Scottish newspapers he had brought with him, a pleasant change from the five minutes flat he gave them on a normal day. They had all gone to press too early to carry any news of the Campsie bomb but were full of gloomy reports of strikes and lockouts and, in the aftermath of the recent Tokyo market collapse, of the sell-off of yet another high-tech Japanese electronics factory to the Unity Corporation. Rosenfeld had been telling the truth: they were shovelling their money into Scotland in a most exciting way.

The brittle-looking stewardess offered him champagne but he opted for a glass of fresh orange juice. As he sipped it, Guthrie felt relaxed despite the traumas of the past few days and the potential strains of the ones ahead. He dozed and when he woke, some time later, the stewardess came up with a message. William Torrance, the Federation's Special Commissioner, was sitting further down the plane and wondered if he could join him for a drink. Guthrie did not feel like talking business but agreed. He could hardly snub the man, since it was Torrance's President he was going over to meet. Indeed he was probably only making the journey in order to shadow Guthrie and brief his people in advance about how the Scottish Cabinet was likely to react.

Torrance ambled up, a large, jovial man with close-cropped, fiery red hair that hinted at his Celtic origins. His prominent chin and incipient jowls gave him away as an American, the result of a childhood where jaw muscles were, he frequently explained, over-developed by an addiction to chewing gum. A third-generation Scots-American and former insurance broker, he maintained his business connections on the side of his work for the Caledonian Societies, a joint role that did not always make him popular with American officialdom in the shape of the US Embassy in Edinburgh.

Somewhat self-consciously Torrance ordered a bourbon and dry ginger. Guthrie, who avoided alcohol on international flights, asked for more orange juice. Torrance opened up, talking inevitably about his golfing handicap which, it appeared, was another major reason why he so much enjoyed his present job. He was cautious at first but, as the journey progressed and a second and then a third bourbon appeared, he became more open about how he saw the Federation's offer of financial assistance being presented to the National Assembly and to the Scottish public without giving rise to media accusations of charity handouts. Guthrie let him make the running, prompting him from time to time to keep up the flow of confidences. In the end, however, Torrance had no more ideas than the Cabinet had already discarded as to a possible way forward.

Suddenly Torrance threw in an unexpected question. 'Would you put the clock back if you could, Robert?' he asked.

'Back? To the United Kingdom?' Guthrie hesitated. He knew Torrance would report anything he said. And more. He'd read all about it in the file.

He thought back to the phone call he had received late the previous night, as he had been packing for his journey. The Duty Officer from the Special Task Force was apologetic, but there was something he ought to see at once. No, for security reasons, the papers had to remain in the office. They were sending a car for him.

By the time he got there it was well after midnight, but the photographs which they had enlarged were still damp. Each page of each letter in the file was there. It had been a neat job, quickly and expertly done, moral scruples set aside in the interests of the security of the State. MacDowall himself had signed the authority and the sentence review which gave maximum remission to the safebreaker from Peterhead gaol.

The most important document in the file was a copy of a coded fax, dated some days earlier, from Torrance to Liam Anderson, the President of the Federation in New York. It gave the background to the approach Torrance had made.

> The recent Glasgow riots between the Reunionist strikers and the Republicans, about which you will have seen full reports, demonstrate the ever deeper and more bitter divisions existing in Scottish society

today. That Scotsmen have died and many others have been seriously injured, is a tragedy which could easily prove a grim template for the future. Civil war is no longer an absurd possibility. The ability and willingness of the Government and of the majority in the National Assembly to contain the present explosive situation is not open to question. But in the long run, the deteriorating economic climate, with more people unemployed than at any time since the thirties, coupled with a severe balance of payments problem, must, if unchecked, lead to disaster. Even the renewed boom in North Sea oil and gas is a shallow phenomenon. Because of her huge international debt and the annual repayments to the English Treasury, that wealth now runs through Scotland as swiftly as the oil in the pipelines.

I am not dramatizing the situation when I say that widespread civil strife could force the clock back. Many, too many, argue that Independence is an expensive experiment that has failed. Significantly, they speak in the past tense. Support for the Reunionist Alliance is growing rapidly and, unless resolute action is taken, they could win the next election. They have many members in the Government, in industry, in the civil service, in the unions and even in the Church. The latest public opinion polls suggest that a majority would not be unhappy to return to the British fold. In this they assume, more than a little optimistically in my view, that they would be welcomed back with open arms. England too has its problems, though conditions are somewhat better south of Berwick. It would be very foolish for anyone to believe that Scotland could go back, warts and all.

Nor is this my speculation alone. My most recent discussions with Prime Minister Keith Sinclair demonstrate that he too is deeply concerned. As you know, my assessment of him has not always been favourable since he has appeared both aggressive and indecisive in the past. I understand his injury has affected him severely, though it has been suggested to me by some of his Cabinet colleagues that the violence of the attack may kindle a fire that was lacking in him earlier. If that is true, Scotland may yet benefit.

Sinclair confirmed my suspicions that Scotland's present ills are not solely caused by the inherent weaknesses of the economy but by the fact that many of those who control the financial reins are supporters of Reunionism. Both through incompetence and by design, a wrecking game is being played. The Finance Minister, Ian Campbell, is suspected of siding with the Reunionists; why Sinclair has kept him in his present post I am at a loss to understand.

I apologize for the length of this report but it is one of the most important I may ever have to write. My message is simple: unless a massive inflow of funds is made available to tide the Scottish Government over its immediate difficulties, it will once again cease to exist as an independent nation. What I am calling for is financial backing not far short of the scale and magnitude that American Jewry provides to the State of Israel. Thus could the nation survive.

If you believe that the Federation can inspire such a level of financial support, we should certainly not give it blindly as we have done in the past. It must not be presented as charity nor aid. It should be tied, secretly but securely, to Scottish Governmental promises to rectify those inherent weaknesses in the economic management of the country. How and when we act must be carefully handled. There is little time to be lost; we must choose our channels with care. It would be counterproductive to go direct to certain Ministers – there are those who are too proud to accept what they would call charity and those who, for Reunionist reasons, would be against it, offering as it would an alternative and unwelcome way to economic stability. Both groups would, in any event, be all too ready to criticize the offer as a new form of US neo-colonialism.

Then had come the final obscure sentence, which, Guthrie remembered, was written by hand at the end of the letter: *I am sending you this on a strictly personal and confidential basis, Liam, since I believe there are certain people within the Federation itself who would like to hijack this plan of ours for their own highly suspect commercial and financial gain. You know who I mean.*

Guthrie was gratified that the Special Task Force had got access to these letters before he left. Knowledge, as always, was power. And now, with care, he had the opportunity to find out what precisely Torrance meant by that final, Delphic sentence.

Torrance continued to talk freely; by now he was more than slightly drunk. He must have had one or two before he had come to join Guthrie. 'In the strictest confidence,' he said, 'I'm extremely worried. That's not as obvious a remark as it might seem. Scotland's future is of great concern to me. Sometimes I feel more loyalty to it than to my own employers. There ... there's something going on at the Federation which I don't like.' His words were slurred.

'Is there?' Guthrie asked gently.

'We pride ourselves in knowing as much about Scotland's economic and political prospects as you do yourselves. It's often easier for an outsider to look in.' Torrance turned to face Guthrie to emphasize his point.

Guthrie nodded, waiting for him to get to the point.

'I end up puzzled,' he went on. 'A new element's buzzing

around which I don't like. Straws in the wind. Someone's out to cause trouble. Friends in the States suggest that a small caucus is being paid to work up discontent among our very own members. I shouldn't mention it, so please keep that to yourself. One of that new lot, a man called de Laski, has been in Scotland all this past week. Then – this is in strictest confidence, please – I've other evidence that suggests our Edinburgh office was broken into. Nothing appears to have gone, but there could have been an attempt to get at our papers.'

The news about the caucus was interesting, just as Torrance's suspicions about the break-in were unwelcome.

'What makes you suspect a break-in?' Guthrie asked.

'Little things. No fingermarks at all on the combination locks of my safe; a pile of newspapers in an attic room that looks as if it's been used as a stepping-stone; the sudden departure of one of our clerks who could well have set the whole thing up.' The last point was a new element to Guthrie, though he had guessed that the Special Task Force must have had inside help. He changed the subject. 'Who are in this caucus? What's their agenda? Who's behind them?'

'Not yet in the picture.' Torrance continued to slur his words. 'Nothing definite. Liam Anderson will give you more of a steer when you see him tomorrow. For God's sake don't mention I've been filling you in about our suspicions. Exceeding my brief, and all that. He wants to put you in the picture himself. While you'll meet the full Federation Executive, Anderson wants to see you on your own. Later. Wheels within wheels, you understand. Not sure how far the rot has spread.'

Guthrie was about to press him further when the loudspeaker crackled and there was an announcement from the captain about the plane running into a patch of bad weather. A few bumpy patches followed and Torrance immediately started looking green. He began to say something more, then, with an abrupt apology about being a poor traveller, he was up and away in a hectic dash for relief.

* * *

Knowledge was power. Guthrie recalled the phrase once again when he reached New York and received the news, by coded telegram, that a series of bombs had, at a stroke, wiped out the Communications Monitoring Station's entire ability to listen in on international messages. It would take weeks before the Campsie site was back in full working order. Coincidence or conspiracy? Only then did Guthrie remember the brief snatch of telephone conversation he had overheard in the executive lounge.

US Ambassador denies 'consular' status

The American Ambassador to Scotland, Mr Gerry Jackson, last night denied that the Edinburgh Embassy was 'a piece of State Department window dressing'.

Speaking to the Edinburgh University United Nations' Association, Mr Jackson said the claim was totally false. He rejected charges that it was merely 'a convenient outstation of the London Embassy', handling only trade and consular affairs. 'It is nonsense to suggest that the Embassy is much less influential than the office of the Commission of the Federation of American Caledonian Societies,' he added.

A Government spokesman said later that they had the highest respect and confidence in the level of American diplomatic representation in Scotland . . .

By our diplomatic staff
(*Herald* report)

As the PM's special representative, Guthrie was greeted in style at the Federation's Madison Avenue headquarters. After the initial pleasantries and expressions of concern about the PM's health and speculation about the riots and the bombings, they all sat round Anderson's office for the next hour, before going through to his private dining room for lunch. Apart from Anderson and Torrance, there were three other members of the Executive there by the names of Lindsay, Carlyle and de Laski.

Anderson, a youthful sixty-five-year-old, was a highly successful real estate entrepreneur; a rich, gangling man who was just beginning to show the first signs of wear. But he was ageing gracefully, and still had all his wits about him. He sat swivelling back and forth in his black executive chair with more of a schoolboy's gusto and enthusiasm than one might expect from the Chairman of Rubin, Corvo and Anderson Inc., and President of the Federation of American Caledonian Societies. From the outset, he was bluntly honest and upfront about the proposal.

When Guthrie had first heard about the offer he had wondered whether the idea could possibly have come from Anderson himself. He doubted it. Anderson wasn't the type to think up sweeping gestures like that. Guthrie knew from the Special Commissioner's file that the idea had been refined in the Edinburgh office, but there was something about Torrance's original letter which suggested that it wasn't entirely his concept either.

Torrance sat on Guthrie's left; on the other side was Lindsay, an elegantly-dressed laird-like man, vague, bespectacled, whom Guthrie found hard to take seriously, since, despite a faultless Caledonian pedigree, he hailed from Alabama. In a drawling voice he put forward some frighteningly hard-right views, but he had been long tolerated because he was a more than generous contributor to Federation funds.

Carlyle, sitting opposite him, was the absolute opposite: a lean-faced, Ivy League businessman with rimless spectacles and rich New England style, he was an unusual bedfellow to find in the largely charitable Federation. Guthrie wondered that the man should have agreed to fill an unpaid post. He recalled for a moment Torrance's remark about wheels within wheels.

Finally, there was de Laski. He claimed that the Maltese in him had left him with his unlikely name but that he stemmed from a long line of prosperous Glasgow ice cream shop proprietors. The rest of his family had come from Inverness. He was sparse, dark and celtic-looking, though it could have been Mediterranean blood. He was wearing a tasteless amount of gold jewellery. The most recent recruit to the Executive, he had not, according to Torrance, come up in the normal way through having been an office bearer of one of their affiliated societies. He had suddenly appeared from nowhere, with impeccable sponsors in the most unlikely places, and had been swept onto the Executive unopposed. He had just returned from a flying business visit to Scotland, he explained, so he was fully up to date with events there. There was something about de Laski's voice that struck a chord with Guthrie, but at that precise moment he could not say why. If, in Carlyle, Guthrie could identify a certain cynical, supercilious style, with de Laski there was immediately something slightly sinister. Fiercely intelligent though he proved to be, as the conversation developed, de Laski emerged as someone who could be tough, if not brutal. He was a man, Guthrie speculated, who would do anything he was paid to do, and do it without question. Carlyle might curl his lip and look down his long nose at any prospect of getting his hands dirty; de Laski would, by contrast, merely wipe the blood off his hands and start all over again. There was, it emerged, nothing the slightest bit funny about de Laski. He was cold and humourless, through and through.

They were an odd mixture but it was an agreeable meal, during which Guthrie learnt little that was new and was offered nothing that would make the package easier to sell to the Cabinet. He did, however, hear the global figure that Anderson had in mind and that made him sit up. That sort of money, spread over several years, would help the Scottish economy to its feet in a highly significant way.

With the exception of Anderson, they all seemed remarkably vague about the mechanics. Carlyle, in a rather distant manner, suggested that they would work out all the details once the matter had been agreed in principle. Even Torrance, who was well aware of the political realities, nodded his agreement to that. But

Torrance, Guthrie realized, had a lot of prestige at stake in having the plan adopted.

When they reached the coffee stage, there was a pause in the conversation and Guthrie realized they were all waiting for him to come up with some sort of reaction. He began by rehearsing the difficulties as he saw them for the Scottish Cabinet, who had to steer a middle course between Republican and Reunionist attitudes. There were many who would be eager to reap the political rewards of condemning such aid, while others would welcome it with open arms but for all the wrong reasons.

It was only when Torrance broke in with a casual remark about Ian Campbell's troublemaking potential, that Guthrie first began to notice the tension between him and some of the others around the table. There had been the odd early signs, but nothing much, a fraction too many forced smiles and pointed remarks that could have been taken in unpleasant ways. He was to be forgiven if he hadn't read too much into it: he was in a strange environment and everyone was being politely paraded there for his benefit. It was not for him to get involved in their internal squabbles.

Torrance's remark broke the calm. Carlyle responded with a censorious, 'Leave that, William. We can handle Campbell.'

Torrance, who again had had too much to drink, failed to take the hint. He went on. 'Sorry, Robert. Mr Carlyle's right. I had thought that Campbell was a problem. Don't worry.' He turned to smile at Guthrie. 'Since I spoke to you on the plane yesterday, things have become clearer. Don't worry about Campbell. As Mr Carlyle says, my colleagues have him all tied –'

'*Enough*, I said, William.' A flush of sudden anger showed on Carlyle's cheeks as he almost shouted the words. The others looked on, saying nothing. Anderson seemed upset.

Torrance paused but was not to be silenced. 'Come off it, Carlyle,' he said with a desperate grin. 'You've got to be honest with Robert Guthrie. He'll cotton on to what you're doing sooner or later. He can only say no, like I did. I tell you –'

It was the dark, intense figure of de Laski who interrupted this time. The threat in his voice was scarcely veiled. 'Would you leave the members of the Executive alone with Mr Guthrie, Torrance,' he said quietly. His soft delivery belied the coldly vicious glint in his eyes. Anderson sat white and silent. Lindsay looked startled: he was obviously not in the picture.

'I . . . you can't throw me out like –' Torrance began. He was flushed and nervous.

'*Out*,' hissed de Laski, half standing as if intending to lean forward and strike the other man. Torrance quickly rose from the table, excused himself surprisingly gracefully, then left the room. There was an embarrassed silence for a moment, then Anderson said:

'Sorry about that. William seems to have had quite a few martinis. He's been working too hard recently, I dare say.' The tension was high. Guthrie nodded in sympathy.

'Out of practice with our hard American drinking habits,' broke in Carlyle languidly. 'It's one thing sipping a good malt whisky late of an evening . . .' Everyone laughed in relief and the tension was broken. And Guthrie's brief spell of euphoria with it.

After the conflicts of the working lunch, the Federation's reception that evening was good-humoured and agreeable. Anderson proved an excellent host and had rounded up a representative company of American-Scots to meet Guthrie. There were the inevitable oddities at both ends of that spectrum: a couple of would-be Scottish chieftains in kilts, straight from their Texan cattle ranches or insurance companies, who would have looked more at home in stetsons or New England suiting, and at the other end was a curiously large number of tough-looking businessmen, most of whom bore Scottish names but one or two with an appearance more akin to some New York gang boss. There was even a black man from Detroit who claimed his grandmother hailed from Aberdeen.

Anderson chatted amiably at Guthrie's side. 'My great secret for someone in my position is that I've never really enjoyed whisky but at least I've trained myself to spell it correctly.' His accompanying laughter was generally echoed by his guests. He was obviously a popular if, tonight, a somewhat nervous host, while Guthrie was, for once, enjoying being the centre of attraction. He had put aside for the time being the problem of what to do about the aid package but looked forward to going into the details with Anderson privately the next morning.

As the party progressed however, enhanced by a slight jet lag, he became detached, even bored by having to listen to lengthy arguments over the location of the forthcoming Alabama Burns' Night celebrations which three of his current court were discussing. His attention wandered to where Lindsay was engaged in conversation with a clean-cut young man at the far side of the room. The man darted off as he watched, and Lindsay turned to look around as one does at a party when one is suddenly abandoned. He caught Guthrie watching him, frowned, and came quickly across to him. Guthrie excused himself from the Burns fanatics as Lindsay whispered in his ear: 'A journalist – you saw me talking to him just now – tells me that Torrance has been involved in an auto accident. In hospital . . . in a bad way.'

'God. I'd noticed he wasn't here,' Guthrie responded. 'How did a journalist . . . Do the others know?'

'Saw it on the news wire. Came straight over to get our reactions. He's looking for an exclusive quote from Liam Anderson.'

'How did it happen?' Guthrie began. Just at that moment Anderson himself appeared, looking deeply shaken. He climbed onto a chair and banged for silence.

'I have sad news for you, ladies and gentlemen,' he announced. 'We've just heard that William Torrance, whom you all know so well, has been involved in an automobile accident and has been taken to hospital, seriously injured. He flew in only yesterday from Scotland to be with us . . .' Anderson held up his hands for silence as a shocked murmur went round the room.

'We're trying to find out more. There's nothing anyone can do. Do please carry on. I'll let you know as soon as I hear anything.'

Anderson clambered down again and came up towards Guthrie.

'I'm sorry,' Guthrie began. 'Should we go to the hospital?'

'They're going to telephone as soon as there's any definite news. But, if you like, do go. I'll get Carlyle or someone to go with you.'

'No point in doing that, Robert.' De Laski had come up beside them. 'He's unconscious. They're not letting visitors near him.'

At that moment the journalist, who introduced himself as Harvey Silt, reappeared, and Guthrie reluctantly agreed to talk to him about the good work Torrance was doing in Scotland. While the interview was in progress, Anderson again went and stood on the table to announce that he had just heard that Torrance had died without regaining consciousness. Without thinking, Guthrie changed to talking to Silt in the past tense.

He questioned Silt as to how it had happened, and was told about a car that hadn't stopped somewhere up on the fringes of Harlem. Guthrie wondered at that. He knew little about Torrance's private life but it was odd that he had been so far away when he should have already been at the reception. His mind went back to the row at lunch and he wondered if Torrance had been out drowning his sorrows. It would help explain the accident if he had been very drunk.

'Off the record, is, sorry, *was* Mr Torrance in the habit of hitting the bottle?' The directness of Silt's question threw Guthrie off guard, as it mirrored so closely what he had been thinking.

'I . . . er . . . I think that's hardly an appropriate question in the circumstances,' he responded sharply, indicating that the interview was at an end. They were alone and Silt persisted.

'Bit blunt, maybe. But this is my bread and butter.' Silt was not going to be put off.

'Your diet isn't to my taste. If you'd excuse me.'

'OK by me,' Silt said blandly as Guthrie made to move away. 'You may like to know,' he lowered his voice briefly, 'that someone's putting it around that Torrance was drunk as hell when the hit-and-run driver got him. But I've got one witness already who's certain he was as sober as you or I. And I haven't even started my enquiries yet, Mr Guthrie.' With that, Silt turned on his heel and walked rapidly away.

Guthrie watched him go, trying to make sense of what he had been told. Who was this man Silt and why should he be so interested in a mere hit-and-run accident? He saw Anderson go up to the journalist and ask whether he still wanted the interview. Obviously the reply was in the negative, for Anderson shrugged in irritation as Silt quickly left the room.

For a few seconds Guthrie was left on his own, then Lindsay and a number of other guests gathered around him once again. Already they were full of talk about collections for wreaths and the organization of the funeral service. Someone asked whether Guthrie could stay on in the States for it, if they arranged it as early as possible. Their morbid intensity sickened him and he gave curt, noncommittal answers. In his mind he was already drafting a telegram to Edinburgh reporting Torrance's death. He needed peace to think.

Alone in a soulless Georgetown hotel room an auburn-haired girl stared disapprovingly at herself in the long dressing-table mirror. Behind her she glimpsed an unmade bed, sign of an unsatisfactory night with someone about whom she now neither regretted nor cared. There had to be more to life; there had to be another way. Exposed to the harsh morning light that streamed through the net curtains, she disliked everything she saw about herself. Yet her semi-transparent negligée revealed details of a very shapely body. Even before she began to apply some make-up, only modest ravages showed on her fine features as the result of a careless night on the town. She had dismissed her temporary partner some time around three in the morning, giving herself a few welcome hours of undisturbed sleep. Now she had to face a busy day, an overdue article to finish for the *Washington Post* and research to complete on two other features which she had been commissioned to write. She paused at her task, still not much liking her mirror image. For a moment she was overwhelmed by one of her brief moods of self-doubt and introspection which she believed she had inherited from her father and his Calvinistic upbringing, with its in-built feelings of guilt inspired by the Protestant work ethic. Yet almost immediately she regained her natural self-confidence. She was not one to brood for long. Life was challenging and usually enjoyable. She had had, after all, a string of boyfriends who had all assured her that she was both good-looking and good company. Now, her long hair, fresh from shower and blow-dryer, cascaded generously over her shoulders in a manner that turned many a male head at the meetings and parties that were part and parcel of her everyday experience. Maybe, Heather Anderson thought to herself, life was not so bad after all.

She put aside her make-up and again picked up the press cutting that lay on the dressing table beside her. A brief, shocking press notice about the death of William Torrance, a long-term friend and colleague of her father's. She knew from the latter's telephone call the previous evening how upset he had been by the accident. She had seldom heard him so distressed and had questioned him closely as to what the matter really was. It had come pouring out. By chance he had mentioned one name: de Laski. It was an unusual name that triggered a distant memory. Before she went out that evening, she had called her New York office and asked them to search through the file of her old press articles. She gave them the approximate date. That research confirmed her hunch: she had come across the same name only once, two years earlier, when, as a cub reporter, she had been sent by her editor to cover a tragic story in the little town of Hulse City, New Jersey. She recalled that there had been a chemical leak from some huge plant and a child had been poisoned. *De Laski.* She now clearly remembered how cold and arrogant that spokesman for the guilty company had been. She had taken against him almost from the start. At each of his press conferences, he had pulled out every imaginable excuse to exculpate his company Unity from the wrong they had done to the people of that little town.

Heather Anderson glanced up from the press cutting to confront her mirror image once again. This time she was less self-critical. As she automatically brushed on light blush to her cheeks and applied liner around her eyes, her mind wandered elsewhere. It was not back to memories of the coarse foreplay and the shabby aftermath to which the bedraggled sheets on the bed behind her were witness. She thought only about the day ahead. For the past three decades her father had worried about her, her ups and downs, her crises of upbringing, of career, of love affairs. Now it was her turn to worry about him. But why should she worry? Why did the odd juxtaposition of her memories of the Hulse City incident, of a man called de Laski and the death of William Torrance, come unhappily together in her mind? She stood up, walked to a wardrobe and carefully selected a dress. The moment she had finished the article she decided she would catch the first shuttle back to New York. Her father needed her.

Hot pursuit still an issue

The Commissioner of Police, Sir Jimmy Mactaggart, met yesterday with chief constables from north of England counties to try to resolve the longstanding dispute over the issue of hot pursuit: whether forces from either country can have the authority, where customs and border posts do not exist, to pursue wanted criminals, car thieves and others, across the border in order to make an arrest. Negotiations have now narrowed to discussing the practicality of so doing, and specifically to prevent the suspect being taken back across the border after arrest without permission from the local police authority.

Note to Editors: Full border customs posts only operate on the A1(M), the A7, the A68 and the A74. All vehicles containing dutiable goods are meant to cross by these routes. Spot checks only exist on minor roads.

(Scottish Press Association report)

When the curtain came down for the interval, Guthrie realized he had appreciated little of the plot. It was one of those unnecessarily brutal plays about an underprivileged youth's struggle in a corrupt world. The director and author had, between them, taken every liberty which current political correctness allowed.

It was the evening following the reception. He sat alone in the second row of the stalls; the seat beside him was empty. Liam Anderson had invited him, but at the last moment his driver arrived alone to deliver Guthrie to the theatre with the message that Anderson had had to attend to some unexpected and urgent business.

It was distinctly odd. It tied in too ominously with the unrewarding session Guthrie had had with Anderson that same morning. When he had arrived at ten o'clock as arranged, de Laski was with the Chairman in his office, and Guthrie sensed that some sort of row had been going on. They both greeted him warmly enough, and from the outset Anderson appeared deeply shaken by Torrance's death. Yet Guthrie sensed that there was something more fundamental behind his anxiety. As they sat down over coffee, it became apparent that de Laski fully intended to stay. After Guthrie had dropped a few hints and Anderson had pointedly ignored them, he realized it was de Laski who was making all the running. When Guthrie made it obvious that he wasn't going to get down to any details while de Laski remained, the latter reluctantly withdrew, saying, as he left, that the Executive would look forward to a full report on their discussions as soon as possible. He smiled coldly as he said it but Guthrie again felt that it was an order with menace behind it rather than a straightforward request.

De Laski's departure produced little or no change. Anderson remained silent and withdrawn. Guthrie told him bluntly that he hadn't flown all the way to New York for nothing and Anderson tried to pull himself together, apologizing for his detachment by referring once again to his shock at Torrance's death. But he remained untypically reticent until Guthrie was determined to force him out of his silence by opening up and putting all his cards on the table. He went over the familiar background about the perilous state of the Scottish economy. Then he revealed how worried Sir Alexander MacDowall was about the latest bomb explosions. When he deliberately turned to voice his suspicions about who might be behind the fomentation of discontent, he realized that Anderson had stopped listening and was scribbling furiously on a pad of paper in front of him. He slipped the paper to Guthrie, at the same time making some vague comment in reply, to cover up the surprised hesitation in the Scotsman's voice.

The note read: *Keep talking. May be being overheard. Delicate discussion comes later. Will explain.*

After he had got over his initial assumption that Anderson had suddenly gone mad, they talked in generalities. Then Guthrie returned to his hotel, content to wait until the evening when Anderson would doubtless give him a full explanation of his warning.

In retrospect, it was inevitable that he would not turn up. Someone, presumably Carlyle or de Laski, was preventing them from meeting privately. They were obviously scared that Anderson would reveal something he should not. Guthrie wondered how this fitted in with Torrance's remark on the flight and what weight he should give to the journalist Silt's suspicions. His conjecturing was becoming dangerously unreal. He needed to talk it through with someone.

As he returned to his seat at the end of the interval, Guthrie's thoughts were distracted by an auburn-haired young woman, who slipped into the empty seat beside him. At first he thought she had mistaken her place but she leaned towards him and said, 'Sorry to surprise you like this, Mr Guthrie. Father sent me. I'm Heather Anderson.'

Guthrie half rose to shake hands but she gestured him to stay seated. 'No,' she whispered urgently in his ear. 'Leave the formalities. Father's in a state. First Mr Torrance's accident and now, unbelievably, he says to tell you he's been banned from talking to you alone.'

'I don't . . .' Guthrie was amazed at having his private speculation so rapidly confirmed.

'I don't understand either. I've never known him like this. He said to say sorry and that he'd be in touch and explain his worries later . . . probably by telephone, once you're back in Scotland.'

'Once I'm back . . .' Guthrie paused as the lights started to dim for the second half.

'That's the message,' she whispered. 'I must go.'

'Hush,' said someone fiercely from the row behind.

'I'm coming too. I've had enough,' said Guthrie with feeling. Then, with much muttering and complaints from those in the audience around them, they pushed past the seats and out of the auditorium just as the curtain rose once again.

As they stood talking in the foyer, Guthrie was able to focus on Heather Anderson. Attractive and cool in a green cotton dress, she had deep concern written all across her face. Her eyes glanced intelligently back at him.

'Father's on his own. I have to get back to him. The Fed used to be such a lively, happy place. Now . . . well, a lot of hard men have moved in, he tells me. Suddenly it's become very different.'

'D'you have time for a quick drink or coffee, or have you eaten?' asked Guthrie. 'If I'm not to see your father again before I leave, there are some questions I'd like you to ask him for me.'

Heather Anderson looked at her watch, then at Guthrie. She liked what she saw. He looked honest and dependable. 'OK,' she said. 'Let me make a phone call. I'm sure he'll understand.'

When she returned, they took a cab uptown to a small piano bar next to the hotel where he was staying. Settling into a corner table they chatted easily with each other on generalities before returning to the reason for their coming together.

'You know Scotland?' Guthrie asked.

'Only indirectly through father. He took the whole family there a long time ago. I was very young and don't remember much about it apart from the rain.' She laughed. 'I've always felt that my image of it was filtered through his rose-coloured spectacles. All tartan, Burns and Scott. I'm sure there's a modern Scotland waiting to be discovered.' It was true, she thought to herself. Scotland had been constantly in the background throughout her childhood. Once or twice, as she grew older, she had contemplated finding out more about the heritage that seemed to mean so much to her father. She would, one day, go and visit that far-off country and challenge or cement the innate impressions she had of it. Other more important things had always got in the way until now. Scotland had had to wait.

'You should come and see for yourself,' Guthrie spoke enthusiastically.

'I might do just that once I've sorted out father's problems. Perhaps he and I could come together.'

'If he is being put under the sort of pressure you suggest, they might not let him off the chain. What's behind it all?'

'I don't have a clear view. Father genuinely wants to help Scotland but the hard men think his plans are too vague and ephemeral. They've more robust aims and strategies.'

'Who are *they*?'

'Don't know that either.' Heather shrugged. 'Hardly met any of them. There's a man de Laski and . . . I could find out,' she volunteered hesitantly.

'That'd be helpful.' As he spoke, Guthrie realized that his answer was prompted by a variety of motives. He would value what she could uncover but it was becoming increasingly apparent to him as he sat beside her sipping his glass of Chablis, that he would welcome a device for keeping in touch. She had a sparkle about her and a warmth of smile that he found instantly attractive.

She glanced at her watch. 'I should be going.'

'Not yet.' He was surprised at his own presumption; he was usually more subtle.

She glanced at him, alert. 'All right,' she said. 'Only a little longer.'

'Tell me about yourself,' he prompted.

'There's not much to know.' She shrugged and grinned.

'Tell me what there is.' He smiled back at her. It was the first time in years that he had found himself so instantly attracted to a woman. He wanted to understand more about her.

'We're meant to be talking business,' she said lightly.

'Business and pleasure can run together.' Guthrie continued to speak with more assertiveness than he felt. He was not normally good at chatting up girls but Heather was proving highly intriguing.

'If you know my father, you know me. Everybody says I'm much like him. Mother died quite a few years ago, so we've remained pretty close. I've a sister but she's married in Santa Barbara and we don't see each other all that often. What else . . .' She paused. 'If you're really interested, well, my first degree was in law at Yale, then I waded into the dreaded career of journalism. It pays well.'

As she spoke she realized that *waded* was a totally inappropriate word to have used. She had gone into journalism with her eyes open because at that time she'd had a boyfriend who was the Latin American correspondent of the *Washington Post*. She looked away briefly as she recalled, for the thousandth time, the black day when the message had come that he had been killed by a bomb in Colombia while working on a drug-dealing story. Even after a decade it still hurt.

Guthrie noted that she had suddenly become subdued but did not pursue it. 'You work for?' he asked.

'Used to be the *New York Times*,' she said. 'Then I decided I wanted to freelance. I write for a range of magazines and newspapers, in New York City and in Washington DC.'

'Subject?'

'Business, law, social. Turn my hand to anything. Like most journalists I rapidly acquire a half-inch-deep knowledge of almost anything. Even wrote about Bonsai-growing the other day. Getting quite expert at dressing up my ignorance.' She cheered up and flashed a warm smile at him.

'Honest of you.'

'It's what all journalists have to do. What more can I say?' She shrugged.

'You stick to feature articles?'

'Do you mean, have I a book in me?' Heather asked. 'No way.

Maybe some day I'll write something longer and more substantial. But not yet. I'll leave that till I'm approaching my anecdotage.' She looked down at her watch. 'Now I really do have to go,' she insisted.

'I'd value hearing what you find out about your father's new colleagues.' Guthrie was surprisingly reluctant to let the evening come to an end.

Heather stood to leave. 'Consider me hired,' she said, and smiled.

Later, before she fell asleep in her tiny East Side apartment on 67th and Second Avenue, she thought quite a bit about the Scotsman she had just met. Here, she felt, was someone who might prove quite special in her life. While he seemed a dark horse and might prove difficult to get to know, she decided, there and then, that she was certainly going to try.

5

MacDowall: the man and the myth

While the country at large seems happy to allow Keith Sinclair more time to recover, the leadership of the nation rests firmly in one man's hands. Sir Alexander MacDowall is like some giant gnarled tree trunk. He has been part of Scotland's national scenery for longer than anyone else. Many people believe that without him the whole fabric of this nation state would crumble away. That would not happen of course, but it is certainly true that, without him, Scotland would lose a sure hand on the tiller . . .

(Profile in the *Herald*)

Three long weeks and Sinclair had had enough. Three weeks of having to learn to do what he had always taken for granted. Three weeks when his arms and shoulders had to undertake all the work that his legs had once done. Above all, it had been three weeks of learning to propel himself around in his shiny new wheelchair. The medical staff had been excellent. They had taught him how to move from bed to wheelchair to bath to toilet. He still had no feelings in his legs. They refused to prognosticate whether it would always be so. Time, it would take time, they kept repeating.

The Prime Minister gave one pooled media interview from his hospital bed. Like a corpse they made him up to look as if he had just returned from a long and expensive holiday. His wife

Nora came and posed, smiling, by his side. He was getting much better, he said. He was dealing with urgent Government papers from his bed; they had arranged his official boxes around him like theatre props to prove it. No, there was no question of his resigning due to ill-health. He would soon be back in charge. Very soon.

And so he resolved. Keith Sinclair suddenly announced that he had decided to attend the Foreign Affairs debate in two days' time. In case anything went wrong or he had a relapse, he warned only Guthrie and MacDowall. His doctors, who were totally against it, were sworn to secrecy. Guthrie and MacDowall clearly showed that they too thought it extremely foolish of him but did not try to stop him.

He made his preparations. He wrote and practised his speech. He would spend the night before the debate at his official residence in Charlotte Square, where it was arranged that a nurse would be on duty to help him.

That morning they wheeled him to a discreet side door of the hospital. His official Rover Ecosse glided across the forecourt and Ingram, his long-time chauffeur, climbed out, uneasily adjusting his shoulder holster as he did so. Special Branch had insisted that he be armed after the attack on him and had put him through a week's small-arms course at Rosyth. Ingram was pleased with the extra wage and status it gave him. It also impressed his wife. A personal protection officer would in future always travel with Sinclair as well.

Ingram came round to help Sinclair with his chair and gave him the news. He presumed it would please or satisfy Sinclair to hear that a man called MacManus had been arrested and charged with the attack that had killed all feeling in him from his waist down.

'He'll no' starve in Peterhead gaol,' Ingram said happily. Sinclair was numb to the remark and to the further information that this MacManus had six children and had been out of work for as many months. The law would take its course, whatever a Prime Minister thought. No one would ask *him* how many years in gaol his paralysis was worth. Presumably judges and jury would weigh it carefully on some scales of justice. Two legs: say twelve years, six apiece. Had Sinclair the opportunity to be on the bench instead, he might be more understanding and tolerant and put MacManus on probation for the sake of his six children. But as the attack had been on a Prime Minister, an example would have to be made. Long years behind the granite walls of Peterhead would not only be just, but would be seen to be essential for the sake of national law and order. So, at the news, Sinclair showed none of the emotion for which Ingram had been waiting. In consequence the chauffeur looked despondent. It was not that he was a malicious man but he was of the Free Church and a believer in an eye for an eye. Fortunately for MacManus the courts could not pass a sentence of paralysis.

On impulse, Sinclair further unsettled Ingram by ordering him to make a detour. He'd been in captivity for too long. On a whim he said he wanted to breathe some fresh sea air. They would go via the East Lothian coast, just for a short while. Ingram and the protection officer seated beside him in front of the Rover glanced at each other but said nothing. A Prime Minister's wish was an order.

When they reached a road that led along by the shore overlooking the Firth of Forth, Sinclair told them to park, then had them help him out of the car and into his chair. He waved them away and wheeled himself as far as he could go, then sat, staring out to sea, collecting his thoughts. After a few minutes he tried to turn the chair but the wheels had a will of their own and, despite the bitterness of the wind, he was pouring with sweat by the time he was halfway to the roadside. Ingram, an unenthusiastic spectator of his sudden lust for exercise and fresh air, left the Rover and came up behind him. But he had a sullen percipience and, sensing Sinclair's mood, withheld his offer of help.

Beyond them both was the sand, the rocks and an advancing tide. Sinclair could see a sandcastle built by some child, which, despite walls well armoured with limpet shells and pebbles, was gradually being eroded as the waves circled it. He sat there for a while, surveying its battle, visualizing it as some form of parable for Scotland's present dilemma. As he watched, the seaward wall of the sandcastle sank gently into an anonymous pile of wet sludge but the central keep remained unharmed. The water was nearly at the highest line of seaweed and the fate of the structure now depended on when the tide turned and whether the wind dropped. So it would be with Scotland.

Ingram meanwhile had returned to the car, impatiently slapping his hands together against the cold. Let him wait, thought Sinclair. The air might bring a touch of colour to his pale, unhealthy face, might dilute the odour of stale cigarette smoke that perpetually hung around him. An odd man Ingram, but he seemed to respect his boss and he certainly valued his job.

Sinclair stubbornly continued to sit there, braced more than numbed by the wind. He only had on a short tweed coat; his legs, in thin camouflaging pinstripes, would be cold if he could have felt them but a touch of refrigeration would add little further damage to what had already been done. To his right the road ran away from the shore. A new housing scheme had not been allowed to spread too far to intrude on the view and a large wooded estate still occupied the landward side, its trees grotesquely bent by the prevailing onshore wind. Beyond, sheltered by the wood, lay the neat black fields of rich East Lothian soil. In that part of the country, life had continued as prosperously as before; some farmers had even gained from Independence, unlike those who lived in the troubled industrial belt to the west, whom Sinclair knew and understood better.

Sitting there, anaesthetized by the cold sea, he felt detached, as if he were uninvolved, as if he could do nothing to alleviate the problems that tore at the heart of the country. But his escape could last no more than a few moments, even if his red despatch box had not been waiting there on the back seat of the Rover, a constant reminder of his high office. Its lid was embossed with a gilt symbolic thistle and the title of his rank but, inside, buff files contained his problems. Neatly and coldly, his civil servants had digested and presented him with their impartial advice, yet the problems were his alone to solve. These were his public tasks, which the public knew about. They and most of his colleagues granted him too much sympathy, too much consideration, for all that had happened to him recently. Even his few close friends knew little of the wreck of his private life.

The rain had been hitting him for some moments before Ingram screwed up courage and disturbed him. 'Are you all right, Prime Minister?' His voice was anxious, more about the Prime Minister's reaction than about his welfare since his master's temper, always uneven, had hardly benefited from his injury.

'Getting wet?' Sinclair's voice was a fraction sharp. 'Very well then. Get me inside.'

He wheeled himself back across the road to the Rover Ecosse and, helped by the protection officer, the elaborate procedure of loading him and his chair into the back began all over again.

Inside the car, he had just pulled the silver top from his hipflask to warm himself up when the car phone began its irritating ring. Guthrie had been getting worried. Where had the Prime Minister been?

They drove into Edinburgh along the bypass. Somewhere by Haymarket railway station they had to stop in heavy traffic. Pulling his body upright, Sinclair moved his legs into a more comfortable position on the black leather seat and thought with gloom about an evening alone with Nora. Why the hell hadn't he taken everyone's advice, left it till tomorrow and gone straight from the hospital to the National Assembly without this extra and unnecessary fuss? His reflections were interrupted by the sight of a man gesticulating outside the car window. He was old, dressed in a greasy gabardine coat and a battered tweed cap, and his face was contorted with dislike. He had recognized Sinclair, and whatever his reasons, his feelings were obvious. He started hammering at the window in his anger. 'No work,' Sinclair heard him shout. 'No work, no food, no home.' Ingram turned sharply in his seat. The protection officer made to get out of the car, but then the lights changed and they left him behind. Sinclair managed to heave himself round and look out of the rear window at the old man who was still waving wildly in his direction.

He had grown immune to most political insults. The majority of them were surface affairs and personal relationships seldom suffered underneath. In any case he gave as good as he got; it was part of the fabric of political life. It was the same with public abuse: every politician had to face up to demonstrations and heckling, but it too was generally of an impersonal kind. It was the other type that hurt him, the individual attacks, on television, in the newspapers and elsewhere, with the conventional wisdom that he, as Prime Minister, was personally responsible for all the misfortunes of the country. That hurt. It was unjust and untrue. Then had come the physical attack on him. It had stilled the critics' voices overnight. The fickle public, led by the press, had shed a guilty tear. Keith Sinclair was suddenly overwhelmed with messages of sympathy and regret. Now when they spoke of him, they set his actions in a less critical light; they prefaced every editorial with sickening references to his disability and his supposed courage in wanting to get back to his desk. He had become a martyr who had fought and fallen for his principles. Others had taken on the role of public bogeymen. Perhaps the old man at the traffic lights hadn't heard about his martyrdom, that the pack were now hunting a different trail. Perhaps he was just more honest than the rest and believed that no politician's principles could have changed so rapidly. Perhaps the old man was right.

His wife Nora was sitting in front of the television set in the small study of their official house in Charlotte Square when he arrived. While the domestic staff were present, she smiled her distant greetings but her eyes were empty. Her thin face, which he had briefly found so attractive, had collected lines of bitchiness around her mouth which symbolized her character so well.

He wheeled himself across the parquet to the open fire. He was wet and cold. Nora rose and pecked a dry kiss at his cheek that failed to make contact, but it hardly mattered. It was all part of their make-believe. He was less anxious about appearances now but was prepared to let things ride. He seldom even lost his temper with her these days. It had always been pointless.

The staff had already converted the morning room on the ground floor into a temporary bedroom to accommodate his disability. He went there to undergo the laborious business of washing and changing and then came through for dinner. The Sinclairs had long adopted the habit, when eating alone, of reading during their meal. Nora had even had two neat mahogany bookrests made to match the furniture. She had given them to him amid much public jollity one Christmas, while his present to her had not stretched beyond the usual convenient cheque. They liked reading and it obviated the need to talk to each other. The housekeeper, Ingram's wife, had got used to serving them in silence; they did not even need to ask each other for the salt, since a grateful constituent had once presented him with two identical Georgian silver cruets.

The meal was mediocre and he drank more than he should. Nora, however, was incensed by the cooking and broke the silence to announce that she intended to give Mrs Ingram a week's notice. He said nothing and went on reading, which she interpreted as his opposition to her plan. She was wrong: he was totally uninterested.

After a few moments she stood up and abruptly left the table. She contained herself sufficiently to hesitate at the door and claim that she had a headache and, for a moment, he thought she was going to stay. She seemed ill at ease, and he sensed that there was something she wanted to say. But he was tired; he should not have touched alcohol on top of the painkillers he was taking. He remarked ironically that it was perhaps she who should see a doctor since her migraines always seemed to time so well with their eating alone together. This was hardly tactful and led to her slamming the door behind her while he returned to his book and the remains of the wine.

Later he asked Mrs Ingram to take a vacuum flask of coffee through to the study and to leave the drinks tray within reach. He wheeled himself through to his desk, intending to work on his speech for the next day. Guthrie had sent him a despatch box with other urgent papers for him to see. He took a little key from his pocket, unlocked the box and began leafing through his letters and files. One was an intelligence analysis of the explosion at the Campsie transmitter. They were still at a loss over the reasons for the outrage. The Police Commissioner was convinced it was the work of political fanatics. He had even rung Sinclair in his hospital bed – the doctors were furious at his insensitivity – to tell him his views.

'You'll have to arm us now, Prime Minister. The force won't stand for much more of this, I can tell you. You'll have to –'

'Discuss it at the National Security Committee, Jimmy, and let me know the result.' Sinclair had been equally angry.

He wheeled himself away from his desk and over to the fire. Out of habit, he poked the remaining embers as best as he could and with difficulty placed the fireguard in front of the fire, intending to summon the nurse to help him to bed. In an alcove off the Adam hallway, an ugly internal switchboard had been installed to enable calls to be put through to any room in the house. On his way to bed he paused to switch the line from the study to the instrument on his bedside table. As he did so, his wheelchair started rolling slightly and by accident and helped by the drink, he flicked the wrong switch. When he got to his temporary bedroom and picked up the telephone to summon the duty nurse, it was Nora's voice he heard. She was talking to someone in terms that were not open to misinterpretation. He did not recognize the man's voice; he was monosyllabic and more discreet than she about their obvious intimacy.

After a few moments, curiosity was overtaken by disgust. He quietly replaced the receiver, wheeled himself back to the hall, threw down the correct switch and summoned the nurse. He had no feeling of betrayal at his wife's unfaithfulness. He had long suspected it.

All the world's a stage

Politics is badly-rehearsed theatre. The National Assembly is, too often, the stage for would-be actors playing to Laurence Olivier's advice that if you can fake sincerity you can fake anything. The best politicians have always stage managed their effects with great care. Churchill, de Gaulle, Macmillan: all could captivate and hold an audience. Keith Sinclair has seldom been able to emulate them but today was a triumph, a personal triumph. Ministers, backbenchers, even Nick Forbes, the left-wing Environment Minister, and never his greatest fan, lined up to congratulate him.

But let us be blunt. Mr Sinclair will be the first to realize that his personal triumph was helped by that most dramatic of props: the wheelchair. It, not his words, had him listened to in silence. It, not his speech, gave him that standing ovation which brought tears to many eyes.

If he does not know, let us tell him it as it was: when he had left the Chamber, the problems and the bitter rancour erupted all over again.

(*Scottish Mirror* Editorial)

It was corporate hospitality at its best: a hundred and fifty of the top movers and shakers in Scotland all invited to a glittering black-tie dinner at Gleneagles by the Chairman of the Unity Corporation. The guest speaker was none other than a former President of the United States, flown over with no cost spared, bribed by an extra hundred thousand dollars into his pension fund for the night's event, followed by some very agreeable days of golf at Turnberry, Muirfield and St Andrews. And why? Because that was the way to get everyone who was anyone to come.

Abel Rosenfeld was a master of the art. He could spin doctor the highest in the land and he knew that every detail had to be perfection. The world-famous Boston String Quartet had been flown in to play before and after dinner, each guest had an expensive, beautifully-wrapped gift at their tableplace and, at the end of the dinner the main speaker, James Fulton himself, stood up to great applause, to hand over a cheque for half a million pounds to various Scottish children's charities. For charity and warmth and friendship across the Atlantic was what the evening was all about.

Robert Guthrie counted himself fortunate to be invited though he did not much relish the long drive home afterwards; he was not one of those privileged enough to be invited to stay at the hotel for the night. He enjoyed the evening, working his way around the room, talking to the captains and the kings of Scottish industry, finance, law and the arts. But as the evening progressed he pulled back and watched Abel Rosenfeld at work: one cool professional watching another. It was only his second substantial exposure to Rosenfeld in action and he relished the experience. He watched this charming, almost sensual fox of a man, admiring the manipulative charm with which the American set about his varied tasks as he worked his way among the guests. Maybe, as was rumoured, Rosenfeld could be duplicitous and two-faced, but Guthrie could not bring himself to dislike him for that. Rosenfeld had resonance, he had character and he always appeared good-natured and imperturbable. What if he was the somewhat insalubrious grease that made the great machine that was the Unity Corporation work smoothly and well? To have reached the position he was now in Rosenfeld had to have more than a well-practised smile.

After dinner, drinks in hand, the two men stood talking, waiting to listen to the music.

'Meticulous,' said Guthrie admiringly. 'Excellent dinner, wines, the lot.'

'The unbeatable amalgam of Scots and American hospitality.' Rosenfeld was at his most charming, stopping short of being too smooth. 'It allows us to say thanks to some old friends and introduce ourselves to some new ones.'

'I see from today's papers that you're looking to take over that fertilizer factory near Livingston?' Guthrie asked.

'Bit premature, but it looks that way.' As he spoke, Rosenfeld's eyes wandered ceaselessly around the room, taking everything in, ensuring that every detail was going to plan.

'The PM is pleased at the confidence Unity is showing in Scotland. We need all the support we can get.'

'That's James Fulton's philosophy. His forefathers all came from Aberdeen – he thinks. He's a bit vague on the detail but he likes it here and not just for the golf. Know what his latest joke is? Thought he was going to tell it tonight.' Rosenfeld laughed. 'There are three types of people in the world: the Scots, those who would be Scots, and . . . those with no ambition.'

Guthrie echoed the American's laughter but, when he was left alone again, he turned his attention from observing Abel Rosenfeld to watching James Fulton at work and play. A big man in every sense of the word; when Guthrie had briefly shaken hands with him at the beginning of the evening he had felt the power, not just in the grip, which was firm, but in the man's whole physical presence. The tycoon had smiled a big smile down at him, each tooth perfectly capped and polished. Now Guthrie saw him from a distance and was glad of the fact: to be too closely involved with the Chairman of Unity would be to be swallowed up. Fulton loomed, towered over everyone there, even the former President. Here was someone who was no mere megalomaniac but a man who was singleminded, abrasive, perhaps crude, but, above all, knew exactly what he wanted, and where he and the company he had founded were going in the future. Here was absolute power personified, both honest and corrupt. James Fulton would, Guthrie guessed, brook no opposition. No wonder his colleagues were said to go in fear of him and his tempers. People would do his bidding, follow or be crushed.

Guthrie went on to speculate about what that one evening must have cost Unity. Hundreds of thousands of pounds had been expended. To what long-term end? He watched a power cluster where Fulton now stood with the former President and with Ian Campbell, the latter bursting with inflated self-importance. Indeed, Guthrie noted, Campbell had been treated as the second most important guest of honour throughout. When the weak got courted by the strong, it was always particularly valuable to look for underlying motives. And, looking around the room, he remembered an expression he had heard once about the massaging of public perception: an *acquiescent society* was one that was willing, for the price of being entertained, to be deceived.

6

Has Independence failed?

Since Independence these few years ago, the *Herald* has always been highly supportive of the Sinclair Government through good times and bad. However we also have a loyalty to our readers. We have a duty to the men and women of Scotland who have lost so much – income, jobs, their previous higher standard of living, and, above all, hope. The question has to be asked: is Independence, this political freedom we have fought for, worth the present penury? No matter where our emotional and historical passions lie, we have to be practical. Has Independence failed?

Some people argue that it is Scotland's size that is the problem. Population has nothing to do with it. A recent report by the *Economist* indicated that twenty-five of the top thirty-five of the world's richest nations, measured in terms of their GDP, have populations of less than ten million. So the truth lies elsewhere.

Hope may be at hand. Scotland has powerful friends of Scottish stock in key positions around the world and, in particular, in North America. In his recent speech to the CBI, Ian Campbell talked about a rescue package, not in the form of third world style aid but through partnership. And partnership would have to mean just that. It can never be the out-stretched hand but an exciting and mutually profit-able treaty between the public and the private sector.

It is hoped that the tragic and as yet unexplained death of that great American friend of Scotland, William Torrance, will not prove a setback for this exciting prospect . . .

(Extract from an editorial in the Herald)

An emergency meeting, held in the main police ops room, was called to consider the impact of the Campsie explosion. The room had been designed with an eye to security, the main feature being its total lack of windows. But there was a work-to-rule among the electricity maintenance men and, while the emergency generator provided sufficient light for the PM to decree that they should carry on and use the room as agreed, the air conditioning was not working properly and tempers quickly became frayed.

The Commissioner's report contained pages of detail about the calibre of the bullet in the policeman's back, the type of explosive used, but nothing, not one single clue, as to who was responsible. Spokesmen for both Republican and Reunionist extremists were widely quoted denying their involvement. Preliminary police and Special Task Force reports indicated that the leaders on both sides were genuine in their protestations of innocence. Meanwhile, both the media and public were clamouring for results.

The mood in the room was tense. The general stuffiness and the fact that the PM, who had decided to chair the meeting himself, was at his most indecisive, added to an already trying situation. Just as the nadir was reached and people were beginning to squabble, Sir Alexander MacDowall quietly took charge of the meeting. The PM, looking totally exhausted in his wheelchair, hardly seemed to notice that he had relinquished control.

'If we accept that the extremists are blameless, Prime Minister, it's either an unknown faction in one or other organization, or . . .' MacDowall waited to make sure he had everyone's attention, 'or, some third party –'

'What are you on about? What third party? We'd know about it,' interrupted the Commissioner with irritation. The two men as usual were intent on rubbing each other up the wrong way.

'– which, though unknown at the moment,' MacDowall deliberately ignored him, 'may sooner or later give itself away.'

'Anarchist? Individual crank?' This time it was the Prime Minister who interrupted.

'Too big for one person, sir,' said the Commissioner. 'Bomb squad believes it was too expertly done for any crazies.'

'What do we say to the press?' asked one of the senior civil servants.

'Nothing, nothing, nothing,' the Commissioner responded tartly.

'If we do that,' MacDowall bridled, 'we'll have both sides blaming the other. They'll be at each other's throats in no time at all. You want a civil war?' he added provocatively.

'Well then,' said the Prime Minister, noting the danger signals, 'my Press Secretary should continue to say that we are working flat out to identify the culprits. On no account do we apportion blame.' He looked round at the sweltering members of the National Security Committee as if, having agreed the press line, the problem was now solved.

'We are now without the benefit of communications intelligence,' said MacDowall softly. He was making indecipherable notes on a pad in front of him and did not look up as he spoke. 'The critical question arises: who could possibly benefit from that?'

'Good point –' the Prime Minister broke off suddenly as if a thought had just occurred to him. The others in the room saw that he had suddenly turned grey with pain. Sinclair fumbled with the wheels of his chair. 'If you would excuse me, I must –' There was a soundless sigh of concern as they stood up politely and watched as he wheeled himself out of the ops room.

With Sinclair gone, the meeting rapidly adjourned to an adjoining conference room with more fresh air, if less security. The move made, the pace of their deliberations sharpened perceptibly. They reviewed the evidence, decided on future security measures, authorized the widest possible undercover investigations including telephone taps where feasible, then discussed getting the Communications Monitoring Station back in working order again.

'There is this rather presumptuous offer by the Unity Corporation of the use of some neighbouring buildings to the Campsie site. I understand they used to house a radar tracking station owned by Marconi. The huts are empty and they're not using them. What do people think?' MacDowall asked.

Although welcomed in general, the possibility was discussed that Unity was doing it in order to buy favours or land themselves some Government contract or other. MacDowall felt an unease about using any commercial facilities on security grounds but no one else seemed to share his concern. Then the controller of the Communications Monitoring Service announced, a trifle shame-facedly, that negotiations with Unity over the property were already under way. Their site was right next door, and it would be extremely valuable in terms of getting the monitoring activities back into operation if the Government had the use of the Unity buildings during reconstruction.

MacDowall curtailed the meeting shortly thereafter. He was not at all satisfied with the progress made but they were all still too much in the dark to do anything else. He put his papers away into his briefcase, making a few notes as he did so, and consequently was almost the last to leave the room. Robert Guthrie, who had remained silent throughout the entire meeting, had lingered deliberately and came up behind him.

'A word, Minister?' he said. 'Not here,' he added.

Guthrie and MacDowall walked together all the way back from the Mound to St Andrew's House and then went up to the Minister's room. It was one of the most pleasant in the building, with a panoramic view of the city skyline. The walls were lined with bookshelves filled with bound volumes of Hansard from pre-Independence days and the few new red bindings of the Scottish National Assembly Proceedings.

They had spoken little on their walk except to talk about the PM's health. 'I tried to stop him coming, but he's still as obstinate as ever,' Guthrie explained. 'You can see how desperately weak he is.'

'I thought you'd leave when he did,' MacDowall grunted.

'We'd arranged . . . he wanted me to stay behind. He's in great pain, you know.'

MacDowall pushed his half-moon glasses a fraction higher up the bridge of his nose. 'Anyone can see that,' he grunted. 'One of our many problems,' he added as if to himself. Then he turned suddenly and looked hard at Guthrie. 'So tell me yours,' he demanded as he went across and sat down behind his desk.

'I don't like it, Minister,' Guthrie began after a slight pause. At face value it was a banal remark.

'Nor I,' responded MacDowall.

'Stating the obvious, I know. But I've come back from New York with a bundle of other suspicions. Eliminate the anarchists, the fringe Republicans, the Reunionists. None of them have anything to gain. They probably didn't even know that the monitoring station existed. Neither has an interest in chaos right now. Both sides know the country's ills aren't going to be solved by such mindless violence.'

'The Reunionists could gain some votes,' MacDowall growled, 'if on top of all the economic problems, serious civil unrest blows up again. Wouldn't take much to drive the fickle electorate into demanding the clock be put back. Scots value their security too much. We'll have the English army marching in to keep order, if we're not careful. I joke of course.' He did not look as if he was joking.

'Agreed. But not now. Forbes and colleagues know the peaceful forces of unemployment will do the job for them. This sort of outrage makes moderate Reunionist supporters, like Campbell, swing Right out of sympathy. You know that, Minister. Neither of them would have anything to do with such violence.'

'Then?' MacDowall prompted the younger man to continue.

'What other group? Not the English. They don't care and they've enough on their plates. So who else might benefit from our instability? Who would have the knowledge and degree of sophistication to believe that wiping out our monitoring capability . . . or, rather, who is communicating the sort of sensitive or hostile information that they wouldn't want the Scottish Government to see?' Guthrie's words were delivered in a quiet, measured voice.

He became aware of the Minister staring at him. He was reminded of his Latin master discovering that he had failed to do his prep. 'You're not suggesting that the Federation of American Caledonian Societies . . .' MacDowall asked.

'Of course not, sir. Not them.'

'Then?' said MacDowall briskly. 'If you've got serious suspicions I want to hear about them, Robert. Now.'

'Look at it this way, Minister,' Guthrie replied softly. 'The police threw an immediate cordon round the whole area. They found nothing, not one single, substantial clue. Not one,' he repeated. 'No traces of vehicles, no strangers in the area. Isn't that odd?'

'An inside job is out of the question. Perhaps they were holed up somewhere very close by.'

They sat in silence. The phone on the Minister's desk rang. It was the Police Commissioner: reports were coming in that the Communications Monitoring Sub-station at Kinloss on the Moray Firth had just shared the same fate as the Campsie one. There was no news yet of any casualties.

'Does the Unity Corporation have a site near there too?' Guthrie asked, when the Minister had replaced the receiver.

MacDowall looked across at him. 'You are not joking,' he said slowly, then went on, 'if you're serious, young man, perhaps you'd better contact the controller of Communications Intelligence. On second thoughts, don't. Get on to the head of the Special Task Force, personally, with authority from me. Ask him to go through their database. See what sort of high-grade messages the Unity boys have been passing to and from their US Headquarters.'

'Minister,' said Guthrie calmly. 'I already have.'

The Government is to ask the Constitutional Court
to increase the number of seats allocated to Orkney

and Shetland in the National Assembly. This follows the discovery that a delegation from the two island councils has been having secret talks in Oslo and Stockholm about developing closer links with them. The councils have made no secret in recent years about their growing disgust at what they perceive as a lack of interest by Edinburgh in their concerns. Councillor Magnus Shettleston said in Lerwick yesterday that Edinburgh and Glasgow had no interest in anything north of the Highland Line. 'In my view, the islands would be better served by increasing their historic ties with Norway,' he said. 'We were long neglected by London and Edinburgh is proving worse.'

Any break-away move could put Scotland's oil fields at risk and the Government's move is an obvious bid to pre-empt such a devastating blow to the national economy.

By our Political Editor
(The *Herald*)

Given a degree of mutual attraction and a belief that they will not be found out, most people will opt for infidelity. So said a French philosopher. True or false, the belief that illicit sexual relations, particularly those involving consenting politicians and others in the goldfish bowl of public life, eventually have a nasty habit of hitting both tabloid and broadsheet is a sounder one. Even the most proper members of society are happy to pass on the news of the indiscretions of others better known and more successful than themselves. *Schadenfreude* is attractive to all.

It was not malicious pleasure, however, but the enhancement of shareholder value and the strategic imperatives of the Unity Corporation that led to a most unhappy episode in the utterly selfish life of Mrs Nora Sinclair. Dressed to kill and with an expensive facelift to match, she thought of herself as a sort of social lighthouse, beaming intelligent conversation and latent sexuality at all around her. She expected to charm, to entice, to fascinate. She had been the wife of an important man for far too long, however, and failed to realize that at social functions she was the centre of attraction solely because of whom she had married. By and large, those who knew her well shared her husband's feeling: they did not like her. To those she liked she could be briefly compelling and she was rumoured to be extremely inventive and progressive in bed. Those whom she did not like, she did not recognize, and the rest she ignored. She was a stranger to being frustrated or bettered in achieving any of her public or private goals. That was why her brief meeting with Abel Rosenfeld was uniquely distressing and deeply unpleasant.

She had been shopping for lingerie in Jenners in Princes Street. While the shop was not known for its risqué fashions in underwear, she knew what suited her and what might appeal to her current lover. She then was due to meet a social acquaintance at the Balmoral Hotel across the road. That lady, who had telephoned her out of the blue offering to subscribe generously to one of Nora's favourite charities, unexpectedly and irritatingly did not show up, and she was about to leave and take a taxi back to Charlotte Square when a stranger came up and sat down unasked in the chair opposite her.

She stood to leave. Doubtless the man was some disaffected voter who had recognized her and who now wanted to hang out his complaints in front of her in the hope that she would have some influence over the Prime Minister.

'Don't go, Mrs Sinclair.' The stranger was smiling. He lounged effortlessly over rather than in his chair, one arm hanging easily by his side. He had an American accent.

'I'm sorry?' she said distantly. 'Do we know each other?'

'You don't know me, Mrs Sinclair. But I know all about you.' She noted the immaculate suit, the expensive tie and shirt and in other circumstances she might have been impressed.

'I really must be going,' she said, moving away.

'No, you don't,' said Abel Rosenfeld, a harder note creeping into his voice. 'The lady whom you're here to meet won't be turning up.'

'I guessed as much.' There was something strange and menacing about this conversation and Nora Sinclair did not think she liked it. Was the man attempting to chat her up? He was dark and what her father used to call Levantine. She did not see him as her type.

'Not coming, so you do have a little time to spare. I need to speak to you. Urgently.'

Nora was as alert as anyone in public life to the danger of strangers, nutters, or those who might wish to hurt her, or get at her husband through her. She looked around the lounge in search of a known face and started to raise her hand when she spotted one of the hotel staff.

'I wouldn't do that, Mrs Sinclair,' he said. 'You see you need to listen to me – in your own best interests. You . . . and Mr Ian Campbell.' The threat of the words was in stark contrast with the smile that had remained fixed on the man's face. He was either a good actor, or a sadist.

She again made to leave, turning her back on him, unsure and uncertain.

'No way will you leave, Mrs Sinclair. Unless you want the story to be all over tomorrow's tabloids. And if you think I'm joking or we don't have proof, well . . . we have intimate letters from you, photographs, and one or two very personal bits of knowledge. Your friend, Mr Campbell, is far from careful with his possessions.'

She turned back to face him. Through her heavy make-up she had lost most of her colour as she collapsed back into the seat she had just vacated. 'How much do you want?' she whispered.

'Come, come, Mrs Sinclair. Do I look like a blackmailer? Do I look as if I need the sort of money you could possibly afford?' The insolence of his words made the challenge even more unpleasant. He was indeed expensively dressed. He was still smiling his switched-on smile.

'Who are you? What the hell do you want?'

'Abel Rosenfeld's the name, Mrs Sinclair.' He made as if to offer her his hand to shake but then thought better of it. 'I work for the Unity Corporation. It's my business to know things.'

Nora's thoughts flashed back to the devastating telephone call from Robert Guthrie, telling her of Keith's accident. She had never told anyone about Ian, so Ian must have been the one to let it leak, damn him. He was good in bed but he was also an idiot. Next time round she would make him really suffer. 'What do you want of me?' she repeated, looking around her to ensure that no one could overhear them.

'Can I get you a drink first, or a cup of coffee?'

She shook her head dismissively.

'You don't mind if I do in that case?' he asked. 'I need twenty minutes of your time, only twenty minutes. I have a deal to propose.'

Twenty-five minutes later, rather than taking a taxi, she started walking back to Charlotte Square. Half-dazed, she needed the time to think. She was both a deeply selfish and totally amoral woman, but now she was angry at being blackmailed in this way. She hated being used. She would have to go along with it of course. As far as she could see there was no other option open to her, no one she could turn to for advice or to confess. No money was involved after all and in time, she consoled herself, she would become used to the duplicity or, she speculated, perhaps it could be called triplicity. She had undertaken, in return for the story of her affair or affairs not appearing in the Scottish *News of the World* – that odious man Rosenfeld had suggested that he knew of certain others of her flings – to provide them with a continuing flow of information and gossip, which she was tasked to entice from both husband and lover. But then, as she walked quickly along George Street, her anger gave way to the need for self-preservation. She would tell Keith everything. He would be angry but he would not want it to get out either. Though she despised him, he *was* Prime Minister. He would know what to do.

Sir,

As a follow-up to your recent reporting of attacks and firebombing of holiday cottages owned by English and European families by ardent 'Scotland for the Scots' fanatics, I believe that such incidents are extremely rare. The one or two cases that have occurred over the past years have, according to police sources, usually been more about conflicts between neighbours than anything to do with anti-Englishness.

I personally have owned a holiday home in Scotland for the last three decades and have never come across any animosity whatsoever. Quite the reverse: I and my family have always been treated with the greatest courtesy and we have many close friends in this beautiful country.

Yours faithfully,

Jennifer Jenkins (Mrs), Sussex

(Letter in the *Press and Journal*)

The ground was frozen hard and the gravediggers had had to use a pickaxe to get through to the softer soil underneath. It was one of the bleakest cemeteries imaginable, set halfway up a hill, well back from the little church through an unkempt wasteland of elder and silver birch trees. Above and beyond stretched the wet, heather-covered moor.

They had built a series of wooden ramps over the drainage runnels on the long ash path to allow Sinclair's wheelchair to be manoeuvred in a reasonably dignified way down to the open grave. From one point of view at least, he was the guest of honour at the funeral.

He arrived just as the cortège came into view. The coffin, draped in a banner with a uniform cap on top of it, was carried by six bareheaded policemen. Somewhere out of sight a drum was beating. The sound, with a messy lack of timing, echoed dully among the gravestones. Some three hundred people, many in police uniform, stood in sober lines around the grave. The policeman's family with other friends and mourners stood in a dark line along one side; the minister, in purple and black, presided from the head of the pit, his vestments fluttering in the wind. He looked flabby and pompous. It would be a pity if he were: funerals could be moving.

Sinclair came to a halt a respectful few yards away, the wheels of his chair resting against an edge of wet turf. Guthrie, who was with him, bent down and needlessly applied the brake. It could not move in the mud. Sinclair adjusted the black tie he had just borrowed from Ingram. In the rush to be on time, his own had been left behind at Charlotte Square.

He was there because the Cabinet had unanimously agreed that the Government must be represented at the highest level at PC Wright's funeral. It was essential to buttress the waning morale of the force by showing everyone that the whole nation was horrified at the outrage.

They were not alone in seeing that necessity. Reunionist and Republican leaders were also there in force, to show that their hands were clean. Sinclair recognized several unusually subdued faces from each faction, ranged behind the orderly ranks of the police contingents. Their presence lent credence to Special Branch reports that neither mob had anything to do with it.

TV arc lights suddenly flared in his face and press cameras flashed. The media had suddenly seen the photographic potential of a Prime Minister in his wheelchair as the coffin passed by. Apart from his brief speech to the National Assembly, this was his first public appearance since his injury and a picture of the half quick and the dead would look good on all the front pages tomorrow. He looked suitably grim.

The minister of the cloth was smug, waxing eloquent and overlong, aware of his brief personal prominence in front of a distinguished captive audience. He departed from the funeral rites to harangue the crowd and, via the television cameras, the country at large, about his righteous horror at the crime. Sinclair

95

sat in growing anger as the man proceeded to debase the occasion with his mixed metaphors and his mock passion. He was a spineless figure seeking vengeance.

Sinclair looked round at the faces of the mourners, all turned to follow the minister's words. Tense, highly charged faces; tears even in men's eyes. The minister was shouting into the biting wind that Police Constable Wright would become a martyr on Scotland's road towards a return to sanity, discipline and moral responsibility. An eye-for-an-eye man even if half the world ended up blind, the man of the cloth turned to urge the arming of the police. The Police Commissioner had his ammunition. Perhaps he had arranged it. Sinclair suddenly felt desperately ill.

The rain came suddenly. It turned the minister from being the centre of Sinclair's irritation into a pitiful, damp buffoon. The end of the sermon came quickly after that, then the last post, blown badly by some local territorial soldier, and dust or mud was shovelled down on mud. Sinclair forced himself to shake the minister's hand, then turned his wheelchair abruptly away to avoid disturbing his short-lived tolerance.

The dead policeman's wife was brought up to be introduced. She was with a boy of about fifteen. Both were dry-eyed, stunned by the event. He shook hands with them in the rain, to the accompaniment of more flashing cameras. He said formal, meaningless things to them but then was left with the wife's parting, bitter remark that her husband wasn't even Scottish; it was her fault he had ever come north of the border.

It was nearly over but then the Police Commissioner appeared from nowhere. He started to praise the minister's sermon to the Prime Minister. He got the brush-off. Guns could wait.

The going back to the car was slow. Guthrie had an umbrella and gallantly attempted to shield Sinclair from the worst of the rain, while at the same time trying to manoeuvre the wheelchair.

Once back in the relative dryness of the Rover, Guthrie climbed in beside him. 'You all right, Prime Minister?' he asked, genuine concern showing on his face. Sinclair nodded, but his Private Secretary knew he was lying.

Ingram drove slowly through the crowd of departing mourners. Some turned to stare in at Sinclair. No one waved. Few did nowadays. Sinclair knew once again that were it not for his accident, and his role as a martyr up there beside PC Wright, he would have already been thrown to the wolves as a sop to the nation's demand for solutions. For the moment, compassion restrained political assassination. It would only be a matter of time.

On the drive back to Edinburgh, Guthrie told Sinclair that James Fulton, the chillingly dynamic Chairman of the Unity Corporation, was coming over to Edinburgh to see him with some sort of major proposition. He'd met Fulton once before, on one of his previous visits, when Unity first started opening up in Scotland. Sinclair had found him a difficult man to fathom; his arrogantly brutal approach to business was unsettling but he claimed Scottish ancestry and so it had always been assumed that his heart was in the right place.

Guthrie suggested that perhaps MacDowall or Campbell could meet Fulton if the PM didn't feel up to it. 'No,' Sinclair said, he was feeling fine. But again he lied.

'What's it all about?' he asked Guthrie, who began to explain about the reports they'd had from Rosenfeld and others that Fulton was thinking of moving Unity's entire global headquarters from the United States to Scotland. Guthrie noticed as he spoke that the PM was not taking it in. Drenched by the rain and soaking from the sweat of his slight exertions, Sinclair was now experiencing an excruciating pain in the small of his back. He assumed it was some localized part of his nervous system reawakening. He shut his eyes and willed the agony to go away. He failed, but must have fallen asleep.

He woke or was wakened by Guthrie just as they arrived back at Charlotte Square. His Private Secretary had a peculiar look on his face though he did not voice his concerns. As he was wheeled in through the front door, Sinclair desperately hoped that his wife would not be at home. He could not bear the thought of facing her in the condition he was in. It was some days since he had overheard the telephone conversation she had

had with her lover and since then he had made every effort never to be left alone with her. It was easily done in the busy life of a Prime Minister, but there was an ominous gap in his programme for the evening ahead. He had no other official engagements. If she were at home, he would not need to feign tiredness: he would simply go to bed.

She was in the study watching some insane comedy programme on television. She complained about the reception, then, 'Mrs Ingram's gone off for the evening,' she announced, getting up and switching off the set. 'I felt I was getting out of touch in the kitchen, so I've made our supper. It's been a long time. You look a bit washed out, so we needn't be late.' She smiled, a fraction nervously.

'Yes,' he said, wheeling himself over and helping himself to a drink from the cabinet. He had no wish to play Happy Families.

'Keith. I need to talk.'

'Yes?' he repeated. It was the last thing he wanted.

'Please, it's important.' The smiled had disappeared.

He looked directly at her for the first time in months. 'Well?' he asked woodenly.

'Could I have a drink too?' She was indeed nervous. Knowing her habit, he poured her a whisky and dropped two ice cubes into the tumbler. He wheeled himself over and handed it to her.

'Well?' he asked again.

After a few moments' pause she said, 'Keith, I've been seeing someone else.'

'I see.' Sinclair was hardly surprised by her news, but she could have spared him the home cooking.

'Please, Keith. I want you to understand. It's not because of your ... your accident. I felt sorry, genuinely. You must realize that.' Her normal, bitchy face had softened and, to his surprise, he realized she was close to tears. Perhaps now that she had brought herself to speak to him, her words were more of a surprise to her than to him.

'I've hardly eaten since breakfast,' he said flatly. 'Can we not discuss this on full stomachs?'

She started to cry at that but he couldn't have cared less. He wheeled himself through to the dining room in silence and she followed lamely behind. In a way he was looking forward to things coming to a head.

The table was set for two and candles were burning in the middle. It was beyond him why she should have thought that such a homespun setting would help things along. Perhaps she had done it not so much to sweeten the pill as to make him realize how he was going to miss her. With Mrs Ingram away, she had to serve him as well, so the personal contact was even more unusual. She had gone to obvious trouble: the soufflé was excellent and she had rifled his wine cellar to good purpose.

The first half of the meal passed in silence. They worked their way through one bottle and then she opened another. Then she began talking, pouring it all out unasked. He didn't interrupt her. She went on about how much in love she was. She told Sinclair how it had started. She announced that she was going down to London to get away from him for a few days to think things through. The only thing she omitted was her lover's name.

After a while he stopped listening but his total silence, far from disconcerting Nora, seemed to give her free rein. She went on and on in a torrent of self-justification. From time to time she repeated the phrase that it was nothing to do with him being a cripple. At last that horrid word registered with him, as it obviously had with her. It left him thinking of the real implications of the term.

'Aren't you going to say anything, react, do something?' He became aware that she was standing over him, coffee pot in hand. She was white and shaking and her voice had suddenly become strident and unpleasant. 'There's something else, Keith. Something happened today. I don't know what to do. You need to help me –' she began.

He looked through her. He was not interested in listening to her problems and he more or less said so. It was a mistake on his part.

He shrugged. 'Help you? What d'you expect me to do? Burst

into tears or something? Sorry, Nora. Can't oblige. Now if you don't mind, and you've got it all nicely off your chest, I need to sleep.' He slowly swivelled his chair round, deliberately turning his back on her.

He could sense an outburst coming. Instead, by accident or design, hot coffee from the pot was spilled in large quantities over his legs, before she rushed hysterically from the room. Had she returned, she would have found him grinning inanely through clenched teeth, as the pain hit him. Scalded, yes. But he had feeling in his legs once again. After that, he must have passed out.

Riotous assembly

Police reinforcements have been drafted into Glasgow from all over Scotland for the opening today of the trial in the High Court of the men accused of leading the Reunionist mob which attacked and killed Republican marchers last St Andrew's Day. Special powers have been granted to the Police Commissioner under the Public Order Act to allow him to set up a security cordon to ensure that demonstrators do not get near the court.

The Speaker had to suspend last night's emergency debate on the economy in the National Assembly for ten minutes after two deputies, Mr Allan Kydd, MP for Tayside East, and Mr Syd Fee, MP for South Central Glasgow, came to blows on the floor of the Chamber.

(Scottish Press Association Report)

Heather Anderson and Robert Guthrie had kept in touch with each other by telephone. She had become increasingly angered and concerned by the fact that her father, a gentle, kindly man, had been totally sidelined by the Federation Executive, an organization that had once been his pride and joy. De Laski was one of the new movers and shakers there. She had not met him in recent times but what she knew about him she did not like. When she had time she dug back through all the press reports she had written as a tyro journalist covering the Hulse City incident when she had first come across de Laski and heard of the Unity Corporation. Then she met up with a man called Harvey Silt, from whom she uncovered the real link between her father's deep unhappiness and the strange events that were rapidly unfolding in Scotland.

At first she thought she was being set up by Silt for some purposes of his own. He was a strangely efficient man and unlike most other journalists she had ever met. He was evasive about whom he worked for and, when she accessed her media database on the internet, the screen showed no story written by him on Torrance's death nor about the workings of the Federation. She confronted him with the fact when he telephoned her to talk about the Unity Corporation.

'I'm working on this article,' he began.

'No you're not. You don't write any articles that I or any of my colleagues have ever heard of.' She was clinical and blunt.

There was a long pause, then: 'Ah. That was careless of me, Ms Anderson,' he said softly. 'You've found me out,' he added. 'If we meet, I will explain.'

And explain he did the next day over coffee at the Pierre Hotel. Somehow she had guessed what it might be, but more importantly, the information he revealed to her encouraged her to redouble her investigations. She set about her task with renewed vigour, with Harvey Silt proving an invaluable collaborator. When Guthrie rang her from Scotland to ask for assistance in providing background information on current Unity operations throughout the US and the rest of the world, she cleverly contrived to get herself commissioned by the *New York Times* to work on a major exposé of them. When she told Guthrie a little of what she was up to, he suggested that she ought to follow up her research by coming to Scotland. It was only natural that she should accept.

7

Lords or Senators

A MORI poll commissioned by the *Herald* has
revealed that a majority of people in Scotland believes
the Assembly should have an Upper House along the
lines of the US Senate rather than a House of Lords.

The findings were 38% in favour of a Senate of
fifty Senators elected for a five-year term and fifty
appointed by an independent commission from a list
of the great and the good, while 20% were in favour
of a chamber modelled on the English House of Lords.
The 'don't knows', however, accounted for 42% of the
replies. The poll conducted last Friday was based on a
survey of 1350 people. (Full details p. 7.)

(*Herald* lead item)

The Prime Minister was rushed back into intensive care that
night. On top of everything else, he had developed pneumonia
as a result of either sitting by the beach or getting wet while
attending the funeral. So MacDowall chaired the Cabinet meeting
the following morning. Guthrie sat beside him, taking notes. As
speaker after speaker droned on about their favourite problems,
Guthrie wondered at the tedious and inefficient process of
government by committee and at the social behaviour of committee men. Men with alert eyes, men asleep, men attentive, men
simply appearing to be so. In this modern Scotland, the only two
women present were the Ministers of Education and Training,

and Health. The few quality people shone; most of the rest were self-important placemen, there because they did not have better jobs to go to. All the mannerisms, inadequacies, subtleties and techniques of a political committee-person were paraded. He watched and noted how a few had their way while most were ignored by their peers. Above all, he marvelled at the art of the chairman, MacDowall, as he silenced the talkative without giving offence and encouraged the hesitant if it suited his purpose. The Minister was usually in control, accelerating or braking the pace to suit his agenda. His carefully-timed interventions formed a science that he had developed to a remarkable degree. In this Cabinet he was no mere *primus inter pares*. He had no equals.

The minutes of the Cabinet meeting were later set out in unemotional and precise terms:

> After lengthy discussion, Cabinet unanimously agreed that, while the security of the nation was at serious risk, until the source of the threat could be positively identified, no value was to be gained by arming the police, placing the Army on special alert, or calling out the Volunteer Reserve. This decision was to be kept under constant review. To take any of these measures would only create wide-scale alarm among the population at large. It was further agreed that this decision should not prejudice the existing authority of the Commissioner of Police to issue arms to members of the constabulary for special operations. It was further decided that the Commissioner of Police, the head of the Special Task Force and heads of the other departments concerned, would be required to meet daily under the chairmanship of the Secretary to the Cabinet to keep the situation under the closest review.
>
> Cabinet went on to discuss the implications of the proposal put by James Fulton, Chairman of the Unity Corporation, jointly to the Financial Secretary and the Minister of Internal Affairs. In summary, his

proposition is that Unity would plan to further invest in, take over or otherwise manage or purchase a number of ailing Scottish companies. This would be in addition to the extensive subsidiaries already under its control. At the same time, they would move their global headquarters from the United States to Glasgow or to a site near Perth. In return, the Scottish Government would have to agree to certain specific tax and other incentives which would have to be offered by the Government to the Unity Corporation for a guaranteed number of years. 'Scotland would thereby become the base for a worldwide economic empire. It would comprise a gigantic public–private sector partnership: a Dollar Covenant,' Mr Fulton said.

[See full report of the meeting in Cabinet Committee Minutes SCC 914/99, circulated separately.]

Robert Guthrie was to reflect later on what the Cabinet minutes, there for posterity, did not record, namely the huge row that developed during those discussions. It exploded into a session of lost tempers, threats of resignation and intemperate personal accusations. It had required all MacDowall's skills to stop several Ministers walking out and, on one occasion, the possibility of two senior members of the Cabinet actually coming to blows. To say that the Scottish Cabinet was deeply divided on the issue, was to put it very mildly. On one side, Ian Campbell had argued that the offer by Unity was, given the apparent collapse, or at best lengthy delay in getting the rescue package that had been proposed earlier by the Federation of American Caledonian Societies off the ground, a godsend. For Scotland it could be all that the Federation had promised and more. MacDowall, as chairman, did not feel able to make his points too forcefully, but others were deeply suspicious of Unity's motives. There was plenty of evidence coming out of the United States that Unity had its own urgent reasons for wanting out of North America. They were under huge pressure from the Federal Government on a number of key fronts, not least over the back payment of substantial amounts of Federal Corporation Tax. Additionally, having been fined hundreds of millions of dollars over the leakage of the poisonous chemical cloud a few years back – the notorious Hulse City incident – a number of other American states were following New Jersey's lead and pursuing Unity in the courts over a variety of alleged breaches of environmental regulations. Unity, by contrast, claimed that it was basically a holding company and financial investment corporation which bought and sold a huge range of subsidiaries for the benefit of its shareholders, so that it was not liable or responsible for the activities of these subsidiary operations any more than it had been at Hulse City.

Forbes, the former union leader turned Environment Minister and the most left-wing member in the Cabinet, was normally at loggerheads with MacDowall. On this, however, he fully supported the Minister of the Interior. He said he was outraged at the idea of Scotland offering refuge to a company with such a murky and suspect reputation. He declared in belligerent tones that it was an attempt at a mega-takeover. Scotland had managed to cut itself free from England after four centuries. Was this to be replaced by selling out to tainted American money? Unity was merely looking for a cheap tax haven. It doubtless also had its greedy eyes on the new *Albion* North Sea oil field as the *quid pro quo* for the deal it was offering. 'No,' Forbes had shouted at his colleagues. 'The whole thing stinks.' There had been silence for a while after that, then MacDowall wisely adjourned the Cabinet meeting for the day, to allow tempers to cool.

Guthrie had kept his own counsel throughout the meeting. As a civil servant, he was there largely to observe and record. Privately he was still very much undecided about whether the Unity package was a good thing or not. What he did feel however was that there should be a much wider public debate on the issues involved. Frustrated by the indecision shown by the Cabinet, when he received the expected folio of information about Unity from Heather Anderson in New York, he decided on a small but critical breach of trust. He arranged to travel to Glasgow to meet privately with a trusted old friend, Billy McKane, the editor of the *Herald*.

Two days later, the *Herald* ran a major feature article, without a by-line, under the headline:

Unity and disunity

There is increasing public anxiety about the huge growth in the activities of the Unity Corporation. Just what is the multinational up to? Although the Chairman of the Scottish CBI and the Presidents of the Edinburgh and Glasgow Chambers of Commerce have welcomed Unity's further investment in Scotland, a *Herald* investigation has uncovered secret deals revealing that its involvement in Scottish life is far greater than the Corporation has ever admitted.

The details give added weight to the concerns expressed by the trade unions and some financial and legal experts about the extent to which Scottish freedoms could be eroded. The investigation, supplemented by research carried out by Strathclyde Graduate Business School, exposes the extensive problems Unity has had in its dealings with the US Federal Government over its tax and investment affairs. For the first time we publish a list of the Scottish companies and assets Unity now controls. It is not complete, because many of Unity's dealings are conducted with a high degree of secrecy, but its scale is undeniably alarming.

Last year Unity acquired the whole of the Arduchan Estate and surrounding farms and forests, making it one of the largest landowners in Scotland. Since then it has completed two well-publicized deals: the takeover of the Nippon and Yamachi computer factories in Bathgate from their Japanese parent companies. They now also own Cragies, the largest transport and distribution company in Scotland, Borough, Jarvis and Abercrombie, the second largest investment house and fund managers and, it is said, employ all the available senior partners in one of Scotland's oldest and most distinguished legal practices, Kennedy-Semple WS. They also own a major stake in Scottish Media Enterprises Limited, Scottish local radio, and control several regional newspapers, including Morrison Press, the leading weekly chain. Although Unity claims its newspapers are given complete editorial independence, the secretive nature of the Corporation's dealings means that nobody really knows whether this is true. The blunt fact is we do not know exactly how much of Scotland it controls. It is time for the Monopolies and Mergers Commission to investigate. (See Business Section p. 23.)

(The *Herald*)

His doctors were angry. Sinclair had tried to do too much. He was equally angry with them. Were they trying to punish him by having that damned rubber sheet under him? Why the hell did they still do it? He had perfect control over his bladder; it was degrading, quite apart from the discomfort. When they had all gone, he'd bribe Sister Rogers.

The private room was cheerful enough, overlooking as it did a pleasant stretch of gardens. There were cards and vases of flowers everywhere, though a futile attempt had been made to keep the news of his return to hospital as low-key as possible. As far as the public was concerned, he was back in for a routine check-up. But Sinclair knew that his doctor, Professor Taller of the Faculty of Medicine, had more surgery in mind for him. The professor had put his plans to the Prime Minister gently, after the latter had told him about the constant pain in his back and legs and the renewal of feeling when he had the hot coffee spilled over him. The professor gave him a long, highly technical explanation, based on the numerous tests he had conducted. It would, he eventually admitted, involve a major operation. The professor was open about it: it offered only a fifty–fifty chance of Sinclair ever getting out of his wheelchair. It would also involve further pain and discomfort and the possibility that he might be worse off at the end. He would certainly be out of circulation for three weeks to a month. As the National Assembly was going into Easter recess, however, it seemed an opportune moment. The Prime Minister agreed, but only after taking soundings from close colleagues that there would be no move to displace or retire him while he was out of the way. He presumed that several Ministers had their eyes on his job but they would not dare make their ambitions known in such circumstances. Aside from his allies in the Cabinet, he could still rally a lot of support in the National Assembly and it would not need too much briefing of a few well-chosen journalist friends to ensure that any move to oust him would be defeated by popular outcry.

Sister Rogers, a pretty little nurse with a soft West Highland accent, came in with tea and a further pile of letters and telegrams, but flatly refused to remove the rubber sheet. So much for his Prime Ministerial power. He lay back against the pillows and began to read through them. Mainly from colleagues and constituency workers, there were a few from members of the public as well. Guthrie would arrange for acknowledgements to be sent later. One, only one, from a crank, was full of wild hatred and abuse. It did not disturb him. People outside public life failed to realize how many anonymous, abusive, often obscene letters public figures received, and how quickly they became immune.

As the days passed, Sinclair monitored events from his sickbed with a growing sense of futility and despair, though it escaped him what action he would be taking had he been physically fit. Guthrie brought him a carefully filtered range of State papers: nothing too detailed or complex that might upset a sick man. Sinclair had insisted however in reading all the Cabinet minutes and had heard about the internal rows that had largely gone unreported. Would he have been able to enforce more discipline, more collective responsibility, than MacDowall? He doubted it. Later he turned to the long article in the *Herald*, wondering who had put the newspaper up to looking at Unity in so much detail and where they had got all their information. It was deeply researched and very compelling. Personally he was still inclined to trust Fulton. Beggars couldn't be choosers and, with a total negative from Anderson and the Federation, he saw little alternative. After all, Unity only had money and commercial clout. They, the Scottish Government, had the ultimate democratic mandate.

In response to Sinclair's question, Guthrie, when he came to see him, reported that he had heard nothing new on Torrance's mysterious death. The Prime Minister shrugged: he was not a great conspiracy theorist and while he agreed with Guthrie that what he knew of Carlyle and de Laski suggested that they were odd people to find on the Federation Board, that did not mean they were malign. He was sorry to hear the news that Anderson was being more or less pensioned off. The chairman had always been a true friend of Scotland.

Sinclair fretted increasingly as he lay waiting for his operation, which his doctor refused to contemplate until the pneumonia had entirely cleared up. MacDowall came only once to visit him but, infuriatingly, refused point blank to discuss any serious business. It could all wait till he was better, the old man said. Yes, he too had read the *Herald* article on Unity. Yes, it was interesting. Yes, he had wondered where all the information had come from. After his courtesy visit, Sinclair was left more irritated than ever.

The day of the operation Guthrie returned, bringing him more letters and a final red despatch box stuffed with official papers. Sinclair had insisted that he be allowed to work right up to the last moment.

'How are you today, sir?' Guthrie asked politely.

'Fine. Apart from this bloody rubber sheet.' Sinclair forced a wry smile.

Guthrie looked worried.

'What's up?' Sinclair asked. 'Hangover or a lovers' quarrel?'

'I don't want to burden you just now, Prime Minister . . .' He hesitated. Sinclair was already shuffling through the papers and Guthrie did not pursue it.

For a few minutes they discussed routine Ministry matters, then Guthrie said, 'I've filtered the contents of your despatch box as much I could, sir, except for the report from Tony Matthews at the Department of Trade. Read it if nothing else.' He hesitated again.

'I'll get round to it.' Sinclair paused. 'Is that what's biting you, Robert?' he asked. He had never seen his Private Secretary so unsettled.

'With you out of action for a while, Prime Minister, I need an urgent steer from you on what you want us to do on the Unity front. As I see it, the arguments are finely balanced,' Guthrie said.

'I'll ring you once I've read it,' said Sinclair. 'I promise you.' Guthrie left and he settled back in bed and to his paperwork.

He opened the box and glanced quickly through the papers he'd been sent. They were mainly routine submissions from his officials asking for his approval for decisions they had, in the most part, already taken. He put them to one side and took out the paper Guthrie had mentioned, the memorandum from Matthews. From the summary it showed that while the short-term economic picture was not too bad, long-term trends were far from encouraging. The permanent officials in the Department of Trade, and Finance, were deeply worried. Scotland was on the brink of a severe international balance of payments problem. They charted a huge and unexpected outflow of cash from some of the largest Scottish firms and industries that had been taken over by foreign-based conglomerates. It was natural, in current circumstances, for managers and shareholders to want to protect their assets and he could not blame Scottish businesses for having sold out for hard cash. Sinclair was no narrow nationalist and he appreciated the need for foreign investment. No country like Scotland could ever hope to be entirely economically independent. Money went where it could obtain the highest return. Yet, setting this all aside, this particular financial tide was flowing faster than was natural. He turned to the appendices. Statistics could be made to lie, but not as easily as the conclusions drawn from them.

It was with fascination if not horror that Sinclair noted that even the *Herald* report had underestimated just how many basic and advanced industries were now under full Unity Corporation control or ownership. Without the impetus an enormous dollar inflow had given the Scottish Government, they would never have had the nerve or strength to go for Independence in the first place. But US confidence in Scotland as a buoyant growth area was one thing; dollars buying the nation up wholesale at rock-bottom prices was very different.

The Prime Minister spent a full hour brooding on the implications of the paper. Had he had his wits about him he would have been even more deeply alarmed. He would have summoned MacDowall and rung Guthrie back as he had promised, to give his support to emergency counter measures, by introducing emergency foreign exchange controls. But a doctor arrived to check his pulse and to give him a pre-operation injection to help him sleep, so he did neither.

The four participants sat in easy chairs in front of a backdrop of pictures and shelves lined with fake leather-bound books. It was meant to impart an intellectual flavour to their discussions. The arc lights were up on the set; in the gloom behind, operators wearing headphones wheeled their heavy cameras around the studio floor to the commands of the producer. In the background, well out of view and close to the door to the greenroom, Abel Rosenfeld stood whispering to his earnest young assistant, Winston Bushfield. Bushfield, a somewhat overweight man in his early thirties, was new to the game of public relations and the massaging of media perceptions but was highly enthusiastic and eager to learn.

'Hush,' said the floor manager, turning angrily towards them. Rosenfeld ignored him. Unity were sponsoring the programme after all and he knew perfectly well that his voice would never be picked up by the microphones at the far side of the studio. The manager was just trying to demonstrate his authority in front of the junior staff.

The studio discussion was already well under way. Three men and one woman were hotly discussing the state of the nation. Much of it was predictable stuff; it was a pre-recorded pro-gramme which would be intercut with documentary footage. The skill would lie in the editing, as Rosenfeld and Bushfield had seen from some of the rushes in the cutting room that morning.

Bushfield's background had largely been with newspapers and his occasional naivety showed when dealing with the disciplines of the electronic media. 'That's not a very flattering archive shot of Keith Sinclair,' he had said. 'He doesn't always look as tired and ill as that.'

Rosenfeld had not even turned to look at his assistant but, for a moment, wondered if he had selected him badly. 'That clip's carefully chosen,' he said. Then he had smiled. 'Remember Winston, the camera *always* lies.'

That was this morning. Now, a professor of Scottish History from Edinburgh, an economist from Strathclyde Graduate Business School, a woman social worker from Falkirk and the Reverend Murdo Morrison, the battling prelate from Forfar, were going at it hammer and tongs. Social worker and economist, perfect role models for two dismal professions, marshalled the traditional arguments of despair and decay. Against them, the saltire of triumphalist nationhood had been raised by the other two against all manner of enemies, domestic and foreign. They were of the do-and-die school, even if they destroyed Scotland with their powerless tartan passions and their bagpipe dreams.

'How does all this nonsense help us?' whispered Winston.

'That's where our gifted film editor comes in again,' Rosenfeld replied. 'A night into day man, he is. Wait and see.'

The four panellists were now onto the esoteric subject of what constituted a nation. The economist was pompously quoting the Peruvian writer Mario Vargas Llosa, that a nation was *a malign fantasy, a political fiction imposed on a geographical reality, usually by force.* Commonality was the only way to economic and political security. Nonsense, said the historian, getting increasingly angry. Cultural nations like Catalonia, the Basques, Bavaria, existed within nation states. Exactly my point, retorted the economist. The Scottish nations – there were several very different ones, he argued – existed most efficiently when a part of the United Kingdom.

It was then that the churchman, who kept talking of *res publica Scotorum*, took up his rod of ire. He more or less said that God was a Scotsman, that the Bible was on the side of nationalism, that the blood of his ancestors demanded liberty. And so on.

'Not my religion, thanks be,' whispered Rosenfeld. 'He certainly worships a god of war. He'll triumph ... unless he has a heart attack first.' The minister had turned a vivid shade of purple.

'What are you so angry at?' asked the social worker in a still, quiet voice.

'Angry? Angry? I'm not angry,' bellowed the minister, 'except at the way this country has been misgoverned.'

'You've a serious problem, you have,' the woman continued. 'You and the professor. You don't have the English to blame any more. You need enemies to frighten the governed. You're like the Americans and the Russians at the end of the Cold War. You want to hate. But there's no longer anyone out there. Independence has even taken the guts out of ancient Scottish–English rivalries. We can happily play football against each other as often as we like now, without the Tartan Army running amok in Piccadilly and Soho.'

The minister almost choked in his fury. By contrast, the Edinburgh professor remained calm, cloaked as he was in the romantic whimsy of nationalism. He was of the damp eyes and lump-in-the-throat school of patriot: culture in a kilt.

'What's all this for?' asked Winston Bushfield once again. He was genuinely perplexed.

Giving in to further angry looks and gestures from the floor manager, Rosenfeld took his colleague firmly by the arm and led him into the cool of the greenroom, where they both collapsed in laughter onto low chairs, to discuss what they had heard. Rosenfeld leant over to the TV monitor and turned down the sound of the studio debate.

'Why do Unity sponsor this trash? I don't understand,' Bushfield continued to question. 'We should be working flat out rubbishing the implications of that *Herald* exposé.'

'Forget the *Herald* article. Most hard-nosed businessmen see us as an asset: a successful company bringing only benefit to Scotland. That was why that Gleneagles dinner was so worthwhile. Sowed the seeds and now they're sprouting.' Rosenfeld was dismissive.

'But . . .' Bushfield was still unsure.

'Let me take you through it,' said Rosenfeld, sipping with distaste at a polystyrene cup of studio coffee. 'Learned it from the British imperialists. When they founded their colonies around the world, they usually discovered warring tribes, rival pashas, hostile lordlings of one sort or another. They imposed what they called *Pax Britannica*, peace of a sort, but a peace that suited them. The Scots, incidentally, were the best sort of colonialists. They were masters of the game. What they really did was maintain full control in a much cleverer way.'

'Tell me,' prompted Bushfield, curious.

'Called it *Divide and Rule*. Played it particularly skilfully in Africa and India. Chief and tribe against chief and tribe. Sultan against Emir, Nabob against Bey, Potentate against Maharajah. They buttered each side up, bribed them, seduced them, told each that they were particularly favoured by London and the Great White Queen Victoria or whoever, then set them at each other's throats.'

'That was in tribal societies –' Bushfield protested.

'What d'you think Scotland is for crissake? I'm not talking about the clans, the tartan nonsense, though we can even play on those rivalries now we control the Federation's Executive. Don't forget your Scottish history: the family of our best ally, Ian Campbell, had a long history of siding with the English.'

'A long time ago,' Bushfield protested, with half an eye on the TV monitor. His voice petered out as he realized the futility of what he was saying. Even with the sound turned down, they could both see that an incipient civil war was building up nicely outside the greenroom on the studio set.

Rosenfeld waved vaguely at the monitor. 'It's so easy. We'll play with the material, cut it, edit it, change emphasis and meaning. Don't forget that a Scot wrote Dr Jekyll and Mr Hyde! In the end, they're sitting fuckin' ducks. The Scots don't need enemies, boy. They have each other.'

8

This is the SBC Six o'clock News.

The English Prime Minister, Mr Barry Lightfoot, arrives this evening for twenty-four hours of intensive talks with the Scottish Government. With an analysis of what both sides hope to achieve from the meeting, here is our chief political correspondent, James Gordon.

'With Prime Minister Keith Sinclair's stay in hospital, it was uncertain whether Mr Lightfoot's official visit to Edinburgh, only the third by an English Prime Minister since Independence, would still go ahead. But given the number of serious issues that need to be addressed, it was decided that it should continue to take place. Sir Alexander MacDowall will lead the Scottish team. Following a working dinner at Edinburgh Castle this evening, informed sources indicate that the main item for tomorrow's meeting will be the continuing wrangle over the maritime demarcation line in the North Sea for purposes of further oil exploration. Basically, should the line run due west from Berwick-upon-Tweed, or should it, as the English urge, follow the general line of the Scottish border in a north-eastern direction? The V-shaped area of difference is huge, but some progress is expected over new Scottish proposals to divide revenues equally from fields operating in the disputed area.

'Another contentious issue is that of dual nationality, a subject on which the English Prime Minister, with his part-Scottish roots, feels particularly strongly. Such has been the degree of intermarriage and of Scots working in the south and vice versa, that the whole question of race is one to which only the most extreme nationalists pay any attention. The acceptability of the separate

Scottish passport and the whole question of border controls are
other issues to be covered at tomorrow's meeting.

'*A spokesman at No 10 Downing Street said last night that*
the continuing dispute over English beef from BSE-infected herds
being refused entry to Scotland was not on the agenda for the
Prime Minister's visit. Mr Lightfoot will be taking one break
however: he plans to spend an hour or so tomorrow afternoon
visiting his old public school . . .

(SBC Radio Report)

For a normally cool and self-possessed man, Robert Guthrie felt
remarkably unsettled as he awaited the arrival of Heather Anderson off the flight from New York. He had seen her only briefly
on the day following their unexpected, post-theatre drink, when
she had again passed on her father's regrets at not being able to
meet up with him before he left. It was the same morning that
Guthrie had received a formal message from the Federation, via
Carlyle, that everything was being put on hold because of Torrance's death. 'Next time,' Carlyle's message was unsubtle, 'since
political decisions will have to be taken at the Scottish end, it
would be more appropriate to elevate the level of your contacts
with us. We would welcome a Ministerial, rather than a civil
service emissary.' Carlyle had not tried to dress up the calculated
snub.

When she appeared at the arrivals gate, they greeted each other
almost shyly, not quite knowing whether their relationship would
develop on purely business lines. He drove her to the hotel he
had booked her into, which was only a few minutes' walk from
his bachelor flat in Edinburgh's New Town. That evening, over
dinner at a fish restaurant on the Leith waterfront, they began
with business.

Her opening remark was startling to say the least. 'The fuss
father's had with the Federation and the way it's now being run
clearly suggest to me that it and the whole Unity expansion
here in Scotland are closely interlinked.' She was being slightly

disingenuous: it was in fact Harvey Silt who had prompted this connection but explaining that to Guthrie could come at another time.

Guthrie showed his surprise. 'Why should they have anything whatsoever to do with each other?' he asked, sipping at his glass of Sancerre.

'Wait for it,' she said with a half-smile.

'What?'

'You remember Carlyle and de Laski?' She paused dramatically.

'Could I forget,' Guthrie responded, failing to grasp what she was driving at.

'They are both also listed as Non-Executive Directors on the main Unity Board.'

'No . . .' Guthrie was genuinely shocked.

'Which means . . .' Heather led the catechism.

'That they probably deliberately pulled the rug from under the Federation's rescue attempt, in order to give free rein to Unity's activities?' Suddenly it was all becoming very clear.

'My guess. And with so much at stake, Torrance, having provided the impetus for their scheme in the first place, could not be allowed to stand in the way,' Heather continued.

'You can't believe that even they'd go that far,' Guthrie breathed.

'Speculation. But I've seen in the past just how far corporate America can go to achieve its aims in various parts of the world. Profits come first; people last. Think of Chile, Nigeria, India . . . What the US companies won't do to keep oil flowing from the Gulf. The way Unity acted in trying first of all to suppress news of the Hulse City incident and then, when it did get out, attempting to avoid the blame, was criminal: buying off witnesses, threatening the child's family and others and so on. But the law got them in the end.'

'I still can't credit –' Guthrie poured them both more wine then ordered a second bottle. He suddenly thought of the conversation he had heard in the airport shuttle lounge. That voice . . .

that voice, could it have been de Laski's? Could he have been talking about the Campsie explosion? He shared these thoughts with Heather.

'OK. Let me take you through something else.' She dropped her voice. 'What if I told you that as soon as they discovered I was working on the *New York Times* article about them, they turned and tried to buy me? De Laski himself called me. I did a quick calculation as to whether, when he offered me a job, he was simply skirt-chasing. He was deadly serious. Wanted me to drop what I was doing and work for Unity, in their public relations department. He'd make it well worth my while, he said. The salary was very, very generous.'

'You should be flattered someone's seen your true worth.' Guthrie attempted a joke.

She looked grim. 'Big business doesn't work that way. They don't pick little people like me. I'm out of their league. This was bribery, pure and simple: they were buying me off.'

'Or they want to get at your father . . .' Guthrie said.

'No. He's no use to them now. But they've tried to get him to get me to accept as well. The strange thing is how hard I've been pursued. This is no simple job offer. People keep ringing me up, producing written contracts, coercing me to make up my mind. They came at me from several directions. De Laski even got on to friends of mine, through other contacts of his, to try to persuade me to accept.'

'You told all this to your father?'

'I don't want to worry him with the detail. He's gradually beginning to get over things.'

'What did you tell de Laski?'

'Strung him along. Said I was thinking of going to Scotland. Would they be interested in my working for them here? I got the feeling they'd turn nasty if I gave a firm no. Or nastier to father. I'm not into heroics.'

'You've got something else?' Guthrie prodded. They were at the coffee stage.

'You came across a journalist called Silt?'

'The man who brought the news about Torrance.'

'He's sharp. He's proved to his own satisfaction that it wasn't an accident, that Torrance wasn't drunk.'

'He was plastered at lunchtime,' Guthrie said. 'Evidence of my own eyes.'

'Maybe so,' Heather responded. 'But when he left your lunch he went straight for a sauna and massage, then spent the next hour or so swimming. He is on record as saying to the health clinic manager that he was out to clear his head. People have gone to a lot of trouble to say he was drunk. The car that knocked him over had to climb onto the pavement to do its work. Silt traced an eyewitness. When he went back to the man to take a verbatim record, he'd disappeared. Silt tracked him down but he withdrew everything he had said earlier. Scared stiff.'

'Dramatic.' Guthrie shrugged somewhat dismissively. He was trying to keep a grip on reality. 'Silt's name keeps cropping up,' he added. 'What's his angle?'

'He's pursuing his own line.' Heather was vague. 'The story hangs together well, doesn't it?'

'I'm not convinced that –' Guthrie hesitated.

'If you're not going to believe me, I might as well –' Heather suddenly flared up.

'Wait,' he protested. 'I'm just trying to get things into perspective. It's difficult for us here in Scotland . . .'

'You've just had a cop murdered?'

'Yes, but –'

'And monitoring stations put out of action.'

Guthrie nodded.

'Unity once did something similar. In Chile, years ago. Didn't want their conspiracies bugged.'

Guthrie stared at her, weighing up the implications of her remark, weighing up Heather as well. He had, in the past, thought of himself as a camera, observing and recording but not getting personally involved with other people. But this time he realized straight away that he would not wish nor be able to stay remote and aloof as far as Heather Anderson was concerned. He had instantly approved of the way she sat, she spoke, she dressed. He admired her style. He noted that she blushed easily and that too he liked. She didn't have the long lacquered fingernails that he so detested in many New York women. He felt himself a good judge of people: in her he detected a challenging mix of resoluteness and uncertainty, of sophistication and North American naivety. Here was someone sensitive and with emotional depth, in part set in her ways, in part open to change. In a brief flash of self-realization, he suddenly thought she was not unlike himself. Or was his imagination running well ahead of the game?

Had Heather Anderson been aware of Robert Guthrie's preliminary view of her, she would have agreed with much of it. She often recognized in herself a varying mix of determination and uncertainty: at times she knew where she was going, at other times she felt deeply insecure and was often perplexed about what she wanted to achieve in the years ahead. She considered herself reasonably intellectual though would have indignantly refuted any suggestion that she showed occasional glimpses of transatlantic naivety. In any event, she, unlike Guthrie, was not a particularly introspective person. She looked outwards, and took people at their face value. In him she at first had perceived a somewhat morose, almost brooding figure who was attractive enough at one level but who was not her type physically. She had always been used to the tanned, athletic male. Here was a man whose pale skin she had glimpsed momentarily between trouser leg and dark socks. She realized from the outset that he felt attracted to her but the fact that he did not immediately press his attentions on her gave her a feeling of security. It was a welcome change from the pressures she had felt from most of her other past suitors. That said, she immediately sensed a mental magnetism: she recognized a first-rate thinker who, later on, might seduce well or indeed be well worth seducing. To her, high intellect had always been the greatest aphrodisiac.

A waitress eventually came with the bill, he paid, and they left the restaurant together. It was a mellow evening and they walked for a while along the dockside then took a cab back to his flat for a nightcap. There they stopped talking business, one thing led to another and in the morning he cancelled her booking at the hotel.

Viewed from the outside, Edinburgh's New Club was in the running for being the ugliest of many of the other fifties' and sixties' architectural follies in the whole of Princes Street. The entrance was a gloomy if discreet door in a wall yet, once through that door and up in the lift, and a visitor was elevated into a setting of old-world charm with some of the best views in the entire city. The rooms, particularly the dining room, were pan-elled with the wood from the original nineteenth-century building and the walls were hung with magnificent paintings and prints. Like many another gentleman's club, its leather chairs were, of an evening, filled with the great and the good, the inebriated and the senile. It was there, late the following evening, that Robert Guthrie tracked down the Minister of the Interior, Sir Alexander MacDowall. He was alone, nursing an expensive glass of malt whisky in one hand and holding a copy of the Scottish edition of the *Spectator* in the other. He looked half asleep.

The Minister only grunted when he looked up and saw Guthrie. Then he waved him into a neighbouring seat. 'What brings you here, Robert? Average age is half a century too old for you . . . Drink?'

'I'm a member too, sir. I'll get one myself if I can disturb you for a moment. Can I get you another?'

'Only if you can afford this stuff.' MacDowall waved his glass at Guthrie.

A few minutes later they were both sunk deep in their leather chairs by one of the picture windows that looked up to the magnificent view of Ramsay Garden and the floodlit Edinburgh Castle. 'Got a great friend lives up in one of those houses,' Mac-Dowall said, pointing. 'He's got an even better view over the New Town, the Firth of Forth and to the mountains behind. On a clear night he can see Ben Lomond fifty miles away.'

'Sir . . . I thought I might find you here,' Guthrie interrupted.

'I'm not a great cook. Wife's away in Inverness. Working late.' The old man rambled on and Guthrie wondered if he was slightly drunk. 'Thought I'd better get some steak and kidney pie inside me, otherwise it would have been fried eggs on toast as usual.'

'Sir . . . Unity,' Guthrie insisted.

'If you must.' MacDowall sighed approvingly as he sipped the malt. 'You know we're not meant to talk business in the clubrooms.'

Guthrie pressed on. 'I'm concerned.'

'*Concerned* is an overused, civil servant-ish word, Robert. You're too young to be concerned . . . or too old.'

'Up to no good . . .' Guthrie persevered.

'Who is? If I had more life in me, with Daphne away, I would be up to no good with the ladies down by Leith Docks. Sadly, as Shakespeare says, alcohol and age increaseth the desire, but taketh away the performance –'

'Unity, sir, please!' said Guthrie again, recognizing that perhaps he had chosen his time badly. 'If you don't mind, it's bad.' He told MacDowall what Heather Anderson had told him.

'OK,' said MacDowall, putting the *Spectator* to one side and reluctantly turning to deal with Guthrie's concern. 'So they move in. They provide jobs. They bring in high spenders. They do what big business has always done and try to bully or persuade the Government. What's wrong with that?'

'They're eating at the heart of the nation.'

'Dramatic words, my friend.' MacDowall smiled. 'Scotland's heart's too big.'

'At the core . . .'

'Some of the core is rotten, I agree. Isn't worth worrying about though.' He shook his head.

'I'm not playing with words, sir. When we think of coups –'

'*Coups?* Another highly dramatic word.' MacDowall raised one bushy eyebrow and stared over his half-moon spectacles at Guthrie.

'It's not just in the third world or the Kremlin that coups take place. Remove a leader and his or her immediate supporters or cronies, and the rest of the fabric of the state doesn't even have to know. It can more or less continue as if nothing happened.'

'You're in danger of trying to teach your grandfather . . .' Mac-Dowall stared accusingly down at his empty glass as if wondering whether his head would stand another.

'I'm convinced that is Unity's strategy.'

'I agree Unity's been playing a dangerous game. They may have been behind some of what's happening . . . even the bombing. But we've got no real evidence of wrongdoing from the intelligence the Communications Monitoring managed to dig up. Scottish democracy is safe. It's all too far-fetched . . .' MacDowall suddenly solved one problem to his own satisfaction: no more whisky. 'I must be away,' he said. 'Tomorrow it'll all be gone with the wind.'

MacDowall pulled himself to his feet and Guthrie, disappointed, stood with him. 'I understand your concern, my boy,' he went on, putting an avuncular hand on Guthrie's shoulder. 'We need to be vigilant. But I don't believe in great conspiracies, nor . . .' he hesitated, 'nor in coups. Now,' he repeated, 'I must be away home to my bed.'

Scotland's European Community subsidies

Some 85% of the people of Scotland live in areas receiving European Commission funding. These EC programmes are aimed at replacing declining industries or supporting areas where there has been a collapse of traditional agricultural or fishing activities. Over the last four years seven hundred million pounds have flowed from Brussels to Scotland. It has been distributed via local authorities or local enterprises to small and medium-sized companies, training bodies, tourist boards and environmental and charitable enterprises. This very generous regional assistance programme, administered by the EC's Directorate General for Regional Policy and Cohesion (DG XVI) provides these structural funds which, under existing Community regulations, must be complemented by private investment or monies from national or local government sources. 'Because all of Europe's regions have to be assisted equally and fairly,' said Director of DG XVI, Alvar Sorenson, 'we cannot be expected, given the vast assistance already given to Scotland, to add substantially to that budget. We have,' he added, 'been pleased to see that funds from the Edinburgh Government and from the new Unity Corporation's major investment programme in Scotland have met the necessary criteria for the EC's regulation on matching capital spending.'

'More than one-third of the structural funds allocated to Scotland are funnelled into the Highlands and Islands,' Mr Sorenson continued. 'These were declared an "Objective 1" area as far back as July 1994. With less than ten people per square kilometre, this region has one of the lowest population densities in Europe. This, combined with its size and location, means it is not only isolated from the major markets of Europe but communities within it are isolated from each other.'

Although these arguments have secured monetary assistance up until now, the European Commission must question whether the Highlands and Islands will be eligible for continued DG XVI funding in the future. At the moment this seems unlikely. Despite many pleas from the Scottish authorities, this will also apply to additional funding to Scotland as a whole, since, while it admittedly has considerable economic problems at present, these are matched by adverse conditions being experienced in other parts of Europe as well.

European Commission DG XVI
(Background briefing paper. No C1871F)

A few days later, it was a morning like any other morning. Sir Alexander MacDowall left home at precisely nine o'clock in his chauffeur-driven Rover Ecosse. His large Victorian house, set well back from the road behind high granite walls, six miles to the west of Edinburgh, was left empty. He kept no help and his wife, Daphne, was still away in Inverness staying with her widowed sister.

A methodical man, MacDowall always sat on the right-hand side of the rear seat of the Rover. His briefcase and the morning's newspapers lay beside him on the left. When he was on official business and had a secretary with him, she always knew to sit in the front beside the driver, to give him maximum space. But, as always for the morning drive to work, he was alone. The only difference on that particular day was that, as he left the house, he realized he had left the book he had been reading in his bedroom and went back to get it, handing his briefcase and papers to his chauffeur as he did so. It was a perfectly straight-forward thing to do. The book, a new biography of Thatcher, he had read far into the night and, while he knew that the day in front of him would be a busy one, he promised himself an hour's relaxation with a sandwich lunch at his desk.

When he came down to the car again he noted, with a flicker of annoyance, that his chauffeur had thoughtlessly placed his briefcase and papers on the right-hand rear seat. He thought about telling the man to move them or to push them across himself but decided not to fuss. It was a beautiful morning. He was getting too old and pernickety. Besides, what did it matter? He climbed into the Rover and settled down on the left-hand seat.

The car turned down the drive, along a side road, then pulled onto the approach road to the M8. He would get to his office, traffic permitting, within an easy twenty minutes. MacDowall disliked speed, preferring to leave that little bit earlier, to be able to sift through the morning papers with minimum discomfort. There was plenty of power under the bonnet but the chauffeur, knowing his boss, drove with due restraint.

A sixties' block of council flats, ten storeys high, stood waiting its turn for demolition: it had been built too close to the bend in the new motorway. A high fence had been built between the two which acted as a barrier preventing vandals from throwing things from the flats onto the motorway. Apart from its position, it was long past renovating. The concrete facings on the building were badly corroded and the whole structure presented a squalid example of one of the high-rise super-slums which the architectural profession had bequeathed to the nation in a prolonged period of collective insanity. Curtainless windows on the second floor indicated an empty council flat. Its previous tenants had won some money in the Scottish lottery, and now lived uneasily with their new neighbours in a neat, red-roofed bungalow in Barnton.

The man in the anorak with his canvas bag containing plumber's tools had been working in the empty flat since shortly after eight o'clock. The peroxided woman in the flat across the stairhead nagged her husband with a stream of bitter invective about council workmen never coming early on occasions when *they* had anything wrong with their plumbing.

Inside the flat, the man in the anorak locked and bolted the door behind him. He went straight through to the desolate kitchen which looked over and down onto the motorway. He had to operate either from that window or from the lavatory; after a quick inspection he opted for the former, which offered him more elbow room. He opened his bag, took out the little radio, and switched it on. There was a slight mush, but it was pre-set. He waited; the radio emitted seven bleeps. It would repeat this every two minutes precisely. Even with the Campsie Monitoring Station out of action, speech was not allowed, preferable though it would have been.

The man opened his bag and took out a tripod. He carefully extended the legs so that the top came just above the level of the window. He glanced at his watch: he had a clear half-hour to go. He pulled the gun out from its case and clipped it on to the tripod. Once the peculiarly shaped silencer was locked in position, he bent over and, aiming at a spot on the tarmac on the far lane of the motorway, adjusted the telescopic sights. The range was rather too great for perfection, but he was no amateur. The gun too was professional. He did a few dry runs on unsuspecting private cars, judging their speed and position on the motorway, lightly pressing the trigger at the precise moment when the drivers hit the centre of the cross in the telescopic lens. At the end of ten minutes, had the gun been loaded, he was confident he would have scored nine out of ten. It was too easy.

Five minutes to nine and a white-and-yellow-striped lorry, amber light flashing, drove up the motorway and stopped just short of the block of flats. Two men in fluorescent jackets got out and started putting up ROAD WORKS signs and distributing red-and-white plastic cones, narrowing the three-lane motorway down to one. This too was according to plan.

The man in the anorak looked at his watch. Not long to go. Everything was in position. Every two minutes the radio continued to bleep. The man took a can of Coca-Cola from his bag, pulled the tag, and drank the contents in one go. As he finished, the radio emitted an urgent and continuous bleep. The target had passed the bridge a mile back up the motorway. The man threw the empty can on the floor, and, as if he had not a care in the world, positioned himself easily behind the sights.

The chauffeur slowed down when he saw the first of the lane closure signs. MacDowall looked up from his *Scotsman*, noted the line of cones, glanced at his watch and frowned. He was already a little late. Each morning he subconsciously noted the time he passed that same ugly block of flats. Ten safe driving minutes from his office. That stretch of motorway was seldom busy but he could be late if there were road works ahead. He was aware of his fussiness increasing with age. What was five minutes more or less to a man in his position? Only the other day he had overheard one of the security guards at the Ministry say that they could set their watches by the promptness of his arrival. Was that a good quality?

Five bullets smacked in rapid succession into the roof of the car. One of them ricocheted and smashed through the side window. Three of them punched neat holes through the leather of MacDowall's briefcase on the right-hand seat. The last bullet, deflected by the angle of the roof, found its true target and embedded itself in his right shoulder. Despite the shock, MacDowall's good left hand continued to hold tightly onto the *Scotsman*.

It was the chauffeur, SAS-trained in his youth to little normal benefit, who cottoned on to what was happening. With remarkable perception, he accelerated rapidly away onto the hard shoulder, knocking down the line of plastic warning cones one after the other. A rear tyre burst or had been shot through, but that was a nicety. The chauffeur only pulled to a stop when they were safely under the shelter of a bridge that ran over the motorway half a mile further on. MacDowall, slouched in the back, ashenfaced but conscious, kept trying to turn to identify where the shots had come from.

'Big block back there, sir. Second or third floor, judging from the angle. You all right, sir?' Then the chauffeur saw the blood. Leaving MacDowall where he was, he jumped from the car, and started trying to wave down a passing car.

Cars and lorries thundered imperviously past, presuming, uncharitably, to avoid the bother of helping a driver with a breakdown. A routine police car patrol, on the watch for speeding motorists, luckily came on the scene. Further valuable moments were lost before the officers, provoked by the choice of language with which the chauffeur described their stupidity, got slowly out of their squad car to inspect the Rover. To do them credit, the speed of their subsequent actions left little to be desired but the assassin's vantage point had been well chosen. The high barrier fence was impossible to negotiate from where they were and by the time other patrol cars got to the building and located the empty flat, it was empty. Even the Coke tin had gone.

9

Lively nights with Nora Sin-clair

Close friends of wheelchair-bound Keith Sinclair,
Scotland's beleaguered Prime Minister, have been
expressing surprise that the lovely Nora has been
straying dangerously far from her husband's sickbed.
Seen dancing the night away at Annabels recently
with an unidentified male Lothario, she sweetly
explained that her husband had sent her off on a
weekend break, away from the cold tensions of Scotland's capital city. We are sure that PM Keith and
his tongue-wagging friends can relax. Nora would
never do anything remiss . . .

(Nigel Dempster's London Diary, *Daily Mail*)

The bare room, deep in the Special Task Force's nondescript
office complex close by the Scottish Office at Leith docks, was
cold despite the heater set into the wall. There was a metal fire
door and no windows and the breeze-block walls added their
own chill. High up, near the ceiling, a ventilator grate emitted a
low hum from the air filtering system. On one wall someone had
sellotaped the centre pin-up from an ancient *Playboy* magazine:
July's playmate, another sexless, bulging doll with unblemished
skin and immaculate hair. A clock on the wall showed ten-thirty.
A trestle table stood against one wall. On it, two or three mugs
filled with blackened dregs, a half-empty milk bottle, some instant
coffee and scruffy paper packets of tea and sugar. The centre of

the room was taken up with a hastily rigged-up and very temporary communications monitoring unit, on which lights flashed urgently. This was far from the high-tech ops facility that the station in the Campsie Hills had long provided, but it was sufficient for this very specific task.

In front of the apparatus, two tubular steel chairs were occupied. One balding, middle-aged man, a pair of headphones clamped over his ears, sat and listened intently. He had a pad of paper on which he jotted notes. To his right, a tape recorder was occasionally adjusted by the other, much younger man. When not required, he sat in his chair thumbing through a copy of the *Nationalist*. He looked bored.

Suddenly, a red light on the panel flashed a warning. The younger man turned, put on his headphones, then he too started taking rapid notes.

A mile away, in a select suburb of Edinburgh, Ian Campbell had just picked up the telephone. He listened for a moment, then said hesitantly, 'Oh . . . It's you. Yes, I'm well, thank you,' he added.

The voice at the other end was slow and deliberate. In the Leith operations rooms the younger man had no difficulty in picking up every word that was said.

'You should know we've moved into phase three, Ian,' the caller said. It wasn't quite an American accent, though speech analysis would later trace the occasional transatlantic vowel sound. 'We're opening up the game.'

'Yes?' said Campbell nervously. He was always cautious on the telephone.

'What news?' asked the caller.

'What about?' Back in Leith, the young man in the headphones made a note that Campbell's voice suddenly betrayed anxiety. His readers liked that sort of background.

'A hunt . . . A shoot. Have you heard what the bag was?'

'My God . . .' There was silence for a moment.

'Are you still there?'

'Yes . . . That . . . that wasn't you, was it?'

'Look – it was you who told us that the old man was our most vigorous opponent.' There was another long pause. The young man tapped his pencil on his pad impatiently.

'Not up to standard,' said Campbell cautiously, composure partly regained.

'Missed?'

'More or less. Back at his desk, arm in a sling, by lunchtime, I understand. Why the hell? Why so vicious? There are other ways . . .'

'Not everyone has your superb lack of principle,' the voice responded evenly. There was a further pause. 'You're right. It was careless. Perhaps he'll be more amenable now. Who said, honour goes when fear plays master?'

'Don't know; not with him, anyway.'

'We'll try. Rather, you'll try.'

'I won't,' said Campbell nervously.

'Yes, dammit, you will.' The voice was suddenly sharp. 'See him today. Report back tonight, Minister.' The title was thrown out without a veil on the sarcasm.

'I . . . I cannot . . .'

The young man in the headphones noted the precise time when the line went dead. He also noted down the vile invective uttered by the Minister of Finance into the dead receiver.

The young man left the bare room, asking his older colleague to keep watch on his line. He'd better get the intercept off without delay. As he had yet to hear about the assassination attempt, he couldn't make full sense of the conversation. But he wasn't stupid and knew that Government Ministers were not usually addressed in such forthright terms. He sat down in front of his computer, and began by typing the word IMMEDIATE in prominent capitals.

Sir Alexander MacDowall was a most determined man. He would not otherwise have reached and retained his present position. Perhaps his most outstanding quality was in assessing and judging his fellow men. With candour and no glimpse of modesty, he realized how much better the Government of the country would have been had he, and not Prime Minister Sinclair, selected and appointed the present Cabinet.

The PM had slipped up drastically on one of his choices: Ian Campbell was, in MacDowall's eyes, an unmitigated disaster. But until that particular day, MacDowall had assumed that the unsuitability of the appointment lay merely in the fact that Campbell was undistinguished in every field. He had been totally lost in the international monetary world, since his merchant banking background had been of a limited bond trading nature that had hardly equipped him for the key role of Minister of Finance. It had become particularly dangerous when Campbell had moved to the critical stage, all too common with weak politicians in power, of coupling incompetence with a certain frenetic activity in pursuing ill-thought-out objectives.

MacDowall, though in considerable pain from the flesh wound in his shoulder and with his arm in a sling, was back at his desk, bravely or stubbornly trying to catch up on his work. Released from a reluctant hospital just after mid-day despite protests from the doctors, he was trying to deal with his papers as if nothing had happened. He was also trying to punish himself by facing up to the bleak realization that Robert Guthrie had been right and he had been wrong.

MacDowall's outer office coped with the flood of anxious enquiries as the news of the assassination attempt spread. He only took one brief telephone call, from the Prime Minister, from his own hospital bed, who congratulated him on his escape. He himself drafted an anodyne press release for the papers, in an attempt to take some of the heat out of the occasion. It wouldn't satisfy them for long, as well he knew. His wife rang frantically from Inverness, insisting on returning home at once. The Commissioner of Police tried to get him on the line at half-hour intervals but, as all he was doing was reporting nil progress in the hunt for the gunman, MacDowall avoided speaking to him.

Then his personal assistant ran into the room saying that Ian Campbell was outside and wanted to see him urgently. In other circumstances he would have had her say that he was unavailable.

But MacDowall had just read the text of the telephone intercept, brought to him by special messenger in an envelope covered with red seals. In any event, the door opened and Campbell came in uninvited, despite the protestations of the two uniformed policemen who had been stationed outside MacDowall's office ever since the attack.

Campbell's face was white and drawn. He began by gushing out his sense of relief at MacDowall's good fortune. MacDowall did not react for some moments, then he looked coldly up from his desk.

'You wanted something, Ian?' His voice was icy but controlled.

'Yes, that is, I came to . . . warn you.' There was a pause.

'A little late . . .' MacDowall stared hard at Campbell over his rimless glasses.

'They were trying to kill you.'

'So I presume. But who? And how could you possibly know?'

'You must be forthcoming with them, more reasonable. You owe it to yourself, your family, the country.' Campbell's voice had dropped to a whisper.

'What are you gabbling about? If you know who, then your duty –'

'You know, and I know, that they . . . that certain people have been trying to persuade you –'

'To give them a free hand to do what they want, to undermine the fabric of the country. Is that what you're talking about?' MacDowall's voice raised itself threateningly.

'We'll go under as a nation. We're done for economically without outside help. I should know.'

'You should indeed, Ian. You should indeed. Did they send you? Are these people, whoever they are, really your friends, Ian? Are they? If so, you chose dangerous bedfellows. It's I who should warn you. Or is it too late?' MacDowall stood up. Despite the bandages and the sling, he felt like hitting Campbell, confronting him with the fact that he had just read the intercept. But that would have given the game away. A huge anger had built up inside him, but it would be pointless to expend it on this creature.

He should have him arrested for complicity but that was not the way forward either. Not yet.

'I'm trying to help,' said Campbell weakly. He was shaking violently and for a moment MacDowall wondered if he was going to cry.

'They've asked me to ... Please be reasonable. It's ... think of it as a business deal. Other people in the Cabinet are being amenable. You're almost alone in standing in their way. They know you're too powerful, so ... so if you won't cooperate, I'm sure they'll try again.'

'I don't need you to teach me what to do, Campbell,' Mac-Dowall said, his voice under control. 'I do not wish to discuss the matter further.'

'I've to tell them you refuse?' Campbell asked.

'There's something you're a stranger to, it's called morality.' MacDowall spoke slowly and deliberately. 'Now, *get out*.'

Campbell started to say something more but then caught the look on the hard, cold face. MacDowall turned away to stare unseeingly out of the window and over the city's grey roofs. Campbell hesitated for a moment, then turned and quickly left the room.

As soon as he had gone, MacDowall collapsed back in his chair. With the back of his good hand he wiped a sudden sweat from his forehead. He was getting old, he had lost a lot of blood that morning, he knew he should be in bed. But one invalid in the Cabinet was enough. Appearances were crucial. He had to keep going. He had to think. Things known or suspected, odd offers of patronage, of money, never direct, never open, never attributable, were recalled one by one. For a long time he had built up a picture of widening corruption. But even when Guthrie had pointed it out so clearly, he had failed to act. It had been a gross error of judgement. It was almost too late.

He presumed that Campbell meant what he said, that the Government had been deeply infiltrated. Who could be trusted? He had to presume that some of his immediate colleagues had already been won over and were now a sort of Mafia, a freemasonry of perjured men. Special Task Force reports had given him plenty of hints of people being picked off, one by one. Not everyone had been approached, only the influential, the self-important, the weak. By such methods the strong became isolated and alone. If Campbell was the main front man, how could he tackle those behind?

MacDowall picked up the transcript of Campbell's telephone call. It had taken enormous reserves of self-control to speak, even in as civilized a way as he had just done, to a man who was in close touch with those who had ordered the attempt on his life. Having the transcript meant he was still one step ahead. But that information was not enough. What should he do? Suddenly he felt old, isolated and very exposed.

For an instant, as the pain in his shoulder rose in intensity, he felt like packing it all in. If others wanted it that way, who was he to stand in their way? He could resign. He could stand aside. Why should he act the hero, the lone barrier against those who were seeking to control Scotland?

The mood passed. It was not too late. Where were the uncorrupted men and women? He would find them. He needed allies, people he could trust.

MacDowall summoned his personal assistant and told her to get Robert Guthrie to come and see him immediately.

When, less than half an hour later, the PM's Private Secretary arrived, MacDowall wasted no time. 'You've seen the intercept?'

'Campbell?' asked Guthrie.

'Bastard's just been to see me.' MacDowall explained what had transpired. 'Robert,' he said softly, 'I'm sorry. You were right. I was wrong.'

Guthrie ignored the remark. 'He should be strung up.'

'I know. But having him arrested would alert the enemy, whoever they may be. They would guess how much we knew. If they've bought up a sufficient number of people like Campbell, we could be the ones to disappear.'

'You don't think . . .' Guthrie stopped, then began talking, telling MacDowall everything he had wanted to pour out that night at the New Club, everything that he and Heather Anderson had found out about the Unity Corporation's worldwide activities.

When Guthrie had finished, MacDowall sat in silence for some considerable time. 'We've waited too long,' he said eventually. 'This is too big for us, any of us here in Scotland. At a guess, London won't want to know. You're going to need your passport, Robert. I want you to fly to Washington. Tonight's flight if you can.'

A large, modern building on the west side of St Andrew's Square that had once housed an insurance company was now the Edinburgh offices of the Unity Corporation. Two whole floors, Abel Rosenfeld explained proudly, were occupied by the Public Affairs and Government Relations Division, of which he was the Strategic Director. Rosenfeld himself had come down to the reception area to meet Heather Anderson when she presented herself, as arranged, at nine o'clock precisely. He was charm itself, escorting her up to his spacious modern office and personally serving her with the best coffee she had tasted since she left the States.

'Mr de Laski's particularly glad you've agreed to join up,' he began. 'It's an exciting job persuading the Scots what's good for them, that they really need us . . . and want us. That's what your father thinks as well, though he may have gone about it in slightly the wrong way.' He spoke warmly. 'We too are *very* sincere about that,' he continued. 'It really *is* in their best interests – and ours too of course. Scotland desperately needs the shot in the arm that only Unity can give.'

'I'm looking forward to hearing . . .' Heather began, forcing herself not to explode at the mention of her father. In the aftermath of the attack on MacDowall and Torrance's death, it hadn't needed Harvey Silt to tell her that she was embarking on a dangerous game. If anything went wrong, if they found out, she too could be in grave danger. If today's plan worked and she managed to do as she had been tasked to do and discover more about the staffing and strategy of the Unity team in Scotland, she would be especially vulnerable.

Rosenfeld's smile disappeared briefly as he interrupted her thoughts, and asked sharply, 'Why did you decide to come over here?'

She was glad she had rehearsed with Silt exactly what she was going to say. She made what she hoped looked like an apologetic gesture. 'Most selfish of all reasons,' she said. 'I've decided I've had New York and journalism up to here . . . Or it's had me. And it doesn't pay enough. I'd like to see what feeding the press news, not being fed it, is like for a change. I might just be good at it.'

'That's why we wanted you.' Rosenfeld's smile had returned. 'Glad to have you on board. Terms are the same, more or less, as you were offered in New York, but you get an additional housing allowance . . . Where are you living at the moment?'

Heather mentioned the name of the hotel where she had booked in for her first night in Scotland. 'Been staying with friends mostly though,' she added quickly. If Rosenfeld decided to check up, she didn't want to begin by getting caught out in an unnecessary lie.

'We've bought up a load of town houses and apartments all over Edinburgh for the use of our senior staff. I'm sure I can swing something,' said Rosenfeld. His well-practised smile had become a permanent feature.

'That's great . . .' She hesitated.

'Look,' said Rosenfeld glancing down at his watch. 'Change of plan. I've got to go through to Glasgow to meet a client. Inconvenient, but I'll get my deputy, Winston Bushfield, to show you the ropes, sign you on, tell you a bit about the job and fix when we'd like you to begin. We'll have to get you to sign a confidentiality agreement. Routine, no more. There's a bundle of politically and commercially sensitive information floating around this building. It could be damaging, even dangerous, if it fell into the wrong hands. You'll find out, for example, that there are a number of quite senior and very blinkered Scots around, who don't see the advantages of what we're doing. One or two actually think we're trying to colonize them or something! We're working on them. Gentle persuasion's the name of the game round here.' Rosenfeld laughed, stood up and, 'Welcome aboard,' he repeated. 'Now, where the hell is Winston?'

Mid-morning and Heather Anderson was sitting alone in a

small studio theatre watching a very professional video which Unity had made to promote a corporate image of itself as both responsible and environmentally friendly.

'We've a number of different versions for use in schools and colleges, for example. Then there's the rather more, how shall I say, impartial version that our television channel managed to get screened at prime time, a week or so ago,' Bushfield explained. 'We brought in a number of worthy Scots to read the lines we wrote for them. It ended up very believable, if I say so myself.' Rosenfeld's deputy, a man not quite as sharp as his boss, had already given her a tour of the department. She had met a number of young men and women, all of whom seemed to have studied at the same charm school as Rosenfeld. Most of the senior people were American but many of the new recruits were Scots. There was a lot of bounce and sparkle in the air; it would be easy, she conjectured, to be taken in by it all. And their product, from TV advertising campaigns to glossy brochures, was top-class with no expense spared. Bushfield led her through the Press department where people, sitting at rows of desks, were monitoring or taking press calls. On a big board at one end of the room were displayed blown-up lists of *bullet points* and *targets* which staff had to adhere to in all their dealings with the media.

'We write opinion pieces here and help with leader writing for some of our own newspapers – where we think our editors might need a bit of a steer or friendly guidance.' Bushfield explained helpfully. 'As Abel keeps saying, editors can create gods and conjure up devils; build reputations and destroy them. Where there's weak government, as in Scotland right now, the media become strong.' Heather Anderson found it difficult to disagree with that trenchant philosophy.

They came eventually to a security door, with a punch key electronic lock to one side. Bushfield went up to it, then hesitated. 'Better leave that for now,' he said, turning away. 'Abel can show you all that stuff when you come in on a permanent basis.'

'What is it?' Heather asked innocently.

'Political Affairs department. Most but not all are still US staff.

We're training some trusty Scots right now but ... loyalty's a strange thing.'

'What do they do?' she persisted.

'Everything from getting Cabinet Ministers to love us, down to the demo team –'

'The what?'

'Shouldn't tell you this, not yet. But what the hell. It's clever stuff. Helping some of those nasty little street demonstrations get hyped up. We call it ICU – incitement to civil unrest. We pay for posters, banners, transport, that sort of thing. We even had a little exercise going to give a bit of discreet help to the anti-white settlers, I mean the anti-English having second homes in the High-lands brigade. But when those weirdos started burning down too many crofts, we stopped that. We don't like undirected violence you know and it might have backfired: spilled over into being anti-US immigrants too! Otherwise, we're strictly impartial.' He laughed. 'We feed both sides: Republicans and Reunionists. What the hell, it's just politics after all. We've got a huge budget for all that. Then there's the Slush Fund. Who was it who said that an honest politician is one who, once bought, stays bought?' Bushfield laughed again. 'One or two of the powerful here in Edinburgh have not been averse to lining their pockets. Politics and ethics seldom mix. The higher they've climbed up the greasy pole, the greedier many of them get.'

'You pay Scottish politicians?' Heather tried to stay calm and collected to stop her astonishment showing.

Bushfield shrugged. 'Someone has to. They only get a pittance from the State. Well, if you must know, the secret is we'll pay them for as long as we need to, then ditch them. In the long run, bought men and women can't be trusted after all.'

Heather Anderson wondered whether Bushfield was still jok-ing, or simply did not see the absurdity of his last remark. 'You can't buy them all?' she prompted. 'No matter how clever you are, some surely ...'

'Yeah, we're clever. But you're right. There are a few hard nuts. They ain't had the training in sleaze of your average New

York politician. But most of them are learning, real fast. Now then, how about lunch?'

Rosenfeld was working on one hard nut at that very moment. He had had the pub in Sauchiehall Street cased for him so he knew a little of what to expect. Despite that prior knowledge and despite having been in Scotland for several years, he entered a very different world to the one he was used to. He was glad he had managed to borrow a nondescript anorak to wear over his Armani suit as he made his way through the smoke-filled gloom. Hard Glaswegian drinkers stared at him suspiciously from behind their marble-topped tables or from their positions propped around the long bar.

Forbes appeared from his corner table to greet him. They shook hands. 'Assume you're Rosenfeld?' said Forbes. His voice was normally broadly accented but he was making an effort to have himself understood by the American.

'Can we go somewhere quiet?' Rosenfeld asked.

'Ma corner's o'er there,' said Forbes, pointing with the back of his head towards a table by the window. 'It's mine. Nobody else uses it 'cept by invitation,' he said threateningly. 'What's yours?'

'What's my? Oh, I see . . . A pint of heavy, please,' said Rosenfeld easily. He had prepared himself for the standard refreshment.

Forbes went to the bar, ordered two pints, and brought them over to the corner table. They sat down, partially facing each other, partially looking outwards into the crowded room. There were perhaps twenty or thirty other drinkers around, almost all of them men. One or two of them nodded to Forbes as he passed but none of them dared come up to disturb him. Forbes was an important man in that community. He was someone you did not speak to first.

'I've heard a lot about you, Mr Forbes,' said Rosenfeld. 'You've a big reputation.'

'And 'ave heard naething about you, Mr Rosenfeld.' There was a pregnant pause. Rosenfeld switched on his smile but immediately realized that it was not going to work. Smiles were out of season. Here was a Glasgow hard man. He would have to cultivate a steely attitude as well.

'What d'you ken about me?' asked Forbes aggressively.

'Want me to be frank?'

'If you want tae talk tae me, truth is an essential commodity,' said Forbes roughly. Neither lips nor eyes showed any emotion.

'Well then. We've got a file on you about an inch thick,' Rosenfeld volunteered.

'Tha' all?' asked Forbes. Was there a glint of humour in his voice as he spoke?

'That's just the file with letters and reports,' said Rosenfeld frankly. 'There's a huge back-up folder full of all your press cuttings.'

'Well then,' said Forbes grudgingly. 'Tha's better. So you ken all about me, then? Or think you do.'

'I know where you come from and I think I know where you're going.' Rosenfeld dropped his voice.

'No great shakes knowing where a come frae. Tha's a' on public record.'

'Agreed. Long-term hard left, past member of the Communist Party, trade union leader, inspired and led a large number of industrial strikes. Great fan of Jimmy Reid and other Red Clydesiders. You're a natural leader of men, so the *Herald* has said on more than one occasion. "Led more walk-outs than most people have had hot dinners," said the *Daily Record*. A great orator . . .'

'Spare the praise . . .' Forbes nodded his head a fraction, briefly basking in the American's words, while not wishing to appear too flattered.

'Since those early days you haven't moderated your views. You've kept your beliefs. You've always fought for a Scottish Republic.'

'A like it,' said Forbes. 'Never reject undeserved praise, a don't. So . . .' He paused. 'Just wha' do you want tae talk tae me about?'

'I realize you've not been a lifelong friend of American

capitalism,' Rosenfeld began. 'But we at Unity Corporation are somewhat different, Mr Forbes. We're here in Scotland because we like what we see. We like the Scottish culture. We like the Scottish labour force, with its high degree of skills and training. We are prepared to work with your particular brand of trade unionism. We believe in a fair deal for the working man.'

'Rubbish,' said Forbes. 'You're just like a' the fuckin' rest.'

'I disagree, Mr Forbes. We're here because we want to be here and want to see Scotland and its workforce thrive. That's why I'm sitting here talking to you.'

'So? Talk,' said Forbes. 'But before you do, why don't you get me another pint.'

Rosenfeld walked uneasily towards the crowded bar but as he approached a gap appeared for him as if by magic and he found the barman ready to serve him straight away. Everybody was watching. 'Mr Forbes's usual, please, and the same for me,' he said in a loud voice, exuding a confidence which he certainly did not feel.

Back at the table, Forbes carried on as if there had been no break. 'A wouldna' be talking to you if you were a Scottish or English capitalist,' he said grudgingly. 'As a see it, there's got to be something driving Unity over here. What is it?'

'Profit motive, stakeholder value, all that sort of thing,' said Rosenfeld. 'It would be wrong to lie to you.'

'You've said that a'for, laddie.'

'I'm being absolutely frank.'

'When somebody says that tae me a start counting the spoons,' said Forbes.

'You won't catch me out, Mr Forbes, I can assure you. I mean what I say.' Rosenfeld leaned forward and again dropped his voice. 'I have a deal to put to you. If you give your support and backing to the Unity move, we'll ensure that full employment becomes one of the driving forces of a weak Scottish Government's industrial and economic policy.'

'You can deliver that? Ma strikers can't.' Forbes sat back in disbelief.

'There are ways and ways, Mr Forbes.'

'Go on,' Forbes urged. 'Gi' us a clue.'

'Money, Mr Forbes. Money. It buys people, it buys ideas, in the end, it buys everything. And we've got the cash to do it. Take yourself, for example. You could so easily be a very rich man.'

Forbes's eyes narrowed only a fraction. 'A'm listening laddie,' he said. 'A'm listening.'

It was cold for late August and the beaters, gathered at the side of the shooting lodge, stood as close as they could to the brazier that was warming their lunchtime soup. More importantly, they all clutched well-charged tumblers of whisky. It was wet and getting wetter, and the day's shoot was only half done.

Inside the lodge, the sportsmen and their ladies were enjoying a substantial picnic lunch. Fulton and Carlyle moved into a small side room as soon as Ian Campbell appeared.

'You've failed?' Fulton looked impassive.

'Yes.' Campbell looked and sounded like a broken reed.

'You're going to need to find some fuckin' backbone, Ian. Soon. You've got the most important job you've ever had coming up,' said Fulton roughly. 'We move to the next stage. Right now. There's not a moment to lose.'

'Sinclair? What about MacDowall?' Campbell whispered.

'They'll be fine. They're invalids. Sinclair's going to be out of action for a long, long time. Until the great Scottish public has forgotten he exists. And as for MacDowall, we're working on that . . .'

'No more shootings . . . No more bombs. Please . . .' whimpered Campbell.

The other men stared at him with contempt, then Fulton said, 'I'll grant you that, Ian. If all goes well, and if you perform your new duties satisfactorily, there should be no need.'

10

Has it come to this?

Anarchy in the streets. Assassins at large in our cities.
Rampant inflation. And, at the top, a vacuum. Prime
Minister Sinclair lies in his sickbed. Sir Alexander
MacDowall is also wounded. We wish them both a
speedy recovery but, in the meantime, Scotland has
to be governed. It demands leadership, particularly
on the business and financial side, to get us out of
our current economic mess. That is why we at this
newspaper believe that someone of the calibre of Ian
Campbell, with his wide experience . . .

(Extract from first leader, the *Edinburgh Citizen*)

Sinclair was released from hospital at nine-thirty that morning.
Ingram and a man called Geoff Dobbs from the Cabinet Office,
who had occasionally stood in for Guthrie when the latter was
away, were waiting at the main door. The Prime Minister was
still wheelchair-bound. Apart from his doctors and the muscular
lady physiotherapist, no one outside the hospital knew that the
operation had proved surprisingly successful and that he had
gained a little power back in his leg muscles. There was still such
a thing as professional medical confidentiality. Sinclair did not
want everyone to know: it was early days and the possibility of
a relapse still remained. It was his private problem and he wanted
minimum public speculation.

Part of the price he had paid for this partial success was a much longer stay in hospital than he had anticipated. During that time, demand as he might, he had not been allowed to keep up fully with his work. He saw only a few key official papers. Guthrie, he was told, was on holiday, taking advantage of his absence, though Sinclair imagined that he might just be keeping out of his way. His personal and constituency mail was being dealt with on a caretaker basis by his office. He fretted of course, but it is always difficult to be forceful in clinical surroundings and his occasional visitors, such as Sir Alexander MacDowall, all in obvious conspiracy with and vetted by his doctors, kept insisting that his health must come first. Sinclair never heard once from his wife. It did not worry him much, but they had been married for many years and time is no idle factor even in bad relationships.

He felt remote and out of touch with reality as he was driven away from the hospital that morning. He was keen to get back to his desk and papers but he was still in so much ignorance that he did not even know what immediate official appointments had been arranged for him. Dobbs, who was sitting in front beside Ingram, began by briefing him on minor matters. He was a morose man at the best of times but today Sinclair felt he was more than usually unforthcoming. He put it down to Dobbs's mood rather than his. The latter talked vaguely about getting up to date on current issues, on the economy and the recent wave of strikes, without actually going into anything in any detail. Sinclair asked irritably where Guthrie was. Surely he couldn't still be on holiday? A fraction oddly, Dobbs told the Prime Minister that his leave had been extended and that all would be explained to him later. Such was Dobbs's off-hand manner that Sinclair decided he would suggest to the Cabinet Secretary that he find a livelier stand-in for Guthrie in future.

He decided to leave further attempts to find out what was going on until they reached the office. With the whole of the rear of the car to himself, he surreptitiously eased his legs, first one, then the other, to prove to himself that their new-found movement had not, in some mysterious way, been confined to within the hospital walls. When he had got them slowly back to a degree of painful life, he settled back in his seat with a degree of satisfaction. Gazing absentmindedly out of the car window, he wondered at the route Ingram had chosen to drive from the hospital to his office. It was raining, and the blackened houses and factories of the industrial area through which they were now passing seemed all the more desolate and grim. How pleasant it would be to get back in harness again. Sinclair felt almost happy at the prospect.

At a familiar crossroad Ingram turned left rather than right, away from the city. Sinclair sat up, immediately alert. He had a job to get back to. What was going on? Had he misunderstood the arrangements?

'Where are we going, Dobbs? I thought we were going straight to my office.' To his surprise there was no response whatsoever from the front, and at first he thought Dobbs hadn't heard him. Raising his voice, he repeated the question. Again Dobbs ignored him. He felt he was dreaming. Had the man gone deaf, or was he asleep?

Sinclair spoke sharply to his driver. 'Where the hell are we going, Ingram?'

Ingram's attention moved momentarily from the road in front of him and, glancing nervously at Dobbs, he broke out with, 'Sorry, sir. Orders is orders. Sorry,' he repeated. To Sinclair's amazement Dobbs reacted angrily by turning on Ingram and telling him to shut up and stick to his driving.

'What in damnation are you on about, Dobbs?' He leaned forward again and bellowed, 'Have you taken leave of your senses?'

Dobbs turned in his seat, and in infuriatingly insolent yet precise tones, said, 'It will do little good getting angry, sir. Things have changed dramatically . . . from today. I advise you to sit quietly. All will be explained to you in due course. You are a sick man, after all.'

Sinclair exploded. 'What the hell kind of explanation is that, Dobbs? I've had enough. Consider yourself dismissed, as from now. Ingram, turn round and drive me straight to my office.'

As he had somehow anticipated, this outburst had no effect whatsoever and his order was totally ignored. Perhaps it was the fact that Dobbs had addressed him as *sir* and not as *Prime Minister* that had triggered an alarm bell. He felt as if he were in the midst of one of those dreams where one finds oneself powerless to prevent some event and so attempts to wake up to escape it.

He sat back in his seat, gripping the leather armrests for mental rather than physical support, and tried to figure out what on earth was happening. He felt sweat build up and slide unpleasantly between his palms and the leather. Had Dobbs been alone he would have put it down to the man having had a sort of brainstorm. But Ingram, a sane but boring man if ever there was one, was in it as well, though he was patently unhappy about what he was having to do.

For a few moments Sinclair remained numb and silent. Then, in what he hoped sounded a composed voice, he asked quietly, 'Where exactly are you taking me? Am I being kidnapped or something?' Once again there was no response. He felt that to continue in this vein would lead to the indignity of his losing all self-control. It had now become clear that kidnapping was the only word to describe what was happening to him.

He tried to relax, to work out a meaning for it all. Perhaps it was he, Sinclair, who was going mad. For a moment he thought of attempting to exert his will by force, using the slight power in his legs. But something held him back. He might need that element of surprise and effort later. Then he realized what he should be doing: if he was being kidnapped, he ought to memorize the route by which he was being taken. But looking around him, he saw he had little need, for they had just driven over the border into his own parliamentary constituency, where he prided himself on knowing almost every road and turning. A quarter of an hour passed. They were now out in open countryside. He recognized many of the individual farms and cottages as they passed. Everything seemed so normal. He switched his attention back to Dobbs. Why would he be acting in this way? What did the man have against him? They had always got on reasonably well, if never particularly closely, on the few occasions that Dobbs had worked for him before. He had always seemed a practical if dull man, with no obvious personal hang-ups. To civil servants, politicians like Sinclair were just factors to be taken into account in the general decision-making process. A bad or difficult Minister was like an act of God. Civil servants didn't take against such people; they merely planned on how to circumvent them. That should have applied to Ingram too, and more so, unless, unbeknownst to Sinclair, Nora had got round to dismissing his wife, their cook-housekeeper. But that was hardly a likely scenario either. Sinclair found himself staring at the back of Dobbs's neck. In the thick flesh at the bottom of the black, closely-cropped hair there was a scar, the mark of an adolescent boil rather than a wound. Dobbs also had bad dandruff.

Sinclair again looked about him curiously as they turned off the main road by a double-gated driveway. This was strange. Or was it? He used to know the big house at the end of the drive so well. It had, for centuries, belonged to the same noble family. Then, like so many, both house and inhabitants had run to seed. The family had scattered and the house itself – more of a castle – had been sold. Then Sinclair remembered, in a sudden flash, that the Unity Corporation had bought it some years ago as the base for their Executive Training School.

The intricately-wrought iron gates had been renovated and recently repainted. The old coat of arms, set in the stonework of the pillars, had been retained, its details now garishly picked out in heraldic crimson and gold. The gates themselves were closed but, when Ingram sounded his horn, a man appeared immediately from the well-kept gatehouse. He was dressed in blue battledress uniform with a peaked cap of the sort that American security guards wear. By his side paced an Alsatian on a short chain. The guard came out to the car, examined Dobbs's identity card, looked at a list he carried, then checked off a name. 'You're expected,' he said in an unmistakably American accent, then saluted and turned to open the gates.

As Ingram drove up the long drive, the gates closed behind them. Sinclair had a momentary glimpse of a high perimeter fence, running both to the left and right away from the gate. The gardens on each side were in beautiful order, so unlike the wilderness of neglect when he had last been there. As they swept up the gravel to the front of the big house, he noticed that it too had regained its old elegance, or more so, since he doubted it had ever looked so immaculate. Two or three expensive-looking cars were parked outside.

Ingram pulled to a halt at the bottom of the steps. Their journey was obviously over. Dobbs got out and started unloading Sinclair's wheelchair as if nothing unusual was taking place. Sinclair made no move, briefly deciding to be stubborn. Then Dobbs pulled the car door open and addressed him sharply, 'I should cooperate fully, sir. It would be unseemly if we had to carry you in.' He stood back and Sinclair decided to retain his dignity and do as he was bid.

Out and into his wheelchair, Ingram and Dobbs carried him backwards up the flight of steps to the main front door. He was facing away from the house for ease of manipulation, and so it was only when they got to the top that he realized there was a welcoming party of two men who introduced themselves as a Mr Carlyle and a Mr de Laski.

'Glad to see you out of hospital, Mr Sinclair.' Preposterously, Carlyle, tall and languid in rimless spectacles, smiled down at him as if nothing was out of order. The *Mr Sinclair* bit was especially jarring.

'Would you mind telling me what the hell is going on? Dobbs here seems to have gone off his head,' Sinclair felt himself blustering.

'We know Mr Dobbs well. He has had a difficult job to do,' responded Carlyle as if that explained everything. 'I – we are sorry if you have been inconvenienced. Please do come inside.'

Sinclair started to say something more but the others had turned and were walking ahead of him into the house and he was pushed unprotestingly after them.

The great hallway was as he remembered it. The ceiling, ornate and gilded, had also recently been restored: stags' heads and suits of armour, doubtless bought up as a job lot with the house, still adorned the walls in ostentatious profusion. The new additions were a reception desk, behind which sat a pretty girl, and beyond, in an alcove that had once held a marble statue, a large control panel for an extensive burglar alarm system. The girl smiled warmly at him as he passed by.

He was wheeled in silence through the hall and into what was still the library. It too was changed, probably for the better. The books looked well ordered and everything else was neater, cleaner, with new chairs and tables scattered about the room to replace the shabby old furniture that he remembered. He was wheeled up to face a large table in the centre of the room. Carlyle and de Laski came round and seated themselves opposite him, rather like an interview board. Dobbs and Ingram quietly left the room, closing the double doors behind them.

'Coffee?' asked Carlyle, pushing a silver tray with cup and coffee pot towards Sinclair. He ignored the offer.

'Very well,' Carlyle said briskly. 'I agree we owe you an explanation first. Civilities, I hope, will come later. Mr de Laski, a fellow director of mine on the Unity Main Board, will enlighten you.' Carlyle sat back in his chair and folded his arms. Sinclair stared back at him uncomprehendingly. His legs had started to ache uncontrollably but the pain actually helped to sharpen his senses and stifle any belief that he might be dreaming.

'A press statement is being released about now by your office to the effect that you have had a relapse and are now in intensive care. You are to remain here for the time being. You will not be able to communicate with anyone outside this building.' Sinclair continued to stare straight ahead of him in total silence, as de Laski went remorselessly on. 'It would be too dramatic to call it a *coup d'état*,' he added. 'Sounds too much like what happens in some tinpot banana republic. Think of it more as a commercial takeover bid with a new board of management almost in place.'

Sinclair must have made some gesture of disbelief, for de Laski and Carlyle turned to each other and smiled slightly, in the patronizing way that adults adopt towards a child who has said something funny or foolish.

'To begin at the beginning would, I think, be unnecessary,' de Laski went on after a moment. 'You must have been aware, even before you went into hospital, that some dramatic moves by Unity were under way. We believe you had even gone to the length of asking for a full report on our activities. To put it in a nutshell, Mr Sinclair, the situation now is that we have, by one means or another, acquired a majority holding in a very large number of your major, and very many of your minor, industries.'

Sinclair listened to the words, fascinated by de Laski's accent and dark looks. He would be a ruthless man to cross. It was hard to pinpoint: an odd mixture of American, Mediterranean and Scottish vowel sounds were mixed and distorted in unexpected ways. He tried to concentrate but his head was swimming.

'By diligent preparation, we have also succeeded in controlling a sizeable part of Scotland's news media. Thus,' he paused, 'we expect to have public opinion largely behind us in whatever steps we, or rather the new Government, decides to take.'

'You were behind the bombings and shootings?' Sinclair heard his own voice, echoing as if from a distance. He was so totally horrified and numbed by the enormity of what he was hearing that he felt an almost complete suspension of belief. De Laski made a brief gesture of assent as if his question were irrelevant. 'Who *are* you?' Sinclair went on. He was aware that his voice had hardly raised itself above a whisper.

'The Unity Corporation, as you must know, is an enormous multinational management group in whose Scottish headquarters you now are. You and your colleagues spent a lot of time congratulating us when we started opening up in Scotland. Our chairman, Mr Fulton, was welcomed by you and your government with open arms. While some other subsidiary companies of ours have been concerned in this exercise as well, the Unity Corporation, fully backed by the new Executive of the Federation of Caledonian Societies – incidentally, we have had to abandon

Messrs Anderson and Lindsay – is in the process of completing the final stages of its strategy. You guessed a little of what was going on but maybe not quite the extent to which –' de Laski paused as Sinclair, in a fit of anger, wheeled his chair round and away from the table.

After a pause, Carlyle broke in. 'Listen to the blunt truth, Mr Sinclair. Such is the extent of our control, that if we were suddenly to decide to pull the rug out from the companies we own or are major shareholders in, the whole Scottish economy would be in grave danger of collapsing. Not to put too fine a point on it,' he paused to emphasize his next words, *'you need us for your very survival*. All *we* need is *your* Government's full backing and cooperation which, with or without your support, we are determined to get. If we do not get it, then we shall ensure that Scotland's predicament, as you call it, is seen as your failure. It is your reputation that will suffer: you, the PM who destroyed Scotland as a nation. Do have some coffee now, Mr Sinclair. You look somewhat strained. Or would you like something a little stronger?'

Unthinkingly, Sinclair did as was suggested and poured himself some black coffee, but he did not touch it. 'Unbelievable,' he said after a moment. 'Like some gigantic Mafia plot.'

'This isn't confederate crime. We are no Mafia,' said de Laski.

'The distinction is hard to pinpoint,' Sinclair responded distantly.

'Most unkind, Mr Sinclair,' said Carlyle coolly . . . 'American multinational companies have been doing this sort of thing for years.'

'In the developing world perhaps. Hand in glove with the CIA as like as not. It was part of your scramble for control in Africa, the Far East, South America . . . I remember Chile, Panama. But, up 'til now, the Americans didn't poach on their friends.'

'We are not the US Government, nor the CIA. We're just a big, big company, buying up assets and support as we have always done. In case you think it's an impossible dream, sir, let me read you a piece from this week's *Economist*. It says, and I quote, "the annual sales of General Electric are still bigger than the net national incomes of all but a tiny handful of countries in the world". Quite a statistic, you'll agree, Mr Sinclair. Now we in the Unity Corporation are not quite as big as GE or General Motors or Exxon or IBM – but we've gone a long way towards it.'

'With Scotland as your latest acquisition? It's bigger than even you must have gone for before?' Sinclair had dropped his voice. He was genuinely curious.

'We got big by thinking big,' Carlyle responded grandly.

'There's a Dale Carnegie cliché,' Sinclair sniped.

'A self-evident truth,' de Laski added. 'Look, Mr Sinclair. We're putting our cards on the table. We respect you personally. We really do. We – I – Mr Fulton likes Scotland and the Scots. I don't want, nor does the corporation want, to hurt you more than you have been hurt already. You have to realize the basic truth: you're going to *benefit* from what we're doing. Yes, you and Scotland are going to benefit.'

'Doing us a favour? How kind! Out of the generosity of your corporate heart?' Sinclair wheeled his chair towards a bow window and stared out at the well-tended lawns beyond.

'Of course we'll also benefit,' de Laski said. 'It's been tricky for all of us in America ever since you – the old United Kingdom that is – joined the European Union. When an independent Scotland worked out its own close relationships with Brussels and we saw how well other American companies and the Japanese had done by basing their major outposts in Scotland, we saw our opportunity too. Last year's collapse of the Japanese economy allowed us to pick up a lot of their assets at bargain prices. You *must* have seen all this going on. It gives us ex-officio membership, so to speak, in the Community. As a by-product, when our move is complete, it will also get the damned US Federal Government off our backs.'

'That doesn't quite add up.' Sinclair was now in full control of his emotions. 'A company as profit-conscious as Unity has to have other reasons for taking over a country as bankrupt and politically unstable as Scotland is proving to be.'

'I could give you a lecture about all our other motivations, Mr Sinclair,' de Laski said slowly. 'Right now I just don't have the time. But consider this: why should we bother about moving into some tinpot principality as a tax haven, when we can have a fully-fledged state like Scotland for the asking? You're going to prove a handy launching pad for our international financial and business deals in the future. I didn't use the word money-laundering but . . . If we overstep the mark anytime, infringe the rules, why we won't need to worry about the Scottish Government getting all upset; we just tear up the rule book. We see Scotland as a sort of offshore fundholder, without government restraints – or at least with only those restraints that suit us. There are lots of other reasons. Many of our subsidiaries will be channelling goods into the European market from now on, without having to worry about paying community border taxes. In return for all our help, Scotland will have to pay its way of course. There may be problems for you. Government spending on social services and welfare – you may have to slash a lot of that. As you said, at Unity the profit motive is our driving force. It will continue to be so even if a lot of people get hurt. That's life, Mr Sinclair. But I assure you, Scotland will benefit in the long run.'

'Materially, maybe.' Sinclair was still battling with the outrageous magnitude of what he was being told. 'It's possible that some people in Scotland could benefit. Doubtless some of your puppets already have. But at what price? We are a proud nation . . .' He turned to face the two Americans, remembering, as he spoke, the famous *Punch* cartoon from the First World War. Belgium had been overrun. The cartoon showed the King of the Belgians leaving the Ship of State. The Kaiser, a leer on his face, was leaning over the side and saying *See. You have lost everything*, and the King replying *Not my soul*.

'Proud nation? Romantic claptrap, Mr Sinclair. It's not worthy of you. You're a practical man,' Carlyle sneered.

'You're obviously practical as well. You get my point. Scotland, having so recently regained its independence, isn't like another big company. It can't just be taken over.' Sinclair spoke with more confidence than he felt.

'You wanna bet, as they used to say?' De Laski smiled.

'You can't use the same mechanisms as you would for a takeover,' Sinclair persevered. 'Replace the board of directors, weed the middle management of its loyalists, that sort of thing.'

'Why not? It's a slower process admittedly. We have to keep the media and the public on side. We'll give your public lots of bread and circuses to keep them happy. We'll not do anything drastic. The National Assembly can continue its chattering, so long as it behaves. But I'm sure you'll agree that mere MPs, the people's representatives, have seldom stopped your administration doing what it wanted. The same was true when you had a UK Government. The Assembly, like the House of Commons, produces little but rhetoric. But,' he paused, 'with people like you around, we have to take rather more care. We have to convince or remove those who matter. As President Lyndon B. Johnson used to say, if we have your pecker in our pocket – a vulgar expression – then the hearts and minds will follow.'

'Nonsense. This is a democracy,' Sinclair said confidently.

'Have the intelligence to smile when you use that word,' Carlyle interrupted. 'Democracy is bunk. You're losing your intellectual detachment, Mr Sinclair.'

'The ordinary shares aren't for sale,' Sinclair ventured. 'Nor is the management.'

'They are indeed,' said Carlyle with a dismissive wave of a well-manicured hand. 'For sale and already bought. Except for one or two. That's why you're here.'

Agreement over Five Nations Championship

In a statement issued last night, Scottish Rugby Union President, Nick Tummell, expressed satisfaction that an agreement had been reached with the other members of the Five Nations Championship over the future division of fees from television companies covering the games. Scotland, having won the championship last year and the Calcutta Cup for the last two, had, he explained, been in a strong position to force the issue to a successful conclusion with the television companies concerned. Mr Tummell also expressed his pleasure that five Scottish members had been selected to represent the British Isles in the forthcoming world championship in Cape Town . . .

(Sports report, the *Herald*)

11

There were a number of people going about their business that day whose actions would have an important part in the scheme of things. One was the journalist, Harvey Silt, who, though apparently not in the mainstream of his calling, worked as a freelance hack for an oddly anonymous agency, which sent him around the world after certain less easily accessible items of news. Silt knew his market. He was good. He was, at one level, a straight, tough, honest, patriotic American, doing the duty he was trained and paid to do. At another level, like many in his profession of deception and subterfuge, he had a skin like an onion. Each layer, could it be removed, would have revealed a much more complex person underneath. He was one of life's plotters, who lived most of the time in a shadowy world where even he did not know, or was not allowed to know, the reasons for or the consequences of many of his actions. Apparently visible yet largely concealed, like an octopus in the shadows below a rock, he was a splendid spy, never revealing all the many tentacles of his trade.

He had only recently arrived in Edinburgh and was not yet sure how pleased he was by his new assignment. He had been there once or twice before and had something of a love–hate relationship with that chilly city. But he had found a hotel he liked and there were one or two bars in Rose Street where he felt as much at ease as he ever felt. When the Scots got drunk, he found them easy to talk to and with the present state of the economy there were always plenty of useful contacts around who were never too bashful about accepting a drink from a comparative stranger in return for a bit of gossip.

This time Silt was on the track of more than gossip. He was building up a dossier on something in quite a different league. It had all started gaining momentum back in New York City, after they had moved him in to discover why the Special Representative of the Federation had been run over and killed. He had reported back to his employers on various suspicious aspects to that case and one thing had led to another. In the end Silt found himself ordered by them to pursue his studies in rather more depth than he might otherwise have done. He used an old ploy: he went around New York claiming that he had been commissioned to write a number of feature articles for a Washington magazine. One of his chosen subjects was the Federation. What he wanted, he said, when he wrote to them asking for help, was a number of interviews with expatriate Scots. These would be generously illustrated with photographs of Scots-American lairds complete with kilts and sheepdogs, standing in front of their Texan ranches or New England mansions. More Scottish than the Scots would be his angle.

His approach to the Federation Executive got him precisely nowhere. He claimed he had been surprised at the total rejection of his offer to publicize the excellent efforts they had been making to help keep Scottish exiles and friends of Scotland in touch with the old country. An icy wall of silence greeted every single one of his requests for interviews with the leading lights of the society. This had the effect of doubling his resolve and he set about arranging discreet meetings with one or two former office bearers. That further fuelled his suspicions. At first Silt warned his employers in Washington that, as with many voluntary organizations, tribal and personal jealousies might just have got a bit out of hand. There might not be much more to it than that. But such was the unanimity of opinion among the former office bearers when he interviewed them about the nature of the new Executive Committee, that he rapidly revised his assessment. Something highly suspect was going on. He tracked down Anderson, the former President of the Federation, and another man, Lindsay, who had personally funded the Federation for many years. Silt spent hours talking to and listening to both these men. He then began to collate his material into a very full report which went way beyond the needs of any magazine article.

Which was why Harvey Silt had been despatched and was now based in Edinburgh in a remarkably well-established way. A discreet office had been rented for him at the top of a building just behind Princes Street; he had been provided with a well-trained, young male assistant, Ryan Sedge, and a secretary. To those who had encountered him in his various roles in the past, it would perhaps be a fraction odd to discover that Silt was now running his own news agency. A scrupulous investigator might have wondered at the market for the product of the *Federate Press Agency*, but there was plenty of evidence scattered about his outer office of a glossy, gossipy nature, to reassure them about the type of material that the agency itself peddled. That was as it should be. Ryan Sedge, Silt's assistant, was a tough, typical all-American boy. The secretary, by contrast, was a Scots girl of minimal curiosity. She was called Deirdre, she came from Kirkintilloch, and she was good at answering the telephone.

One morning early, Silt was sitting in his inner office with Sedge when the telephone rang. He picked up the receiver. As always, Sedge listened in on the extension earphone.

'It's tonight,' said the voice. For Silt and Sedge there was no need to ask who was calling. 'They've got Number One,' the voice at the other end of the line went on. 'Straight from the hospital. Earlier than we anticipated. They're after Big Mac again, so we're going to have to provide him with extra protection that he doesn't know anything about. Or we may confront him with all the facts and give him a chance to run to the bolthole. Have you traced Guthrie?'

'Yes,' said Silt, casually. 'Sort of.'

'What d'you mean?' said the voice, displaying a certain irritation.

'He's in Washington DC.'

'The shit he is,' said the voice. There was a click and the phone went dead.

After a moment, Ryan Sedge turned to Silt and shrugged: 'That's it. We came in too late. It's all over and they've won.'

'No way. No way,' Silt repeated enigmatically. 'I would say we've just begun.'

Silt's brief conversation dramatically changed the nature of Robert Guthrie's visit to Washington DC. He had gone, as arranged, to the State Department to see one of MacDowall's contacts. But the people there did not want to know about Scotland's problems with the Unity Corporation. They could not, or would not, help Guthrie identify others in the Federal Administration who might side with him in his attitude to and suspicions about that huge company. The Scottish Ambassador and his small team in Washington were, MacDowall insisted, strictly out of bounds, since no one in Edinburgh could be sure where their loyalties might lie and whether they might have already been got at. Guthrie felt dispirited and alone. Why not just pack it in and accept that the Unity takeover could be the best news for Scotland after all? Why had he bothered to come? Why was he trying to play the hero? He again realized that America was just too big to worry about small dots on the world map like Scotland. It had its own spheres of interest in the Pacific rim and in Central and Southern America. Even Canada had to struggle for a place in US political thoughts. He knew from his time in the States that US newspapers as distinguished as the *New York Times* and the *Washington Post* could go for weeks hardly even mentioning Europe. Why should little Scotland get a look in?

Robert Guthrie was nothing if not introspective. He spent a long time thinking things through. The question that now faced him was where was he going and why? What was he really looking for, for himself and for Scotland? Abel Rosenfeld's arguments, expressed all those months ago over lunch, had, even then, been highly plausible and filled with good sense. Now, despite all the dirty tricks, they had even more validity. Then there was the money aspect: as a bachelor, Guthrie lived quite well but doubtless he could triple his salary if he moved to the private sector to join Unity. His background in the higher reaches of the civil service, with his detailed knowledge of the workings of the Scottish Cabinet and Government and of the Prime Minister's office, meant his value to outsiders would be huge. There remained only the small matter of his conscience.

He decided to walk back from the State Department to his Georgetown hotel to pack his bags. His flight left at eight that evening. He would phone MacDowall and admit defeat, then, maybe, a film or a museum visit before the long trip home. Unnoticed, a long black limousine pulled up beside Guthrie as he made his way along the sidewalk. Immersed in his own thoughts, he paid little attention to it. Two men, both large, athletic, with close-cropped hair, jumped out and started walking, one on either side of him. Guthrie felt a sudden surge of panic but realized that these were no thieves; this was no street mugging. These must, he thought in a flash, be Unity heavies, who had somehow tracked him down to the States. Who else could possibly know that he was here? Moral and practical decisions which he had been agonizing over were about to be taken from him. All these thoughts and more crossed his mind in an instant and he decided to make a run for it.

Both strangers were strong and powerful. And they had the advantage of surprise. They gripped his arms and pulled him quickly down into the car. They did it so efficiently that it was obviously a well-practised manoeuvre. It was discreetly done. The few other pedestrians on the street would hardly have noticed a thing, least of all because Guthrie did not even have time to shout. He was thrown back onto the wide leather seat of the limo and the two men slotted in to wedge him securely on either side. Only then did one of them speak.

'Good afternoon, Mr Guthrie. Sit quite still, please. We want you to take what we have to say very seriously.' The man paused as the limousine glided forward, then he began to explain.

Guthrie had been firmly advised to change his plans and fly into Prestwick via Amsterdam. They handed him the new flight tickets they had arranged for him. He had half expected Heather to be waiting for him at the airport, but instead it was Harvey Silt with his assistant, Ryan Sedge, and there was a third man, a tough-looking driver, sitting in the battered and anonymous Ford outside the terminal doors. Things had, as they had warned him, changed dramatically.

As they set off for the hour's drive north, Silt passed Guthrie a selection of that morning's Scottish newspapers. He picked up the *Herald*. The banner headline shouted GOVERNMENT PURGE. Similar stories dominated the *Scotsman*, the *Record* and the *Press and Journal*. The detail was thin but there were unconfirmed reports of Ministers resigning, being replaced and of some senior officials being summarily dismissed. The *Herald* complained, in a long front-page editorial, about a veil of secrecy having been thrown over these critical events. It trumpeted the cause of open government and vigorously pointed to the dangers of what it euphemistically called 'hidden hands' corrupting the nation's destiny.

'After the first editions hit the streets,' Silt explained, 'the English radio stations started running reports that a heavy mob of unidentified thugs went to the *Herald*'s offices in Glasgow and did a lot of damage to people and equipment. Apparently the Editor's gone missing . . .'

In the front passenger seat, Ryan Sedge turned up the car radio as he heard the SBC newsflash:

It has just been announced from Charlotte House that the Prime Minister, Mr Keith Sinclair, has tendered his resignation to The Queen on the grounds of ill health. The Finance Minister, Mr Ian Campbell, has been invited to form a new Government.

Mr Sinclair, who is recovering from injuries inflicted when he was struck by a brick thrown by a demonstrator last St Andrew's Day, had suffered a serious relapse, according to Charlotte House spokesman, Mr Geoff Dobbs. The former Prime Minister had been transferred to the intensive care unit of the private hospital in Clydebank. His wife Nora is at his bedside.

At an impromptu press conference, Prime Minister Campbell

told reporters outside Charlotte House that he was 'deeply sorry to be taking over in such tragic circumstances. Keith Sinclair has made a huge political contribution to Scotland before and after Independence, and the nation would always be grateful for his great dedication.' The new Prime Minister is to make a full statement to an emergency session of the National Assembly in two hours' time on the current political and economic situation.

Here is our Political Editor, Magnus Reid.

'The Prime Minister is expected to announce a major package of economic reforms intended to boost the Scottish economy when he speaks to the Assembly for the first time this evening. It will, I understand from informed sources, include the announcement that the American Unity Corporation is to move its corporate headquarters to Scotland. I will be reporting live from the Assembly as it happens.'

As Sedge turned off the radio, Silt turned towards Guthrie and said, 'We half expected that. That means you're out of a job too, Mr Guthrie.' Then he smiled a thin smile.

Contrary to the Scottish Broadcasting Corporation news report, Nora Sinclair was, at that precise moment, not by her husband's bed but in bed with the new Prime Minister of Scotland, Ian Campbell. But their pleasure was to be short-lived, their passion unfulfilled. As they were beginning to get into the swing of their imaginative foreplay, the door of the PM's bedroom in the official residence in Charlotte Square burst rudely open, and in walked Abel Rosenfeld and two of his staff. The American looked down with distaste at the couple trying to hide their nakedness under the bed sheets. He ignored their shrill protests, silencing them with an impatient wave of his arm.

'You intend to lead a back-to-basics, Victorian values, moral crusading Government, Mr Prime Minister. Remember that's what your speech says . . . the one you should be rehearsing right now, downstairs, with Mr Fulton and the others. They don't like being kept waiting.' Rosenfeld turned away in disgust and snarled to his assistants, 'Get that bloody woman out of here. Use a back entrance. I don't want to see her again, nor,' he paused, 'hear a squeak from her, if she knows what's good for her.'

When he had finished with the newspapers, Guthrie turned and asked, 'Where are you operating from?' He knew the partial answer from the surprise briefing he had been given in Washington DC. But now, driving through the peaceful, domestic Ayrshire countryside, it all seemed so unreal and far away.

It was Ryan Sedge who answered. 'First-class headquarters, sir,' he said. 'Custom-built. One of your huge subterranean Cold War nuclear bunkers. They were constructed to act as regional military HQs if the Soviets ever overran Britain.'

'I thought we filled them in or sold them off years ago. They were enormously costly to keep. Weren't the majority of them bought up for storage dumps?' Guthrie was intrigued.

'The former British Government did just that, sir,' Sedge continued. 'But they kept one or two for unforeseen emergencies. Then there's ours...'

'Ours?' Guthrie was puzzled.

'When the US Government moved out of the Faslane Polaris Base on the Gareloch all those years ago, we agreed with the then UK Government that we would be allowed to keep and maintain it on a ninety-nine-year lease.'

'So...' Guthrie was astonished. He had never seen papers on this during his entire time in the PM's office but then, if they were old Top Secret files, as like as not they'd be buried away in the classified archives in London.

'We're confident the new junta and the Unity boys don't know anything about it. We've been keeping it discreetly stocked and supplied by submarine for years. "Care and maintenance basis" we call it. Recently it's found its use,' Sedge added helpfully.

'Who's working there?' Guthrie asked, fascinated by what he was being told.

'CIA staff mainly. Ever since the secret Presidential Directive you've been briefed about. And an NSA Monitoring Unit. A few out-of-uniform US naval guards, admin staff, cooks and so on.

Now your people have started joining us. A dozen or so of them have come in so far, but only once they've been screened. They're already calling it Resistance HQ. Quite a party spirit building up!'

'That astonishing briefing in Washington had to be curtailed because I had to catch that earlier flight. Tell me more,' Guthrie prompted. For once he felt both ill-informed and out of his depth, and he did not like it.

'We – the CIA team – are under the direct command of Admiral Muller, our Director for Europe. You met him briefly in Washington, I believe,' Silt broke in. 'He's already explained to you the US Administration's secret agenda on Unity. That damned company has broken too many rules. We want to pull them apart. They owe the US Treasury nearly two billion bucks in back taxes, and, on top of that, they've polluted more North American states than a dozen other key US companies put together.' Silt paused. 'I'm not telling you what you know already, Mr Guthrie, am I? You've heard from my colleagues that we're particularly riled at the way Unity's been behaving overseas. They've acted just as badly elsewhere, though in some Third World countries like Nigeria, where they own a lot of mines, their corruption doesn't show. They've been steadily making a load of enemies for the United States right around the globe. The Secretary of State is particularly against multinationals starting up their own countries. That led to the Secret Presidential Directive, as I said. We're out to take 'em apart. Finally.'

'Keep talking,' urged Guthrie. 'What's been happening here on the ground while I've been away?'

'Scottish media have only glimpsed a fraction of what's really going on. The wave of Unity-prompted arrests was perfectly synchronized. For example, we know that three men came for the Secretary to the Cabinet yesterday, at seven-forty-five precisely. There was no struggle. He was alone, dozing in his chair, and the men were all American security people. He's being held incommunicado.'

'The hell he is,' Guthrie breathed. 'Where's the PM? Where's Sinclair?'

'As you heard on that newsflash, they're saying publicly that he's in that Unity-owned private hospital at Clydebank,' Sedge said. 'We think he's much more likely to have been taken to their Perthshire HQ. They have that place so well fortified with new high-security fences and so on, it's a Scottish Fort Knox. That's where Fulton, de Laski and the others are holed up. It's their command and control centre.'

'How d'you know all this?'

'You may not know but your Special Task Force were all CIA-trained after Independence. Meant to keep them a breed apart from the old MI5 and Special Branch hands,' Harvey Silt explained. 'They've stayed loyal . . .'

'Loyal to whom?' Guthrie was increasingly confused. 'When you have something approaching an incipient civil war, it strains every loyalty.' It reawakened his own doubts about where Scotland was heading: siding either with Unity or with the CIA was not the easiest nor most obvious of options.

Silt stared thoughtfully at him for a moment. 'No civil war yet, Mr Guthrie. Scotland would be united if it knew the whole truth.' His voice sounded confident enough. 'On the wrong side so far there is the Unity team and a few key quislings they've bought up, like that creep Campbell. Special Task Force has always only reported to MacDowall,' he added. 'Despite the evidence from them, Sir Alexander was at first reluctant to believe the scale of the deception, even after they shot him. When we'd found you'd been sent to Washington by him, we moved in to back up the Special Task Force reports and confronted him with all the facts. He saw he had to get out. Immediately. He's now at Resistance HQ. Seems to be enjoying the army camp life.'

'Who else?'

'This'll come as a surprise to you, sir. One of the other stalwarts at Resistance HQ is Sir Alexander's lifelong political enemy, Nick Forbes.'

'Forbes, the Environment Minister? He used to be a Red Clydeside union leader.' Guthrie was totally astonished.

MacDowall had always hated him more than anyone else in Scottish political life. 'What bedfellows ... How come?'

'He and MacDowall are getting on great guns. Soulmates with a common cause and one ambition.' Silt smiled. 'They got rather drunk together only last night.'

'How come he's on board?' Guthrie pressed.

'Rosenfeld, Unity's front man, tried to buy him. Thought he had. Forbes led him on until he heard what their whole game plan was. Then he went straight to MacDowall. We got both of them away just in time, otherwise they'd have been pulled in. Search warrants out.'

'Search warrant for Sir Alexander? Who's doing the arresting?' asked Guthrie. He could still hardly believe what he was being told.

'True, sir. The regular police so far, though there are plenty of signs of dissent. But most of them believe the propaganda they've been fed. Think they're doing their loyal duty.'

'The Commissioner?' Guthrie asked. 'Surely Sir Jimmy –'

'He's personally been sold a line by Campbell: told there was a plot by the Reunionists to take over the Government by force while Sinclair was incapacitated. Ironic isn't it? Campbell has also promised to arm the police, we believe. That helped sell the lie. We've also got Billy McKane, by the way. As Editor of the *Herald* he was a real threat: they came to pick him up but we were ready and spirited him out. He's beginning to coordinate the media strategy, the counter-propaganda, for when we're ready to go.'

'And Heather Anderson?' asked Guthrie nervously. Washington had told him what she had been tasked to do.

'She's just reported in, Mr Guthrie. She's safe. She's being debriefed at this very minute.'

'The next step?' Guthrie asked.

'We've got to spring Mr Sinclair,' said Silt quietly. 'We need him. He's the linchpin.'

The entrance to the secret bunker was cleverly concealed among a thick plantation of trees that ran along the side of the Gareloch to the north of Faslane. There were only two entrances: one was via a set of discreet steel doors deeply embedded in a man-made hill-side that was planted over with heather and bracken; the other was accessible only by sea – a deep underwater channel allowed supplies to be brought in by an American mini-submarine. Inside the bunker itself there were miles of tunnels with rooms off them, containing operations and communications centres, basic sleeping and living accommodation, store rooms, kitchens and power generators. All was totally self-contained as it had been designed to be back in the sixties. The British Ministry of Defence had never quite solved the problems of damp and the ventilation system left much to be desired but, by and large, the several dozen men and women who were already there lived comfortable enough lives.

In the depths of the bunker, two people faced Heather Anderson across the trestle table to debrief her when she was brought in to report. MacDowall, remote but kindly, sat flanked by Billy McKane from the *Herald*.

'Did you see Rosenfeld again before you left?' asked McKane.

'No. Bushfield took me out to lunch and gave me a pretty full briefing on their media activities. I don't think he held much back on that front, though he continued to be cautious, even nervous, on the political aspects. Said it was more than his job was worth to talk. He was very pleasant,' she added hesitantly, throwing a quick glance at MacDowall. 'I didn't like doing it. I'm not cut out to be a spy.'

'You did very well, Miss Anderson,' said MacDowall reassuringly.

'I hope you don't want me to go back. I might crack and reveal all . . . The Unity people were so plausible and convincing, some of them. I got quite scared that I might succumb . . .' She smiled nervously.

'Have you told them?' McKane asked.

'Not directly. I chickened out. I told them I would take a day to read the literature they gave me, waited, then I telephoned Rosenfeld's office and left a message that I'd changed my mind. I bet he'll be furious.'

'He is,' said McKane. 'Don't be shocked.'

Heather looked at the man questioningly as he turned and threw a switch on a tape recorder that stood on a side table beside him. The sound was crackly but the words were distinct.

BUSHFIELD: *The bitch. I bought her lunch.*

ROSENFELD *(shouting): She must have given you some fuckin' hint.*

BUSHFIELD: *Not a thing, Abel. Sweet as pie. Maybe she really has changed her mind.*

ROSENFELD: *You hope . . . but given her parentage and the* New York Times *background, I smell a rotten stitch-up. (Pause) How much did you give away?*

BUSHFIELD: *Only what you told me to, Abel. I promise.*

ROSENFELD: *The media campaigns?*

BUSHFIELD: *A bit. The video, advertising, a little on the soft feature and editorial writing . . .*

ROSENFELD: *Shit . . . Political affairs?*

BUSHFIELD: *No way would I. She . . .*

ROSENFELD: *Thank God for that. Where is she now?*

BUSHFIELD: *She only checked in one night at that damn hotel. We're out looking.*

ROSENFELD: *It doesn't smell nice. Have her picked up. Firmly. Nicely. Keep her right out of harm's way. If she turns difficult though . . . I don't want anything going wrong. Not now.*

Even in the comparative safety of the bunker, Heather Anderson gave an involuntary shudder.

At the same time as Heather Anderson's briefing session finished Silt was dropping Guthrie off at Queen Street railway station in Glasgow. There he caught a train to Edinburgh, where he made his way to his flat in the New Town, unpacked, made himself something to eat, then, after long and careful thought, telephoned Abel Rosenfeld at his Edinburgh office. He was put through at once.

'Can we talk?' he asked hesitantly. He had to fight hard to

camouflage his nervousness. It was a dangerous step he was taking.

'Sure. Where are you?' Rosenfeld responded cheerfully. 'Hear you've been travelling.'

'With no joy,' came the terse reply.

'So . . . talk.'

'Face to face,' Guthrie insisted.

'At your disposal. Shall I come to you?'

'I'd prefer it. I expect you know my address.'

'It'll be on the Unity database, but why don't you give me it again. Be with you in half an hour.'

Guthrie had prepared coffee and the two men sat facing each other in his book-lined living room.

'Fine library you've got. And paintings . . .' Rosenfeld looked round the room approvingly.

'Thank you. Mainly inherited,' said Guthrie. His nervousness had not gone away. By contrast Rosenfeld did not seem to have a care in the world.

'So?' asked Rosenfeld, sipping at his cup of coffee.

'You remember our conversation at that Glasgow restaurant?'

'Of course.'

'Well . . .' Guthrie hesitated. 'I wonder . . . would you still like my help?'

'Delighted to have you on board,' said Rosenfeld, smiling broadly. This news had the potential of making his day. 'You'd be particularly useful in dealing with Mr Sinclair.'

'That may be more difficult. He has firm principles.'

'So we're discovering. No flexibility at all.' Rosenfeld gave a slight sigh.

'What would you like me to do?'

'You may know already. You're out of a job. Ian Campbell doesn't seem to be your biggest fan. We'd like you to come and work at our main headquarters . . . on political strategy.'

'I know too much about Mr Campbell. Fear breeds dislike.'

'Ah . . . could that be anything to do with Nora Sinclair?' asked Rosenfeld with a wink.

'You know?'

'Not only know; put a stop to it, I can tell you. Don't want any sleaze factor with this new government.' Rosenfeld gave a dismissive shrug.

'Moral mission?' Guthrie asked, impressed despite himself. Rosenfeld had never once stopped smiling.

'Moral? You've got to be kidding. This is all to do with image. Image is the key in this game.'

'Right,' said Guthrie, standing and offering Rosenfeld more coffee. 'I'll turn up tomorrow, shall I?'

Rosenfeld shook his head. 'Right now, I'm afraid,' he said quietly. 'Why don't you go pack some things? I'll wait here. You'll be staying with us for some time, just to be on the safe side, you understand. I've got a couple of men in my car outside. They'll come and help carry your suitcase.'

Guthrie forced himself to smile back, suddenly aware that if he had not volunteered, he'd have been taken along in any case.

12

Property boom on the way Halifax reports

A new survey by the Halifax Building Society shows
that house prices in Perthshire and the Central Belt
have risen dramatically over the last few months.
Analysts suggest that this is largely due to the demand
for top-quality housing for American and other senior
executives who have started house hunting in the
Perth–Stirling area, in advance of the move by Unity's
Global Headquarters to Scotland.

(Property Section, the *Scotsman*)

It was a perfectly agreeable bedroom and certainly no prison cell.
Sinclair had been there since the confrontation with Carlyle and
de Laski which had ended about midday. A waiter in white
jacket and black bow tie had brought him an adequate meal at
lunchtime and he was promised dinner at eight. He had a plentiful
supply of light reading material in the room but the improba-
bilities of his own existence gave him too much to think about
to be able to cope with the demands of mere fiction. Warned not
to leave the room without summoning one of the guards, he
lay flat on his bed and waited. He saw no value in pointless
histrionics.

It had come as an immense shock when he finally grasped the
enormity of the truth. Only now was he beginning to come to
terms with it. The realization that an internal coup had apparently succeeded, here in Scotland, required immense reserves of

understanding. What they had claimed about their takeover of important sectors of the country's industrial and manufacturing strength was, he had already accepted, true. He knew too that many major land holdings which had come on the market over the past two years had been snapped up by them, perfectly legitimately. But they were now clearly on the way to a wholescale erosion of the political fabric of the country as well, replacing it with their own carefully trained puppet regime. They took great pains to explain to him just how much they had already achieved and how they were now trying to isolate or remove the *stalwarts*, as de Laski called them. Most people could be bought if the price offered was high enough. So it always was with political life. There were only a few people like himself who were powerful yet honest, impossible to win over, circumvent, or corrupt.

Unity had planned it all so carefully that Sinclair found it difficult not to envisage them succeeding. There would be no more violence, they promised. The attempt to assassinate Mac-Dowall was, he was assured, arranged and plotted at a low level. Mr Fulton and the Unity directors had been shocked. Violence was out. Character assassination was simpler and just as deadly.

For some time he remained aloof, fascinated yet remote and detached from this fantastic exposé. At the outset he was confident of his own moral position and what he would do to expose them once he regained his freedom. It was then that de Laski coldly started on him. Calmly and efficiently, he produced files of documentary evidence of Sinclair's supposed complicity in the whole operation from its very beginning. The most damning material came in a neatly filed dossier of evidence of which he was given a copy to take away and study. Over the past year to eighteen months he had, according to these papers and accounts, accepted each and all of Unity's proposals one by one. At the same time, according to cleverly forged letters, he had made it a condition that he be allowed to filter off sizeable sums for his own use.

Sinclair began to laugh, to ridicule the absurdity of the accusation. But he soon lapsed into a shocked silence, particularly when de Laski placed in front of him all his private bank statements for the previous year. These gave the impression of being totally accurate in every detail, except for the large regular monthly payments into his personal account. With the aid of an employee at his bank, his own copies of his bank statements over the same period had been removed from his house, and the altered versions substituted. It was all so devastatingly efficient. Everything had been thought of, down to the last detail. Had he not been so numbed by that stage, he might have cracked. They sent him away to his bedroom to think things over.

'You have total freedom of choice, Mr Sinclair,' Carlyle summed up.

'Like the freedom a poor man has to dine at the Ritz,' he responded with more panache than he felt.

'The Ritz is pleasant enough,' came the laconic reply.

Later that day, Sinclair was again summoned. The intervening hours had passed slowly, then, just before six, de Laski came in and insisted that he come and watch a special programme on television. It would, he promised, be of considerable interest. The waiter helped him into his wheelchair, and steered him back to the library. To Sinclair's horror, Robert Guthrie was already there, ensconced in a deep armchair by the fireplace. So he had been bought too. Guthrie stood up nervously. He looked pale and ill-at-ease.

'What the hell are you doing here?' asked Sinclair, coldly.

'We live in interesting times, sir,' Guthrie said faintly.

'That's an ancient Chinese curse,' Sinclair began. It explained why Guthrie had stayed away, had not come to visit him in hospital recently. He had always trusted his Private Secretary. Now he felt doubly betrayed. Then de Laski came in and started talking before he could tell Guthrie exactly what he thought of him.

'Sorry to bring you together in what cannot be relaxed circumstances. For some reason we have only one television in this part of the building. I'm confident none of us would like to miss the PM's statement. Drink anyone?' de Laski asked.

He pressed a bell and the waiter reappeared. Sinclair coldly declined the offer. The set was on with the sound turned down. A cowboy film was in its final throes. The hero, wordless and wounded, was lying in a girl's lap. In the background, some crook was being dragged away by the sheriff's men. Gradually the scene faded and the titles were superimposed. De Laski went forward and turned up the sound as the gruff, reassuring figure of a programme announcer, whom Sinclair knew well, came on screen to say that the channel, in common with all other Scottish radio and television networks, was about to broadcast a special live message from the new Prime Minister. Then, incongruously, they started to play 'Flower of Scotland'.

'Good touch, don't you think?' Sinclair heard de Laski whisper in the background. He addressed his remark to Carlyle, who had appeared behind him in the doorway.

The picture faded and Ian Campbell came on screen. Sinclair knew his former colleague only too well and could see, despite the make-up, that he was as nervous as hell. He began to speak, haltingly at first, then more fluently as he focused on the teleprompt in front of him. His tie was askew, which added to the uncertainty of his performance.

'I am speaking to you this evening in the aftermath of a great crisis. Behind the scenes, evil forces were seeking to destroy the whole fabric of our society. So organized were they, that, for some time, the continuing independence of Scotland was under threat.' Campbell hesitated for a moment, nervously brushing away a lock of hair from his brow. 'I am speaking to you as your new Prime Minister. As an emergency measure, I was asked to replace Keith Sinclair only this morning, after certain grave facts had been brought to the Cabinet's attention about the behaviour of some of the highest officers in the State. Full details of all these facts will be issued shortly in the form of a White Paper, which will be available free at your local Post Office. I will not go into all the disgraceful details here. Suffice it to say that a conspiracy of the very highest order was under way, similar to the notorious events of 1707, to subvert Scotland's constitution and to sell this country back into the Union.

'We have managed to nip this in the bud. The attempted coup d'état has been thwarted. You will all know that there has been considerable industrial and civil unrest for a long time past. I do not have to remind you of the murder of several members of our security forces, of the blowing up of our communications stations, and of numerous other acts of sabotage and criminal nuisance. We now know that these incidents were part of a carefully orchestrated plot which, but for the vigilance of our security forces, would have succeeded.

'Many well-known names have, tragically, become involved in this seedy plot. It is difficult but necessary to apportion some blame to my predecessor, Keith Sinclair, for much of this. He is, as you know, a very sick man and perhaps much of the root cause lies there. Who are we to judge?' Campbell paused for a moment and managed to impart a moment of drama into what he was saying.

Sinclair heard his words as if in a dream, then stopped listening altogether for a moment. He glanced across at Guthrie, wondering how he could have the cheek to sit through this evil parody. But Guthrie slouched unmoving in his chair, his eyes averted. How could someone as apparently honourable as he be corrupted by the Unity line? Perhaps it was money: he had been bought by foreign gold. At the thought, Sinclair sat up straight in his wheelchair, anger welling inside him with such force that he realized that if he had pushed down with his hands on the arms of the chair, he could have stood up unaided. This shock made his mind all the more alert to the danger that he was in. He glanced down and saw that his knuckles had turned white with the strain, and it took some moments before he could bring himself to relax his fingers. No one else had noticed his reaction. They were all intent on listening to the treacherous words of Ian Campbell.

'Your government has decided, with great reluctance, to introduce, as a temporary measure, limited internment under a new martial law decree. I have instructed that the police be issued with arms; they have orders to shoot if their lawful commands

*are not obeyed or if they otherwise need to act in the execution
of their duty. Full details of these new regulations are contained
in the Government's White Paper.*

*'I can assure you that, at the first moment it becomes advisable,
we will wipe all these regulations from the statute book. This is a
free and democratic country. We must safeguard our inheritance.
Good evening and God bless Scotland.'*

They were all left staring at the flickering screen. Sinclair saw
that even Carlyle and de Laski were overawed by the implications
of the broadcast, though they must have had a full hand in its
drafting. Then the familiar figure of the announcer was on the
screen once again, introducing a special programme on the day's
dramatic events. Much of it had obviously been prepared well
in advance. Film of the Clydebank riots was followed by flash-
backs to the blowing up of the Communications Station. There
was a reconstruction of the attempted assassination of Mac-
Dowall and, finally, up-to-the-moment shots of the arrest of
certain top political suspects, all unnamed, all with their
faces disguised. Surely this sort of stuff wouldn't fool anyone,
Sinclair thought to himself. Yet it was convincingly done. Expert
editors had created a most competent propaganda film. Again
Sinclair's hands strained in frustrated rage on the arms of his
wheelchair.

On the TV screen, the most recent shots were of the new Prime
Minister. The commentator poured out insidious stuff about how
deep the rot had spread. On and on it went, myth after fiction,
until even Sinclair did not know what to believe. Parts of the
programme were genuine: sections on the economic state of
the country, for example, had been inserted to give those who
might harbour suspicions undeniable facts on which to cut their
doubts. The programme makers knew that if you're going to lie,
lie big and lie often.

At last Carlyle stood up and turned the television sound down,
remarking that he imagined they had all heard enough. Sinclair
moved his head a fraction to glance once more at Guthrie, who
looked as if he had not moved an inch.

Carlyle stared down at Sinclair. 'You,' he said coldly, 'we do not need to hold as a prisoner. You are your own captive.' He looked pointedly at his wheelchair. Sinclair again felt a surge of anger, but this time he ensured that no trace of what he was feeling showed.

Guthrie gave the first signs of movement since the television programme had begun. Shifting slightly in his chair, he opened his eyes wide and stared round the room. Carlyle had turned away. The moment his eyes were averted and with de Laski standing by the television set, Guthrie briefly turned in Sinclair's direction and stared back impassively. Sinclair shook his head with a mixture of sadness and disbelief. Why, he asked himself, had Guthrie of all people sold his soul to the enemy? That hurt most of all. Sinclair's further conjecturing was cut short as de Laski turned, and in a brisk voice said, 'To your room, Mr Sinclair. *To your room.*'

The Commissioner of Police, Sir Jimmy Mactaggart, fastidious and rigid but at heart an honest man, was deeply troubled. He did not know where to turn nor whom to go to for guidance and advice. He had tried to talk to his wife but she was up to her eyes with the Rural Institute fête and failed to see the dimensions of the problem that her husband faced. He had never been able to stand or get on with Sir Alexander MacDowall but since the Minister of the Interior's disappearance, which in itself had added greatly to the Commissioner's unease, his instructions had been relayed to him by a medium-ranking civil servant, a certain Geoff Dobbs.

It was neither right nor proper. He had long demanded that the police be armed; now they had given in, almost without a murmur. Now that he had that strength, however, he was afraid of being asked to use it. Things could so easily get out of hand. That, coupled with this whole new police-state apparatus of internment and martial law that had just been announced by Campbell, reminded him all too vividly of the time when, as a young constable, he had been seconded to the Royal Ulster

Constabulary in Northern Ireland. But that was then and this was now. And this was Scotland.

He sat at his desk, sipping at his glass of weak tea, staring at the two lists of names that he had been handed by Dobbs. One was of people already detained under the emergency measures though, as a matter of practice, most of them were merely under house arrest. Among the names were people he knew so well, people with whom he had sat at meetings, people whom his wife and he had met at theatres, at receptions, had heard speak at Burns' Suppers and other gilded occasions. The Secretary of the Cabinet – was he really a conspirator? Jock Reid, the morose Permanent Secretary at the Ministry of the Interior – had he really tried to undermine the fabric of the State in collusion with Sir Alexander MacDowall? One of his own Chief Constables, the Head of News and Current Affairs at Scottish Television: there were twenty other key names there. Some names, some conspiracy.

Then there was the second even more unsettling list, names for whom arrest warrants had been issued, people whose whereabouts were not currently known. A distinguished catalogue: MacDowall, Forbes, McKane of the *Herald* . . . Were they all traitors? Whom could he believe? Who was telling the truth; who was lying? What was the truth and who said it was the truth? All those questions, taken together, amounted to why the Commissioner was so troubled.

He thought about summoning his chief constables and senior deputies to an emergency meeting. But to what end? They, he knew, were looking to him for guidance and advice. They needed leadership. But in what direction? The force was even more deeply divided and demoralized: two of his most senior men had wheeled in to see him first thing that morning to list their bitter complaints. He listened, he sympathized, he said nothing. He remembered the old phrase about evil triumphing when good men remained silent.

Where did his own loyalties lie? They lay with the State, of course. But who, what was the State? Campbell was the First

Minister, yet the Commissioner had little time for the man. He was weak and recently when the Commissioner had met with him he always seemed to have a coterie of strange American businessmen hanging around him. That was something else he did not like. His policeman's nose, out of training from lack of recent practical experience, sensed things there that concerned him deeply.

He would have brooded about it for longer, would have given himself time for further reflection, had not his secretary, an indomitable woman in her mid-fifties, come in bearing a piece of paper held in the tips of her fingers as if it was unclean.

'This,' she announced, 'was pushed through my letter-box last night. Then, believe it or not, I saw another copy lying on the floor of the top deck of my Number 23 bus this very morning.'

The Commissioner of Police took the pamphlet from his secretary. It was a sheet of cheap, recycled A4. At the top was the one stark title QUISLINGS, set out in bold capitals. Below it was a short, brutal statement about corruption in high places, about a so-called *coup d'état*, about the illegality of certain recent arrests. It went on to ask a number of all too pertinent questions. One in particular the Commissioner had been asking himself more than the others: Where is Keith Sinclair? Then, at the end, there was a final paragraph entitled WE NAME THE GUILTY MEN. He saw his own name stand out prominently underneath.

The Commissioner of Police stood up behind his desk and stared back at his secretary, who was watching with a look that betrayed both anger and concern.

'Ring the Prime Minister's office. I'm on my way over. If he's busy, I'll wait. I'll wait for as long as it takes.'

Two hours later, Mactaggart was shown into the Prime Minister's office. Dobbs and an American called Carlyle, to whom he had been briefly introduced before, were there as well.

'What's the problem, Commissioner?' asked Ian Campbell. Unease was written all over his face.

'For you alone, sir,' said the Commissioner stolidly.

'I'm sure you don't mind if . . .' Campbell hesitated, waving vaguely in the direction of the other two men.

'Alone, sir,' the Commissioner repeated. It was most irregular that he had to repeat his request.

Carlyle started to say something but the look the Commissioner threw at him, one that occasionally shook the most recalcitrant of his police deputies when he wore it, silenced the man in his tracks and Carlyle and Dobbs reluctantly left the room.

'Damn cheek,' muttered the Commissioner not quite under his breath.

'Valuable advisers, Jimmy,' said Campbell weakly, using his Christian name now that they were alone. 'I've actually appointed Mr Carlyle as one of my unpaid political or rather economic consultants. Prime Ministers throughout British history have always had kitchen cabinets in Downing Street, so I don't see why I shouldn't.'

The Commissioner ignored the piece of self-justification and thrust the duplicated pamphlet forward. 'Have you seen this, Mr . . . er . . . Prime Minister?'

''Fraid so. Rubbish-bin fodder, Jimmy, that's all. There is a number of different versions floating around. We're trying – correction – your officers are going to be tasked with finding out where they originate from. I've just signed the warrant . . .'

'Prime Minister . . .' The Commissioner was not the most intelligent of men but he had an innate sense of justice and fair play. 'Would you mind telling me, in your own words, precisely what the bloody hell is going on?'

'You heard my speech, Jimmy . . . my message to the nation on television.'

'I did, sir. But it doesn't smell right.'

'Things are very difficult at the moment, Jimmy.' Campbell was even more ill-at-ease now. He looked nervously round the room as if wondering who else was listening.

'To be blunt, I don't like it at all, sir. It isn't right. Where's

Mr Sinclair? Where's Sir Alexander, Guthrie, the Secretary to the Cabinet? Who is this man Carlyle?'

'Everything will be fine, Jimmy.' Campbell was sweating profusely, even though it was quite cool in the office, 'Believe me, it was a close-run thing . . .'

'What was, sir?' The Commissioner's feeling that things were worse than he had feared was growing by the minute. 'I have to tell you, sir, my senior officers and the general staff at Scottish Military Command are deeply –'

'We just need to get through this next week or two . . .' Campbell interrupted breathlessly.

'No, Prime Minister. You listen to me.' The Commissioner could hardly believe what he himself was saying. 'I've had enough of this. I tell you what I intend to do . . .' He paused, and watched with astonishment as Campbell, in desperation, put his finger to his lips, pointed around the room, and then held his hand cupped to his ear. There was no mistaking the message: the walls were listening. But the Commissioner's anger was riding high. He didn't care who the hell was listening. 'I intend, this very afternoon,' he continued, 'to summon a meeting of all my senior officers and the Defence and Military High Command if they wish to come, which I am sure they will, to discuss and question the, to my mind, dangerous and undemocratic moves you have recently taken. I can assure you that the fact that we are having that discussion, and the outcome of it, will be made public. Enough is enough, Prime Minister. I will . . .'

The Commissioner paused, open-mouthed, as the door of the Prime Minister's office suddenly burst open and in came three well-built young men, all in dark business suits, each carrying a handgun. Beyond, in the outer office, he glimpsed the strained faces of Carlyle and Dobbs surveying the scene.

'Sir Jimmy Mactaggart, you are under arrest,' said one of the young men. His American accent was unmistakable. 'Put your hands above your head.'

'This is not happening,' thought the Commissioner to himself. 'This is some outrageous nightmare.' Brave man that he was, he chose anger rather than caution, and rushed at the young man who had threatened him, in an attempt to disarm him. But the American was faster. He had a momentary picture of the horrified face of Campbell staring at him before a sharp blow to the side of the head knocked him unconscious.

'You're being moved, Mr Sinclair.'

'What?' It was seven in the morning; he had slept badly and was hardly awake.

'There's an ambulance picking you up in one hour. Be ready.' De Laski turned on his heel and left the room. Sinclair sat up in bed. What the hell was going on now? He had been a prisoner for nearly three days, three days of enforced idleness, speaking to no one, seeing no one except for the man who brought his food and who helped him when he wanted to wash and dress. He hadn't set eyes on de Laski or Carlyle again, let alone Robert Guthrie.

The waiter came in with a breakfast tray and announced that he had been told to help Sinclair pack. That was a minimal task since his lack of everything, except what he had had with him in hospital, had been one of the more irritating factors in his captivity. The hour passed. De Laski reappeared.

'Where are we going?' Sinclair asked lamely.

'You are going into hospital. A specially secure unit at our place in Clydebank. You'll be very comfortable. The press are irritatingly curious as to where you are. We wouldn't want them to think that you are anything other than physically incapacitated and having the best medical attention.' De Laski smiled distantly, paused, then went on, 'Your own doctor, Professor Taller, has had to be warned. He has been talking publicly about his concern for your whereabouts and welfare. There's a lot of sympathy for you out there, despite our best endeavours . . .'

The ambulance was waiting outside. Beside it, to Sinclair's surprise, stood a shifty-looking Ingram. He could not bring himself to look at the man directly but he sensed his unease. The wheelchair was manoeuvred for him onto a mechanical lift by the back doors of the van and he was slowly raised into the rear. Ingram and a second man, a guard of some sort Sinclair supposed, climbed in after him and the doors were firmly shut from the outside. The windows were totally covered in frosted glass so he was unable to see out nor could he see who was seated in the front of the cab.

The ambulance drove off. He felt it stop shortly thereafter, presumably for them to be checked through the main security gates. It started again but, half a minute later, it stopped once more. He heard the sound of scuffling and what sounded like a curse or a quickly suppressed shout of anger. In the back of the ambulance, Ingram sat impassively but the security guard looked decidedly jumpy. Sinclair wondered if there had been some sudden change of plan: was it all much more sinister and could they be taking him off somewhere to eliminate him?

His speculation was interrupted as, suddenly, the rear doors were wrenched open and there stood Robert Guthrie with a serious-looking gun in his hand. Inside the vehicle, Ingram had somehow also got hold of a gun and, pushing past Sinclair, forced the security guard to put his hands behind his back, then snapped a pair of handcuffs over his wrists, while Guthrie, who had produced a black cloth bag, pulled it roughly over the guard's head. By this time the ambulance had started to move forward again, and Ingram had to reach out precariously over the road to pull the rear doors closed.

'Hold on tight, sir,' barked Guthrie. 'Make sure the wheels of your chair are securely locked. Now comes the tricky part.'

To Sinclair's bemused astonishment, Ingram was efficiently bundling the captive guard up and onto one of the stretcher beds and strapping him in. His former chauffeur looked over when he had finished his task and caught Sinclair watching him. He gave a sudden unexpected smile. 'Expect you'll forgive me and Guthrie when we're through with all this, sir,' he said happily.

In the driver's cab someone had switched on the ambulance siren. Then Sinclair felt the thrust in the small of his back as the vehicle reached for its maximum speed.

13

Scotland's lost leaders

Many people in England fervently wish that some of their political leaders would quietly get lost. Without naming names, to quote W. S. Gilbert, 'they'd none of 'em be missed'. But losing leaders north of the border seems to be getting quite a habit. Mystery, in particular, surrounds the whereabouts of former Scottish Prime Minister, Keith Sinclair, and Sir Alexander MacDowall, the Minister of the Interior. Both men were victims of violent assaults, Mr Sinclair's attack, by a demonstrator, leaving him confined to a wheelchair. The attempt on Sir Alexander's life has never been fully explained and no one has been arrested nor charged. Their disappearance from public life has not been explained. Where are they? The new Prime Minister, Ian Campbell, must surely know. So far his Parliamentary performances have been nothing short of disastrous yet somebody in Scotland is taking robust decisions about where the country is going. Mr Campbell has a lot of explaining to do. We can only hope that the policies his government are pursuing will rescue the Scottish economy from its parlous condition. It is not in England's interest that her northern neighbour should be . . .

(Editorial, *The Times*)

Deep inside the bunker there were bound to be occasional tensions in the barrack-room atmosphere, sleeping, eating and working underground, with too little exercise or recreation. But overall there was a splendid spirit of camaraderie, driven as they were by their common cause, waiting excitedly for the time to make their move.

The arrival of Prime Minister Keith Sinclair among them – and that to them was still his title – greatly lifted their spirits. Because of his frail health, most of the coordination and the chairing of meetings continued to be left to MacDowall, with Robert Guthrie remorselessly driving and plotting from behind. The Scottish and US teams worked well together. Admiral Muller – Joe to his staff – came and went from time to time. Otherwise they kept their external movements to a minimum, leaving the bunker only at night. Fortunately there were few towns or villages nearby; the forest was privately owned in the name of a rich American banker and it was relatively easy to keep the whole place under wraps.

The most valuable resource possessed by the Resistance Cabinet, as they had started calling themselves, was access to the clandestine radio and telephone intercepts. They also received transcripts from the bugging devices which the Special Task Force had successfully planted in various key areas of their headquarters building from Unity's earliest days in Scotland. If there had been one catastrophic loophole in Unity's otherwise meticulous planning for its *coup d'état*, it was their belief that, having destroyed the Government's Communications Monitoring Station in the Campsies and the second sub-station at Kinloss on the Moray Firth, they could talk openly without having their conversations monitored or bugged.

Guthrie and Sinclair were particularly gratified and amused at being able to listen to the verbatim reactions of the Unity godfathers after the PM had made his escape. They sat in the operations room as the Special Task Force's operator played them the relevant tape. They easily identified de Laski and Rosenfeld from their voices. Special Task Force said they believed that Fulton and Carlyle had also been in the room.

DE LASKI: *What's the fuckin' excuse?*

ROSENFELD: *Let me take you through it.*

DE LASKI: *Get on with it.*

ROSENFELD: *Someone outside, probably Billy McKane of the* Herald *or another of those fugitives working for MacDowall, arranged for Campbell's office to be bombarded with press calls asking about the state of Sinclair's health. That's why, remember, we all, repeat all, (pause) agreed to move him to the Clydebank hospital.*

DE LASKI *(angry): We know.*

ROSENFELD: *We trusted Ingram. That was a big mistake. Number one. He took our money and ran. Guthrie fooled us too. We thought ... OK, OK, I thought he had been won over too. We had checked it out; his story of having got nowhere with the administration when he was in the States was true. Now we know he's been shacking up with Anderson's daughter. Dangerous liaison ...*

DE LASKI: *Get on with it.*

ROSENFELD: *We know where Guthrie cut through the perimeter fence. Trouble on that was we are fortified as hell to stop people getting in ... not breaking out. The night guards have been sacked. Between them, Guthrie and Ingram arranged for one of their men to take the place of our regular ambulance driver. In the circumstances, our US guard sitting in the back didn't stand a chance. We found him, or rather the police found him, tied up by the roadside.*

DE LASKI: *So many fuckin' excuses ... Sinclair?*

ROSENFELD: *Vanished. They'll have had a bolt hole ready. We've a general search out but we'll be lucky ...*

DE LASKI: *Get lucky or you're in deep shit, Rosenfeld. D'you realize the danger to our whole fuckin' strategy of having that bastard on the loose? If he ever got an opportunity to rally the nation we could have a bloody civil war on our hands.*

ROSENFELD: *I'm working my butt off . . .*

DE LASKI: *Which ain't good enough. And (pause) I don't want him caught. Sinclair alive is dynamite. Wipe him away.*

ROSENFELD: *He's sick . . . a cripple, in a wheelchair.*

DE LASKI (sneering): *So was President Roosevelt. Franklin D. helped win the last German war out of a wheelchair. Now, get out and don't come back till you've done him.*

(Door slam. Silence.)

FULTON: *I thought you said he was good.*

DE LASKI: *Rosenfeld is good. He just had his eye off the ball.*

FULTON: *Unguarded moments kill. Keep after him.*

Then the tape went dead.

Not all the news filtering into the bunker was as entertaining or as positive. By and large, the Unity-controlled Scottish press had given an enthusiastic welcome to Campbell's speech and to the economic announcements he subsequently made. News of the thousands of extra jobs that were to be created by Unity's move to Scotland was also widely and understandably applauded, though in some of the independent press and in the London newspapers, disquiet was expressed at the degree to which the Scottish economy was becoming dependent on one huge conglomerate. The London *Financial Times* carried a two-page spread, largely drawing on the earlier *Herald* disclosures, showing how extensive Unity's Scottish and worldwide operations were. Its editorial, on the other hand, was cautious: 'As long as Unity remains benevolently inclined, Scotland can only benefit from the inward investment currently being injected into her ailing economy. But is any conglomerate truly warm-hearted in the long run?'

The London Government could hardly be blamed for keeping their distance after the way in which Scotland broke from the Union. They were fully aware, from the reporting by the English High Commission in Regent Terrace, of much of what was happening north of the border. But since Independence, they had taken infinite care to avoid taking any action that might be construed as meddling in the Scottish political scene. At best, they were benevolently neutral; there was no way Sinclair's government in exile could, overtly or covertly, run to them for help. The English media and the EBC, the successor to the BBC, were equally circumspect in their coverage. One thing that the London Government had begun to do, however, was to introduce stiff restrictions on foreign owners of firms operating inside England. They were determined to avoid a similar Unity operation sweeping in south of the border.

The council of war held that evening, with Prime Minister Sinclair in the chair, was a grim occasion. Admiral Muller attended along with the Deputy Chief of Mission from the US Embassy in London. For obvious reasons, the US Ambassador and his staff at the Embassy in Edinburgh were being kept right out of it. If anything went wrong, they would be left with relatively clean hands in their future dealings with Campbell and his backers. The outcome of the meeting was unanimous in one respect: they agreed they could not simply come out of hiding, even with public backing from Washington and London, and expect to have Sinclair reinstated. As Billy McKane, the deposed editor of the *Herald*, argued plausibly, it would be too easy for Campbell and Unity to portray Sinclair to the media as a sick and unbalanced man, with the crowd around him as a bunch of discarded has-beens.

McKane went on to argue for a major PR offensive, though admitting that they would need some sensational news peg to launch it. Waiting for Campbell or Unity to slip up was no serious strategy. There was little hope of stirring the Republicans or the Reunionists into precipitate action, since their leaders were reported to be reining in their troops and waiting on events. Both parties wanted to see how Campbell's promised reforms worked out before leaping into the attack. The other main problem was that most of the Scottish media, including the *Herald* under its new puppet editor, were behaving like sheep: they would need a dramatic lead to make them break free once again.

Guthrie and McKane were detailed off to work out a proactive public relations strategy. They found a quiet corner one evening and, over a few measures from a bottle of vintage Macallan, debated how they were going to operate. 'If we're going to feed stuff to the world's press, we'll need an American voice on the telephone,' McKane said, so Guthrie went off to find Heather Anderson to ask her to join their propaganda working group. They sat facing each other round a wooden trestle table and worked well into the night.

'News manipulation,' McKane began. 'I've been subjected to it all my life, so I should know how it operates.'

'How many news targets are we talking about?' asked Heather.

'Not all that many,' McKane speculated. 'If we concentrate on, say, a dozen, we may be able to build up ... let's see ... the *Financial Times*, *Wall Street Journal*, *Handelsblatt*, *Nikkei*, *Neuer Zürcher Zeitung*. That'll do for a start.'

'We need to feed them a lively story with the right slant and appeal,' Guthrie interrupted.

'Yes,' said McKane. 'It's got to have the ring of truth about it. It's got to stand up when cross-checked. It's got to be topical and newsworthy. There's only a certain size of news hole for editors to fill every day. If there's a war, a major scandal, or a huge natural disaster on the go, most other news stories get buried or spiked. Timing is crucial.'

'Are we just talking about feeding the financial newspapers ... the print media?' Heather asked.

'No way.' McKane sipped at his glass. 'Electronic as well. Reuters, AP, UPI, the satellite and internet channels. Look, let's draw up a list of London, European, American and Far Eastern media outlets we want to hit, people who are going to be interested in the Scotland–Unity thing in the first place.'

'If I was sitting in Tokyo, let alone New York with its well-known news insularity, I'm not sure I'd be hooked by the happenings of a faraway country of which I knew nothing and cared less.' Heather shrugged.

'She's right, Billy,' said Guthrie. 'How do we get them even to answer the phone?' He stared across the table at McKane.

The big Glaswegian folded his hands together thoughtfully. 'I'm working on it. What would I do if I was editor of the *Wall Street Journal* or the *South China Morning Post*? I'd junk any story unless it was either big enough, affected local interests, or could potentially hit my readers' pockets. We can't, on what we have to go on at present, run with the first two. To my mind we have to work up a "multinational in financial scandal" line, particularly aiming at countries where Unity have business interests. It's our only hope.'

'But how?' Heather asked.

'Markets are fickle things,' Guthrie broke in. 'Even the most hard-nosed City analyst or fund manager and, certainly, the teenage scribblers who seem to write most of the financial pages, are just as susceptible to rumour and sentiment as the man in the street. They think they're experts. They're not. They're also notoriously lazy.'

'Journalists? Lazy?' McKane laughed.

'Come on,' Guthrie continued. 'You know some of them pick up press releases and company hand-outs and run them verbatim or with very little editing. That's why the financial PR companies make so much money. Even if they've spent a lifetime watching the Unity Corporation, they still don't know what's really going on inside. They read the news releases and annual reports like everyone else, get the soft-soap treatment from company spokesmen and strategists like Rosenfeld and guess the rest. That right, Billy?' He looked to the deposed Editor for his approval.

'Yeah. That's the theory,' said McKane. 'And if one paper runs a story in a big enough way, the others will too. We're all scared stiff of losing out or having missed a big scoop. I've done it myself often enough.' He nodded, then added acidly, 'Now all we need is the headline to feed.'

Apart from letting themselves get bugged, Unity had one other surprising weakness which the Resistance Cabinet tried their best to exploit. Unity had failed to pay much attention to international opinion. A country, like a multinational, could only do that for so long. From the file of cuttings from the world's press which Heather had been collecting over the months, critical reporting of what had been happening in Edinburgh could soon be ripe for exploitation.

As the week passed, however, nerves in the bunker began to fray. Knowledge was one thing; lack of action another. Admiral Muller arrived and reported on the latest negative attitudes in London. The English had been approached informally by Washington but were determined to stick to their passive role. Behind the scenes, the London Government had a cold, clear view of where their best interests lay and they were adamant that they were not going to come off the fence and start criticizing the Campbell regime. The English Foreign Secretary, however, equally informally, did volunteer that the Foreign Office might be able to put on a bit of discreet pressure if the issue became internationalized through the UN in New York.

Thus, after much lobbying by friends of Scotland like Anderson in the USA and like-minded men and women of Scottish descent in Canada, Australia and New Zealand, the Canadian Delegation to the United Nations reluctantly brought the issue before the Security Council. It was listed on the Council Agenda as 'The present state of Scotland: a matter of urgent international concern'. Certain European countries and Guatemala, which had had past experience of Unity's ruthless behaviour, spoke at the subsequent debate. But it was all very low-key and there were more important issues before the Council that week. It ended up with mere words: people listened but nobody heard. The matter did not reach a vote; there was no credible reason for one. Scotland may have its problems but they were insignificant in comparison with the conflicts that were destroying other parts of the globe. The issue raised few headlines in the world's press.

Most of the Scottish and English newspapers were smuggled into the bunker and monitored closely. Where Sinclair or Mac-Dowall's names were mentioned and, with a few exceptions, there was a growing lack of curiosity about where they might be, they were treated with ridicule or contempt in the Unity press.

They were dubbed the 'Has-been Men', who were now branded as having been fully responsible for the economic chaos that Scotland had bravely tolerated for so long. Under Ian Campbell and his newly appointed Cabinet, things were looking up. Members of the Resistance Cabinet complained among themselves about how gullible the Scottish people were, without appreciating the first rule of State propaganda: lies are sanctified by constant repetition.

Tensions rose again with the frustrations of communal living, particularly since a number of those who had sought refuge there had abandoned normal lives, wives and families in the process. One evening a punch-up was only just avoided between Nick Forbes and Billy McKane. They were sitting round the communal table eating the very passable evening meal which the US staff had as usual cooked for them, when Forbes opened up with an unexpected torrent of complaint.

'It's the capitalists what got us intae this mess in the first place,' he volunteered loudly. Guthrie, watching him from across the table, could see how Forbes as a younger man would have gone out of his way to pick a fight in some Sauchiehall Street pub. 'You lot . . .' he pointed rudely with his fork at MacDowall, 'shoulda have seen it comin' a long, long time ago.'

'I've freely admitted that,' said MacDowall, carefully avoiding taking offence.

'If you hadn't rallied your men to take the law into their own hands, creating industrial relations anarchy, you wouldn't have driven the Japanese and the Germans out, leaving the vacuum for Unity to fill,' McKane burst in angrily.

'Don't you bloody –' Forbes began, then checked himself. 'OK, OK. Here we are fightin' amongst ourselves. Tae what purpose? We're tryin' tae act like a government in exile, and a fat lot of good its daeing for us or for Scotland.'

'We've kept our principles,' said MacDowall gently.

'Principles are fine but expediency makes far better strategy . . .' Forbes went on.

'What exactly are you saying, Forbes?' asked McKane with a

note of growing hostility in his voice. 'Are your principles beginning to evaporate?' he challenged.

'A don't need learnt by the likes o' you, McKane,' the former
union leader shouted back across the table. 'All a'm saying is
maybe it's time tae accept what's happened. Maybe we should
at least put out feelers towards Campbell . . . work out some
compromise. A dinnae like being bribed any more than the next
man, but we have tae live in the real world.'

'Quitting are we?' McKane provoked with increasing fury.

'A'm nae quitter and naebody's gonna call me one neither.'
Forbes half stood, with MacDowall, who was sitting beside him,
trying to restrain him. 'Maybe it's just a matter of jealousy.
Campbell and his cronies have won. We've a' lost our power
base. Is there ony mair tae it than tha'?'

Heather Anderson watched the scene and in particular Robert
Guthrie's reaction to it. His face was impossible to read, showing
no reaction one way or another. What was he really thinking?
she asked herself. Forbes kept it up, as if deliberately wanting to
antagonize the others round the table, though some of them at
least must have privately shared some of his concerns.

'After a',' he said, 'how many o' our country men and women
have protested at the changes? Have there been ony mair demonstrations? Have there been new strikes? Are the workers any
worse off?' He looked round defiantly. Admiral Muller and the
other CIA men watched, waited, kept their distance and their
own counsel. This was an argument for the Scots to sort out
amongst themselves. 'The figures may have been rigged, a grant
you that . . . but unemployment seems to be droppin' month on
month. If the Scottish people dinnae care a damn what sort o'
government they have . . . and they've put up wi' a lot worse
over the years . . .' he again looked round accusingly, 'then why
should we play the heroes? We all may bloody genuflect at the
words *patriotism* and *democracy* but . . . need we play the
Braveheart scenario as well?'

Disappointingly, Forbes did not get fed any further angry
response and maybe, having got it all off his chest, he felt the better

194

for it. Suddenly he looked round the table, slightly abashed at his own outburst. Then suddenly he smiled. 'Och it's just me sounding off,' he said. 'Dinnae worry folks. A'm wi' you a' the way.'

If some relationships were fraught, the personal one between Robert Guthrie and Heather Anderson was not able to develop as fast as it might otherwise have done within the tense confines of the bunker. Men and women slept in separate dormitories; there was little opportunity for the development of a more passionate affair. That they were increasingly attracted to each other both of them knew: it was, Guthrie remarked to her when they were briefly alone one night, rather like a Victorian romance; they could look but not touch. In any case, they were all kept very busy, he on planning the international media campaign, she constructing from information largely provided by the CIA an ever more detailed chart of everything that was known about the Unity Corporation and its subsidiaries. In the main ops room, which a thoughtful sixties British Government had provided with wall charts and world maps, a huge picture of their intermeshing company network was being produced.

As she worked, she watched with increasing admiration as Guthrie gradually took more and more control. He was not a demonstrative person and she was never quite sure what he was really thinking, but she noted that he tended to get his own way in the end. Away from the old constraints of the government and civil service rankings, he deliberately used his close relationship with MacDowall to mastermind the overall strategy to attempt to undermine or shake confidence in Unity's global financial position. With Guthrie's knowledge, which dated back to his study of capital markets when he was a student at Harvard, he, McKane and Heather started work, using the secret CIA communications network to spread rumours by telephone and fax about Unity to specially selected correspondents, analysts and brokers in stock markets, finance houses and the business media around the world. They realized that they would not always meet success and that many people would fail to return their calls or would ignore the stories they were being fed. But enough of it stuck. International market sentiment is, at the best of times, a fickle thing. Rumours coming from all directions at once eventually built up a rewarding head of steam, and the scale of the reaction grew. At Unity Headquarters James Fulton spent his time shouting at Rosenfeld, asking him where the hell the largely false stories were coming from and what he was doing about it. Rosenfeld tried his best. He partly guessed who was behind it but was baffled at the way such intelligent and believable lies were being fed in all over the world. That, to him, suggested a high degree of organization. He was particularly worried by one day's hard-hitting rumours which were fully reported in the next morning's *Financial Times*.

Shares depressed by London/Wall Street jitters

Shares in Unity Corporation suffered again yesterday, both in London and New York, as market traders and analysts reacted adversely to rumours of the company having overstretched its debt position. Confidence was further undermined by reports of boardroom conflicts between Executive Chairman, James Fulton, and some of his senior colleagues over future strategy. This particularly referred to the controversial move of their entire HQ to Scotland, given the current insecure political situation there. Negative reports were reflected in the FTSE 100 Index and in afternoon trading on Wall Street where the Dow Jones Index was also affected.

Further rumours hit Unity's share price in Tokyo and Zurich. This followed suggestions that the company's debt position could only be rectified by massive management restructuring and cost controls, with the closure of several factories in Scotland where overproduction of personal computers has flooded the market. This would, market analysts speculated, undoubtedly lead to the loss of thousands of skilled and semi-skilled jobs in an economy that is already suffering badly.

Shares eventually tumbled twenty pence on the London market to close at 612p, in spite of the group's announcement that all was well and that no significant management restructuring was antici-pated. Relations between Mr Fulton and his board were, it was emphasized, excellent. Further losses are nevertheless expected overnight, coupled with a poor response to the new Scottish Government Bonds offer, with investors reluctant to take positions with so much uncertainty in the market.

(Report, *Financial Times*)

Later that day and gradually during the following week, market stability crept back and the Unity share price largely recovered. Rosenfeld even got a grudging 'well done' from Fulton but in his bones the latter felt it was only a temporary respite.

Guthrie and McKane were, by contrast, increasingly gloomy. Rumour had helped briefly but, even in the unstable world of financial markets, more substance would be needed to do serious damage to the Unity position.

Silt was very much against what he considered Guthrie's foolish move. He encouraged Admiral Muller to have a word with Sir Alexander MacDowall, but the latter had merely grunted that the bunker could not be a prison. If Robert Guthrie and Heather Anderson were fool enough to want to go off for a twenty-four hours' break to Guthrie's remote highland cottage that was up to them. Silt was angry. If they were picked up and interrogated, even if force wasn't used, they could so easily give the whole game away. And this was no game. He decided that they would get CIA protection, whether Guthrie wanted it or not.

They disguised themselves to the extent that Guthrie wore

sunglasses and Heather tucked her distinctive auburn hair inside an unfashionable silk scarf. Even Silt admitted that they weren't high-profile enough to have squads of Unity bother boys scouring the remote highlands for them. They drove north of Tarbert, then westwards along the top of Loch Long through majestic glens to the head of Loch Fyne where they turned south towards Inveraray. It was a cool, clear day and Heather's first view of that part of Scotland found it at its very best. Halfway down the side of the loch and round a sharp bend, Guthrie, who was driving along as if he did not have a care in the world, suddenly braked and pulled off the main road and into a hidden side lane among a plantation of Scots pine. He quickly switched the engine off and waited.

'What is it?' Heather was taken aback.

'We've had a tail for most of the way,' said Guthrie, impassively. Behind him, in the driving mirror, he saw a dark car speed past the road end without stopping. 'It's probably our friend Harvey Silt trying to mother us, but I don't want to test my theory. I hope this car's springs are OK. This wasn't the road I intended to take.'

They drove on the potholed track for several miles, up and away from the loch, crossing several streams and cattle grids. When they reached the highest point, Guthrie stopped the engine and they got out of the car to admire the view. To the east, they looked down on the glistening waters of Loch Fyne; to the west were more lochs and mountains and the distant, misty sea.

'Beautiful,' murmured Heather, reaching out and taking Guthrie's hand. 'Not a house, not a person to be seen.'

'That's half the trouble,' said Guthrie, coming close and putting his arm round her shoulders. 'It would spoil it in so many ways but there ought to be loads more tourists. We need them. The strikes and the troubles have driven them all away. Scotland's done so much harm to itself these past years.'

'They'll come back,' said Heather, kissing him gently on the cheek. 'In the meantime, we have it all to ourselves.'

'Wait till you see my little surprise,' said Guthrie.

Down the other side of the hill, they turned onto a cart track which led to a metalled minor road. The Ford's springs had lasted the journey, but they were both glad to have left the bumps and holes behind them. Guthrie drove a few miles more until they reached the crest of another hill with, below them, the sea and the misty islands of Jura and Islay beyond.

'So peaceful,' Heather said. 'Where now?'

'There.' Guthrie pointed up and to the left where a neat, white-washed cottage stood out amid a clump of windblown trees. 'That's my spiritual home.'

They continued down the hill, then turned up to stop on a patch of grass beside the house.

'Peat fires, cold water to wash in, and only porridge to eat?' asked Heather. 'I think I can put up with all that for this view.'

Guthrie went up to the front door, produced a key, unlocked it and swung it open into the shade beyond. He frowned slightly to himself but said nothing. There was a smell about the air in the cottage that was unfamiliar and unwelcome, but a quick tour reassured him. They were alone.

Later they walked for a while on the moor above the cottage, relishing the freedom and the fresh air after the stuffy days in the bunker, then they went back to the croft, where he lit a fire in the open hearth. Heather looked around: it was much better equipped than he had pretended. There was a fridge which he filled with the provisions they had brought with them; there was a cupboard well stocked with wine and whisky; there was a heating system that provided hot water for the bath that they took together when they had finished their long afternoon of making love.

That evening, intoxicated by their burgeoning relationship, he cast discretion aside and took her to dinner at the Crinan Hotel, at the western end of the canal. He realized that they were playing a dangerous game but didn't realize how much . . . He did how-ever take the precaution of checking in advance with his friend the hotel owner, who told him that there were few other guests staying that night. No: no one had booked in unexpectedly. They were given a table at the window of the seafood restaurant with a panoramic view that looked out at a rose-red sunset, which matched any famous sight in the world. They ate local prawns and lobster and drank ice-cold Chablis, until even the genial, jovial, rubicund landlord started looking at his watch and yawning pointedly.

It was past midnight when they drove back slowly along the canal to Lochgilphead then across the hill to the cottage. A full moon rode high and bright in the western sky. At a bend in the road Guthrie suddenly cut the engine, dowsed the car's headlights and stopped.

'What's the matter?' Heather asked amorously, reaching out to touch him. 'Can't you wait till we get there?' She nuzzled against his shoulder, beginning to seduce him with her hands, body and lips.

'Hush,' he said quietly, winding down the window. 'Look . . . Over there.' He pointed up and to the left to where his cottage lay.

'What is it?' she asked anxiously.

'A light. I thought I saw a light.'

'What of it?' she said.

'A light where there shouldn't be one,' Guthrie responded. He thought for a moment then he shrugged. 'It's gone now. Maybe just moonlight reflecting on something.'

With her warmth beside him, wisdom and caution were further swept to one side as he considered the alternatives: returning to a hard, steel-framed bed in the bunker, or going to bed with Heather. There was no competition. Again, he comforted himself, the Unity people weren't going to go all out looking for such small fry as them. Sinclair, yes; MacDowall and Forbes, yes; not a mere civil servant. He started the engine again and drove slowly on up towards the cottage.

That his judgement had taken a back-seat was particularly highlighted by his entire neglect of the Rosenfeld factor. Guthrie knew him well enough, he should have realized what the man would be feeling right now. He should have weighed up how seriously damaged Rosenfeld's ego would have been by what had happened. The American's confidence in his own judgement of character had proved to be disastrously flawed. It would not have needed de Laski and the others to tell him the error of his ways. To have misjudged Heather Anderson was one thing: a serious enough lapse but one that he could have dismissed as a temporary crack in the vanity of his self-confidence. But he had, within a few days, compounded his mistake threefold: Ingram, the driver, a minor but crucial figure; then, folly of follies, he had also misread Forbes, and, worst of all, Robert Guthrie. Everything had been going so well: he had become careless as a result of his easy success in buying up so many others in the Scottish establishment. These were very big mistakes, especially since they were almost home and dry. Rosenfeld was a man driven by the need to win. He was determined both to learn and benefit from these unforgivable lapses of judgement. He had a new mission: Robert Guthrie was still to experience the pain of similar failings.

Inside the croft the lovers sat by the peat fire for a while, sharing a gentle nightcap, exploring each other, building up passion and desire for the night to come. Eventually, they prepared to go to bed. She was in the bathroom brushing her teeth, he was stripping naked, when he heard the noise from outside. It wasn't caused by the wind, nor by animal nor bird. It was a human noise, a boot tripping on an unfamiliar stone perhaps. It sent shock waves coursing through his body. He switched the lights off, quickly dressed again in the dark, then went and told Heather to do the same.

'Let's hope it's just Harvey Silt. But if we're that important to good Americans, we might be to bad ones too. I don't intend to play heroics and wait and find out,' Guthrie whispered urgently.

'What do we do? Wait for them to come . . . bar the door . . . make a run?' she whispered back.

'Let me think,' said Guthrie. With the lights off, his eyes had grown accustomed to the gloom but, when he looked cautiously out of the window into the darkness, the moon had sunk so low on the horizon that he could see very little by its faint light. But he did notice that the wind had risen a little and that inspired a possible solution. 'I hope your shoes are strong,' he said. 'It's rough country around here.'

Crouched behind a dry stone dyke in the lee of the croft, the senior of the two Unity heavies who had been staking out the place put a call through to Abel Rosenfeld's Edinburgh apartment. The bell woke him and he was curt and bad-tempered.

'They're back and in the cottage,' said the man in a low voice.

'Both? You're quite sure?'

'Sure. Only one entrance. Watching that now.'

'Anyone else around?'

'No way.'

'Haven't spotted you?'

'No way,' the man repeated. 'What now?'

Rosenfeld was angry and tired. 'Do what you're paid to do,' he said. He put the receiver down and went back to an untroubled sleep.

Behind the dyke, the man swore under his breath and loosened his gun in his shoulder holster. As he did so, his colleague, resting his back against the wall for support, knocked over a loose stone, which rattled noisily down onto a pile below.

'Shit,' said the man.

'Great,' whispered Guthrie inside the croft. 'Perfect wind direction.'

It had not rained for several days. The paraffin-soaked rags thrown out of the door and window quickly lit the grass and dried bracken, causing an immediately rewarding burst of flame, and then, better, a thick choking smoke. In other circumstances Guthrie would have felt guilty at fireraising, but he hoped it would burn itself out soon enough when it reached the burn.

Climbing rapidly out of a window on the far side of the house, Heather Anderson and Robert Guthrie ran up the hill, away from the smoke, leaving croft, car, and, they hoped, whoever was out there looking for them, far behind.

Soon they reached the small copse of pine trees which had

been Guthrie's goal. There he intended that they would hide till first light, before trying to make their way back to the bunker. Below them, they heard the noise of someone running and a shout as someone ordered them to stop. But whoever it was was a long way behind, they surely could not see them in the dying light of the moon's rays.

They threw themselves on the pineneedle-covered ground. Both of them were gasping for breath.

'Safe here,' whispered Guthrie.

'Sure are,' said a male voice close beside them, then the reassuring figure of Harvey Silt appeared from among the trees. 'Clever move, that bush fire. Quick thinking,' he said approvingly. 'Redeemed yourself, Robert. Nearly didn't need our help. C'mon now. Quick. We've got a four-wheel drive waiting on the far side of the wood.'

14

Leaked letter scandal

Leaked love letters written by crippled former PM Keith Sinclair's ex-wife, Nora, to an unknown stud – rumours say he too is a prominent politician – have been offered to the *Scottish Sun*. Editor Kenny Thomas said that the offer had been rejected and no money had changed hands. The kinky letters contain no-holds-barred details of lurid sex scenes between Naughty Nora and her beau ... (see p. 5 for further details).

(Front page lead, Scottish Sun)

The rains came heavily to that part of Africa. Slowly and inexorably they washed away at the treacherous slag and dross at the base of the huge man-made mountain. It was a famous place, emerging as it did from the jungle and swamp land that surrounded it. On its topmost slopes there was money to be made by the tribesmen and women and children, picking at the ingots which, rejected as not having enough copper content to please the mining company, could still be taken by the basketful, all the way down to where the middlemen would buy them and smelt them in little home-made furnaces.

But it was on the lower slopes, where thick vegetation had covered the tip and given a false sense of security, that tragedy stuck. When the local people saw rye grass and thorn bushes they had felt it safe to build their thatched huts and mudbrick hovels. There they could cook and eat and sleep and their many children could play up above the steaming heat of the jungle below.

For the rest of the world, the small screen captured almost more than the reality, for reality was too great in scope, in dimension, in horror. The outside world would merely have heard of another tragic, Third World disaster, somewhere in the back of beyond, if it hadn't been for a London-based television crew that had been filming close by. They were there to capture on film secret evidence of the persecution of the local tribespeople by the military government that still ruled so brutally in that desolate part of sub-Saharan Africa. They had already taken a lot of footage of the evil, sulphurous wasteland that surrounded the oil rigs and other extractive industries along the Niger Delta. So they were right on hand to film the pathetic attempts that the survivors made to pull the hundreds of bodies from the thick, stinking, brown slurry. One image said it all: a tiny black face and a single hand stretched towards heaven from out of the all-encompassing mud.

In the safe depths of the bunker on the shores of the loch, the men and women there watched the moving, tearjerking footage on the evening news. It came as item three after the Cabinet reshuffle and the rumour of threepence more on income tax. They all turned as Admiral Muller walked in to the concrete-walled room with a look of grim satisfaction on his face.

'Ladies and gentlemen,' he said. 'We have 'em now. That there . . .' he pointed at the flickering television screen, 'is a Unity-owned mine.'

Everything was detailed like a military operation. D-day was chosen: budget day in the Scottish National Assembly in Edinburgh. Two days to go, and there was still much to do, and not everyone could know each detail of every plan. At one point during the frantic preparations, Heather Anderson, by chance, climbed up to the external steel doors of the bunker late one night and, after checking with the duty guard, went out for a welcome breath of fresh air. She stood in silence for some time until suddenly, she noticed the silhouette of a man standing close by the dense bank of trees. It was totally silent outside; a bright moon sailed clear of the few clouds in the sky. For a moment she was frightened and moved back in the direction of the doors, intending to alert the guards that someone was loitering about outside.

But then she clearly heard Robert Guthrie's voice. He was speaking on a mobile telephone. With shock and disbelief in her heart, she heard him tell someone unknown about the precise arrangements that had been made for Keith Sinclair's secret move to Edinburgh. The exact timing and the registration number of the ambulance were carefully spelled out. When she heard his last fatal words, an icy chill spilled through her and she almost fell. 'This is your only opportunity, Abel,' she clearly heard Guthrie say. 'If you don't act, you will have lost.'

Slowly and quietly Heather Anderson slipped back down into the depths of the bunker. Breathlessly, she rushed along the long echoing concrete corridors, in and out of rooms until she found Sir Alexander MacDowall and forcefully pulled him into a side room. Tears streaming down her cheeks, she sobbed out the horrible treachery she had just overheard.

Early the next morning, on the misty and deserted A814 between the Gareloch and the A82 that runs down the west side of Loch Lomond, an ambulance, amber lights flashing, drove at high speed, its driver expertly negotiating the many twists and bends. He was a well-trained professional, but even he felt his heart hit his mouth when he saw, in his driving mirror, the powerful black Jaguar suddenly appear from out of a side track, and swing in behind him. Even at a distance he could see it was full of dark-suited men.

The chosen spot was just round the next bend: maybe two hundred yards to go if they had accurately picked up Guthrie's bait. Yes, there ahead, an identical black Jaguar was drawn up, totally blocking the road. The ambulance driver did not slow down, but switched on his siren instead. Still the car did not move. Fifty yards short of the road block, by a deep gully between two clumps of trees, he screeched to a stop, opened the door of the cab and, with well-practised skill, jumped out and down into the gully, rapidly disappearing into the mist. He had deliberately left the handbrake off and the ambulance in first gear, so it slowly began to move off the road, over a shallow ditch, before gently nose-diving down towards the gully.

The car ahead had sprung into life. The car behind halted a few yards from where the ambulance was continuing its slow descent. Men from both cars jumped out, all armed with semi-automatic guns, all ready to fire.

'No,' shouted Abel Rosenfeld holding up his hand. 'Perfect. Just perfect. No bullets wasted.' He made a sudden gesture and another man pulled what turned out to be a flame thrower from the back of the car.

'Now,' shouted Rosenfeld. 'Now, damn you,' he repeated.

A huge jet of fire spurted from the flame thrower and hit the ambulance side on. It took only a few seconds before that vehicle of mercy, siren still sounding, amber lights still flashing, red cross visible to the end, was torched into a fireball of oblivion.

Less than half an hour later, Rosenfeld and his men were found cautiously making their way through the dense screen of fir trees that hid the entrance to the bunker. They had all donned camouflaged overalls and now looked more like commandos than businessmen. When they reached their goal they stayed in hiding among the trees while one man, obviously well trained in military tactics and fully briefed as to exactly what he was meant to do, crept forward through the undergrowth until he reached the fortified door of the bunker. Deep inside, a small group of nervous men and women secretly watched his progress on a hidden monitoring camera. They saw that the man was carrying a neat brown briefcase which he placed strategically at one side of the entranceway. They saw only part of what happened next: as they watched he bent low and did something to the handle of the briefcase before running rapidly back to the shelter of the trees. Five seconds later those in the bunker did not see the huge explosion or, once the dust had cleared, how the entire entrance to the bunker had totally disappeared under the weight of falling rock, earth and mud.

Outside, Rosenfeld's men knew full well that this would not be the end of those in the bunker. They were probably all quite safe, hidden deep inside, well away from the entrance. The bunker had, after all, been built to sustain a nuclear attack. It would need more than a briefcase of semtex to touch them. Rosenfeld realized that only too well. But they were surely entombed for some considerable amount of time. And time was what Unity needed right now.

Less than an hour after that, thirteen-year-old Piggy McNeish, the little boy with the fascination for submarines, who was playing truant from school and was up in his hillside hideout watching for any shipping passing along the loch, did not see the small submarine as it slipped out of its secret underwater entrance to the bunker. It did not surface then. It did not surface for nearly three hours until it was around the far side of the Kintyre peninsula. There, at a discreet, well-chosen cove, it surfaced briefly to allow all the key figures from the bunker to be ferried ashore in rubber dinghies to where a number of undistinguished cars and vans, their engines running, were waiting close by the beach.

The next morning, the Scottish National Assembly prepared to go into full session. Crowds of interested onlookers lined the street from the Old Scottish Office building all the way to Regent Terrace, and up and around Calton Hill. Television cameras were everywhere. This budget day promised to be a crucial event for the Government and for Scotland. What Ian Campbell, who had decided to lead the debate himself, had to say would determine how much support or opposition the Republicans and the Reunionists would give to his proposed legislation. There was an atmosphere of high expectation in the country at large.

Inside the Chamber there was an equally expectant hush. Everyone stood as, preceded by the Officer of the House carrying the great Mace of State, the Speaker processed to his seat. The members' benches were crammed to overflowing and the public, press and VIP galleries were packed. Following prayers read by the Moderator of the General Assembly of the Church of Scotland, the Speaker tapped his gavel for silence and announced that, prior to the business of the day, the Prime Minister had a special statement to make.

Rumours were whispered all along the back benches. The more observant MPs noticed that Ian Campbell was wearing a black tie and that a weeping woman in a highly fashionable, broad-brimmed black hat had taken her reserved seat on the front row of the VIP gallery. Nora Sinclair held a delicate handkerchief to her eyes and dabbed them dry. Further along the front row sat an imperturbable James Fulton, flanked by de Laski and Carlyle.

Ian Campbell rose to his feet. An expectant hush fell on the Assembly. Television monitors focused in on his tired, uncertain face. In the TV and radio control rooms and in the press lobby, the news had just broken. There was a terrible excitement in the air.

'Mr Speaker, Moderator, Honourable Members, it is my sad duty to rise and inform this House that earlier this morning I received the tragic news that the former Prime Minister, Keith Sinclair, has been fatally injured in a road accident. As we did not have the full details I felt it would be wrong to release a statement any earlier. His widow Nora . . .' Campbell briefly looked up to where she was sitting, a piece of additional theatre staged by Rosenfeld to add a further human interest touch to the tragedy, '. . . has been very brave and insisted on being here for this sad announcement. As you know, Keith, my old colleague and a dear friend, was far from well. This morning he was being taken by ambulance to hospital for further surgery when the vehicle appears to have left the . . .'

There was a sudden commotion as the sound of raised voices came from the back of the Chamber. It caused Campbell to hesitate as he asked everyone to rise to their feet to observe a minute's silence. High up at the back of the visitors' gallery, Robert Guthrie and Heather Anderson appeared to survey the scene. Outside, Abel Rosenfeld had seen what was coming and was going berserk.

Below, by the entrance to the floor of the House and directly in front of the Speaker's chair, a small procession, pursued by a cluster of press, nervous police and security staff, appeared. Keith Sinclair MP, propelling himself in his wheelchair, entered the Assembly Chamber, flanked by Sir Alexander MacDowall MP, and Nick Forbes MP. In the stunned silence that greeted the appearance of the three men, Sinclair rose from his chair unaided, and the three Members of Parliament dutifully bowed to the white-faced Speaker.

'Permission to address this House, Mr Speaker, as an elected member of the National Assembly.' Sinclair spoke in clear, ringing tones. In the TV control rooms, the editors were going wild.

Campbell was still on his feet, but only just. He knew he should demonstrate delight and joy but his acting ability failed him, and he slipped helplessly back into his seat. Glancing upwards he saw but did not register the varied reactions of Nora, Fulton and the rest. From his chair he made a feeble, unnoticed gesture to the Speaker, as if to have Sinclair banned from being heard. But then came the bewildered cheers, the shocked cries of greeting, the shouts of happy disbelief.

The Speaker gavelled the Chamber into silence. Press lobbyists and others thronged every door. Sinclair took a silver-topped walking stick from Nick Forbes and, walking unaided to the rostrum, began to speak.

Newsflash
Channel 2 News has just acquired exclusive footage, taken by an unidentified amateur cameraman, of the ambushing and destruction of the PM's decoy ambulance on the A814 road north east of Gareloch. The faces of those concerned have been disguised for legal reasons. Viewers may find some of the following footage distressing . . .

(Lead item, SBC Six o'clock News)

Unity: is there a future?

Rumours on Unity Corporation Inc. hit markets heavily yesterday, leading to collapse in globally quoted stock prices. The Nigerian mining disaster had already severely dented confidence. Despite a rushed statement from Unity Chairman, James B. Fulton, expressing fullest confidence in future company profits, failed expansion plans in Scotland, linked with complaints by Federal authorities that Unity's move there was an elaborate tax dodge and route out of expensive civil litigation following the Hulse City incident, downed market confidence to zero. Lawyers in Delaware and Illinois quote claims of toxic waste treatment which could run to billions. This exacerbated negative trading positions on Unity stock in London, Zurich and Tokyo.

(Tape item, *Wall Street Stock Report*, Wednesday)

Fears follow Unity collapse

Confidence among Scotland's business leaders has plummeted following the virtual collapse of the Unity Corporation operations in Scotland, according to a report by the Scottish CBI. The sell-off of Unity subsidiaries may have alleviated some of the worst effects but their decision now not to establish its corporate headquarters in Scotland is a major blow. The Scottish Trade and Industry Department says that the proposed IMF loan, guaranteed by the US Government, with the waiving by the European Commission of this year's payments by Scotland into the EU Budget, should be of huge assistance in tiding the country over through the coming difficult months.

(*Financial Times*, Scottish edition)

There were many repercussions. One of the smallest and least consequential found Keith Sinclair waiting in the hallway of the house in Charlotte Square, surrounded by suitcases. His overcoat, briefcase and walking stick were all close at hand. Ingram would be arriving at any moment to take him to the airport. Many of the Cabinet would be at the VIP lounge to see him off. He hated fuss and was not looking forward to it. Sir Alexander had telephoned to say that he would certainly be there; he had proved a popular choice as the new Prime Minister. Others would be present too, including Guthrie and his fiancée Heather Anderson; he had already bought them their gift and had wished them well.

They had all pressed him to stay on but he told them that he wanted time. He had accepted with alacrity the Harvard offer of a visiting professorship for the academic year. The duties would be more honorary than onerous and it would give him the opportunity to record all that had happened. He had arranged to get all the Scottish newspapers airmailed to him so that he could keep in touch and watch progress.

He was surprisingly unconcerned about what charges, if any, they were going to bring against Campbell. If it were up to him, he would have let that fool slip quietly away to London and into well-merited obscurity. Nor did he much care what the CIA and the Washington administration between them were doing with Fulton and his cronies. His had been a short skirmish in a long war. And why should he waste any time thinking of Nora?

He looked around him, bidding a mental farewell to his official home. He would not miss it nor the constant comings and goings, the VIP visitors, the demanding flow of official red boxes, the tedious memoranda and correspondence. Thinking of letters, he glanced down and saw the one, written with an almost childlike hand, that he had just read; he had laid it to one side but it had fluttered to the floor under a table out of his reach. It was from the widow of PC Wright and had been posted from Devon, where she had returned with her son. It was short, poignant and appeared merely to thank him for having attended the funeral.

She wrote that in the end the local people had been very kind, kinder than they had ever been to her during her long exile in Scotland. They had brought her meals, they had helped her pack up and helped her on her way. But even then, the majority had still appeared distant and unconcerned. Why shouldn't they? They had their own lives to lead, their own problems to face that left them remote from others' tragedies in life.

Mrs Wright's simple remark caused Keith Sinclair to ponder once again about the attitude of the people of Scotland during these recent shattering events. They all had their own preoccupations. Ninety-five percent of them watched the news on TV or read about great events in the newspapers, then shrugged and sighed and got on with their lives. The fortunes of those at the top of public life were of passing interest but of no real concern. Sinclair recalled an expression that Robert Guthrie had once used about the 'acquiescent society': one that let most things happen provided they were left reasonably content and untroubled. So it would always be.

Sinclair reached unsteadily over for the bottle of whisky that stood half-empty on the hall stand, intending to pour himself a pre-journey drink. He knocked the glass over and it rolled onto the floor, where it cracked but did not break. With difficulty he retrieved it from under his chair and poured himself out a fair measure. It would help the pain, if not his nerves. He bent his head back, shut his eyes for a moment and remembered once sitting in the rain by an East Lothian shore. He saw waves and a child's sandcastle almost washed away. But the tide had turned just in time, and the white pebbles and the shells remained.

From outside came the sound of a car.

Another repercussion was felt later that same Friday. It was the Bank Holiday weekend. Glasgow Airport was packed with people queuing for their charter flights to the sun. There were still many Scots, Robert Guthrie thought to himself, with sufficient time and money to be able to go off and enjoy themselves. As he pushed his way through the throng towards the exit doors, he experienced a brief feeling of loss. He had just seen his old boss, Keith Sinclair, leave for his year of self-imposed exile among the academics of New England. Heather had flown out an hour later on the London shuttle to meet up with her father and spend a day or two with him while he attended a conference in Oxford. They would both come up to Scotland later to stay with him after the long weekend.

And he was about to begin a new career as the freshly appointed Permanent Under-Secretary in the Ministry of the Interior. He had, he understood, been personally chosen by Sir Alexander, who thought him too senior for the role the new Prime Minister wanted his own Private Secretary to play. MacDowall wanted a safe pair of hands at his old Ministry until the security situation had returned to normal.

Guthrie was about to leave the terminal building to find his car, when, out of the corner of his eye, he spotted someone whom he recognized. He could so easily have turned away, pretending not to notice. It might have been better to go home and forget all about Abel Rosenfeld. But something made him pause and turn, and go towards the American who was staring straight ahead of him as he tried to steer an unwieldy luggage trolley, piled high with suitcases, through the milling crowd. Just as he reached him, the suitcase on top of the pile slipped off and fell to the ground, causing two others wedged beneath it to follow suit. Rosenfeld stopped and began to rescue them. Guthrie, unthinking, bent to help him.

'Thanks, I can . . .' Rosenfeld began. Then, as he straightened up, he recognized Guthrie. He was slightly red-faced from his exertions, which might have camouflaged any embarrassment that he felt. On the other hand, Rosenfeld was not a man who embarrassed easily.

'Come to see me off, have you?' Rosenfeld smiled a shameless smile. 'Make sure I leave the premises without the family silver?'

'Mr Sinclair's just –' Guthrie began woodenly.

'Never did have that follow-up lunch,' Rosenfeld went on as if it was the most natural thing in the world. 'If I didn't have to check in all this damn luggage . . . I always used to travel light; it must be age,' he sighed theatrically, '. . . I'd suggest a cup of airport coffee.'

Guthrie shook his head. He was, he realized, much less at ease than the American.

'No? You could have paid this time.'

Guthrie was forced to smile. 'Which flight?'

'The last one.'

'New York?'

'Paris. Keep out of the States for a while, till I see what way the wind blows. Think that's wise, do you?'

Guthrie ignored the question. 'I heard you and Fulton had one great bust-up.'

'Wonder how you picked that up, Robert. Wait . . . Stupid of me. You know, it was only towards the end that we flew some technical sweepers in from Stateside. They found your clever devices. Foolish, very foolish of us.'

'We thought so too,' said Guthrie, wondering why he did not bring the conversation to an end. 'Staying on with Unity?' he asked.

'Yep. Still on their payroll. They can't afford to let me go elsewhere. Too many skeletons I can rattle. If you hear of any coups needing fixed up . . .' He paused. 'Of course, that ain't funny . . .'

Guthrie made to leave.

'So . . . doubtless you think we lost.' Rosenfeld wasn't looking at him and seemed largely intent on steadying the top suitcase in its precarious position on the trolley.

'A common view . . .' Guthrie confirmed.

Rosenfeld shrugged dismissively. 'It always seems to matter who wins and who loses,' he said. 'That's what life is all about.'

'Life's really about perceptions,' responded Guthrie. 'Politics in particular is all about perceptions. You lost the perception too.'

'Have it as you will,' said Rosenfeld. 'If it makes all of you happy to think you've won, that's fine by me. I'll probably never come back to Scotland after all. Pity, that. I like the scenery and the golf . . .'

'Come back in a few years' time and you'll see what we've made of the place,' Guthrie said aggressively. He was more than a little irritated by Rosenfeld's cold-hearted detachment.

'With whose help?' came the impertinent question.

'It has to be on our own . . . in the long run. Sure, everybody needs some help and Scotland is part of Europe, after all. With American and European funding we'll achieve prosperity. It may be a tough battle but we Scots have a resilience.'

'That nonsense is unworthy of you, Robert. Most resilient Scots left centuries ago. You know that.'

'We're good at breeding new talent. We'll make it work. It's not a game, you know.' Guthrie was tiring of the conversation and of Rosenfeld. He turned away.

'Game? All right,' Rosenfeld called after him. 'Let's agree that both sides can claim victory. How about that? Call it quits? That's hardly unusual in political life, is it? The faithful can believe what they want to believe. But if you're going to win out, you Scots have got to stop slanging each other. You're better than the Irish at being your own worst enemy. You've got to stop carping at success, ditch the Scottish habit of envy that so stifles much of your initiative. Every time anyone puts their head above the parapet too far, sneering figures come along and snipe at it.'

'It happens in other countries too,' said Guthrie defensively. He might agree with much of what Rosenfeld was saying but was not going to admit it now. Then he nodded. 'OK,' he said, grudgingly. 'We didn't win outright.'

'Wait a bit. You'll worry me if you start agreeing with me! It makes me feel I'm losing my dispassionate sense of judgement,' said Rosenfeld, still smiling as he stared up at the departures board. 'Did you win at all? Did you, Robert? Did Scotland? Hey . . . look, sorry . . . It'll have to be some other time. With this crowd around, I gotta rush and check in. I'm not going to miss the last plane out.'